Kingsley Amis

Russian Hide-and-Seek

a melodrama

Penguin Books

Penguin Books Ltd, Harmondsworth,
Middlesex, England
Penguin Books, 625 Madison Avenue,
New York, New York 10022, U.S.A.
Penguin Books Australia Ltd, Ringwood,
Victoria, Australia
Penguin Books Canada Ltd, 2801 John Street,
Markham, Ontario, Canada L3R 1B4
Penguin Books (N.Z.) Ltd, 182–190 Wairau Road,
Auckland 10, New Zealand

First published by Hutchinson 1980
Published in Penguin Books 1981
Reprinted 1981 (twice)

Set, printed and bound in Great Britain by
Cox & Wyman Ltd, Reading
Set in Intertype Times

To Margaret and Brian Aldiss

1

The sheep clustered by the infant oak-tree looked up suddenly and turned their heads. Something was coming towards them over the close-cropped turf, coming fast. At the same time a low noise that might have been the beginning of a storm grew steadily louder, and there seemed to be a vibration underfoot. The sheep swung abruptly aside and started to run.

What had alarmed them was not one being but two, a pretty five-year-old black mare with a fine head and good bone, and in the saddle a young soldier, fair-haired, pink-cheeked, with light-blue eyes that sometimes had the look of not fully taking in what they saw; they had that look now. He rode with great dash and some carelessness, but the mare had been schooled by the regimental farrier-major himself and would have been equal to much less prudent horsemanship. She was remarkably well balanced, the most necessary of qualities on occasions like the present, a full gallop across ground broken by badger setts and tree-roots.

Man and mount came up with the sheep, which had not had the sense to scatter and were moving in a series of aimless curves. The young man amused himself for a time by circling as closely as he could round the bleating, flinching group. He laughed and shouted and swore at his victims. Then one of the ewes, more enterprising or more fearful than the rest, broke away at a tangent, only to attract the rider's whole attention. Quite soon, harassed, jostled and more than once nearly sent sprawling, the solitary sheep ceased to run and let out a sound not unlike the cry of a human infant. At that, the young man wrenched his horse's head round and made off at top speed, not slackening till he reached the side of a road a couple of hundred

7

metres off. Here he halted and sat motionless with face lowered, biting his lips and swallowing every few seconds. When he reached out his hand to lay it on the mare's neck it was trembling violently. He sat on while a mule-drawn waggon full of mangolds went by. The two men in it touched their caps to him, but he appeared not to see them at all. At last he gave a deep sigh and raised his head. His eyes were full of tears.

After walking his horse a kilometre or so along the road the young man turned off to his right and went through a small churchyard by a path that ran among ancient gravestones, some of them fallen. He dismounted to negotiate a low gateway of brick and stone. To his left front was situated a grand house in the style of the early eighteenth century; ahead and to his right were extensive gardens with trimmed shrubs and hedges, ornamental steps leading up to a stone summerhouse, a large artificial pond and hundreds of tree-stumps – oak, holly, pine and, most noticeable of all, cedar: the specimen that in former times had stood at this south-east corner of the house had measured nearly two metres across at its thickest part. Other trees, mainly oak and ash, were still entire, but none was much more than twenty years old. Not that the young man could have identified any of them or estimated their age; to him they were trees or what was left of trees.

He hitched the mare to a miniature temple with stone pillars and a wrought-iron roof bearing a weather-vane. It was early in the evening of a fine July day, warm and tranquil, but he showed no sign of tranquillity. He hurried up the steps and into the house, where he raised his voice and called in a peevish tone. Very soon a white-haired man with a large moustache and lined cheeks came bustling up. He wore a brown frock-coat and had a pink kerchief round his neck, and he was sweating slightly.

'Good evening, your honour.'

'Send somebody to take Polly to the stables, will you?'

'Where is she, sir?'

'Where she always is at such times, in the name of Heaven – down by the little temple.'

'Yes, sir. I'll see to it. Leave it to me, your excellency.'

The young man walked up the hall and reached the foot of the impressive staircase. Here stood a pedestal surmounted by an alabaster urn, perhaps the survivor of a pair. On the floor above, past the empty niches at the stairhead, in the gallery that ran the full width of the house, displayed against some inconsiderable remains of panelling, were three further objects from the past: a painting of two largely naked male children and a lamb, a large tapestry showing a meeting between two exalted persons of antiquity, as it might be a legendary king and queen, and the portrait of a woman in her thirties, no doubt a long-departed member of the family once in possession. These and the urn had been discovered by chance only four years earlier, in a papered-over cupboard. Everything else in the building that was portable, even if portable only at the expense of truly herculean effort, had gone.

Such abstruse relics made no appeal to the young man in his present mood, but he strode along the gallery, a tall slim figure with at the moment a firm gait and upright bearing, and reached the great window in the east front, that by which he had just entered. Through the imperfect glass (it was not the original glass) he looked down with the same half-attentive gaze as when he was galloping towards the sheep, and indeed his mind's eye was not so much on what he saw as on what he knew had once been there: the pond in the shape of a semi-circle with a step in its margin at each side near the base and a metal statue in its middle, beyond this an avenue of slender trees – cypresses, four hundred metres away a small lake exactly in line, below the window and round the pond carefully-trimmed blocks of yew hedge, stone statues, a low wall with diminutive stone lions along the top. The pond and the lake were still there, of course, but nothing else was. Shadow covered the nearer part of the outlook as the sun went down on the other side of the house.

He turned with his habitual abruptness and went into the room that had been on his left. Its floor was covered with canvas on which heavy, dark-coloured rugs had been thrown. On the walls there were numerous pictures of far more recent date than the two in the gallery: landscapes under snow, peasant merry-makings, still-lifes with much use made of unflippant materials like bread, potatoes and onions, military scenes. There was a birchwood dressing-table, a birchwood writing-table, a birchwood bookcase half-full of novels by forgotten writers, plays, collections of poems and army manuals, birchwood chairs, a birchwood bed. On the writing-table stood an opened bottle of white drinking-spirit and an elaborately-engraved glass. The young man poured himself about a tenth of a litre and took it down in a single swallow. Coughing hard, turning red in the face, he undid the bone buttons of his high-necked grey tunic, wrenched it impatiently from his shoulders, flung it aside, dropped face down on the bed and lay without moving from his first position.

After no more than a minute there came a gentle tap at the door. He spoke with his face against the bolster.

'Who is it?'

'May I see you, Alexander?'

'All right, come in then, mummy.'

A good-looking woman of fifty or so, rather short and stooped, entered the room carring a raffia flower-basket full of pink roses. She frowned in a way that indicated more anxiety than annoyance and no disapproval at all.

'Alexander, I don't think you should just lie there like that when your mother approaches you.'

Soon, but not immediately, the young man lifted himself up from the bed and kissed her without much warmth. 'I'm sorry, mummy, I was miles away. What you call day-dreaming.'

'You do too much of it. I wish you'd grow up.'

'That's not a very nice thing to say. Or accurate either. I'm twenty-one and an ensign in the Guards.'

'I know you are, darling, and I'm sure you're very good at your job, but you do spend a lot of time wool-gathering. It stops you noticing what's going on in the world and taking life seriously. Look at the hours you waste mooning over that silly old window-pane.'

'Mummy, you're not to call it silly. It means a great deal to me.'

10

'No doubt, but exactly what does it mean to you?'

'I don't understand.'

'I suppose you think of yourself as . . .' She stopped speaking.

'Please go on.'

But she did not. Far off within the house there was a faint crash of breaking glass or crockery. The inveterate wool-gatherer grasped his mother lightly by her silk-clad upper arms and, with a tender but vague smile, inspected her at some length. There was an air of great solicitude in his voice when he said,

'You're tired, poor little mummy. You work too hard. You really must do less yourself and make those lazy good-for-nothings below stairs do more. It's a positive disgrace.'

'I've only been cutting roses,' said his mother.

'But in this heat . . . Oh yes. How pretty they are.'

'They're quite pretty. Not as much so as they must have been, you know, before. It's the mildew, like last year. Such a shame.'

'That rascal Mily idling as usual.'

'There's nothing Mily can do. He has a hard enough time looking after the vegetables.'

'With three men under him?'

'There's nothing anybody can do. Well, I must go and see to these flowers. I dare say they'll look well enough on the dinner-table. Oh, now that reminds me; of course, that was why I came: your father wants to know whether you'll be dining with us tonight.'

The young man sat down heavily on the edge of his bed. 'Oh, merciful God.'

'What is it, darling? You're quite free to have something brought you up here if you'd rather. You don't imagine your father would try to compel you? You know that's not his style,' she said in a neutral tone.

'No, it's just that the whole idea sickens me.'

'But why? So many things seem to do that.'

'Life's so boring. No wonder I day-dream.'

'You can go and live at your regiment any time you like.'

'Thank you! It's even worse there.'

'Well then. Anyway, this is just a small party, I promise you. The Tabidzes are to be here . . .'

'Is that supposed to be an attraction?'

'You've always said how much you like them. Or at least respect them.'

'Hm.'

'And – what's he called? – Theodore something. From the Commission. I remember you said you'd met him playing croquet. I thought he might be nice company for Nina. And Elizabeth, of course.'

'Mummy, please spare me a lecture on Elizabeth.'

'What else am I doing? Are two words a lecture?'

Alexander said nothing. After another silence, his mother said,

'I must go. I have a lot to do. If you don't want to decide now, would you at least let Anatol know by seven o'clock whether you intend to come down to dinner or not?' There was a faint severity in her tone and manner which grew fainter when he turned his blue-eyed gaze upon her, but had not vanished altogether when she added, 'So that he can lay the right number of covers.'

'Yes yes.'

'Your father would be very glad of your company. And so would I.'

'Thank you, mummy.'

He opened the door for her, closed it after her carefully and strolled over to his bookcase. With an experimental air, as if quite ignorant of what he might find, he took down and opened a large thin volume bound in dull purple. He sighed heavily and frowned, turning over the pages with an air of great finality. Eventually he read aloud,

> 'Down the wind drain the last leaves,
> Snow garbs the naked alders; a grim sun
> Yet holds out hope of what the blood wishes,
> Thrills it with memories of heat-dozed lawns,
> Messages of lust suffusing all.'

He shut the book with a loud slap. 'Shit!' he cried, whacking it back on the shelf, or rather trying to force it between its neighbours while perversely not using his free hand to hold them apart; 'the jackass hasn't the least idea. Will any of them ever even begin? If only somebody would tell me what I feel!' A step sounded just outside the room, but he added in a loud, trembling voice, 'If only! If only!' The knock that followed was much firmer than that of ten minutes previously, and there was nothing at all tentative about the demeanour of the girl who came in, Alexander's sister Nina.

She was nineteen, of medium size, not thin, auburn-haired, rather pale, with good features but too friendly an expression to be considered beautiful. Her flowered cotton skirt, white blouse and wide-lapelled mauve waistcoat, also of cotton but woven like satin, had been chosen with care and effect. She looked at her brother with a smile in which, as often with her, affection was joined with amusement.

'Talking to yourself again,' she said in agreeable, slightly guttural tones.

'Was I?' said Alexander loftily. 'What if I was?'

'Nothing whatever, my dear, I assure you. Mummy asked me to come and see you, as you'll have guessed.'

'I don't guess that sort of thing.'

'Not you, no. She said you're being difficult about dinner tonight. I'm here to persuade you to say you'll come. What's holding you back, anyway?'

Alexander hesitated. At last he said, 'I don't much care for sitting down at the same table as Director Vanag.'

'What makes you think he'll be coming?'

'He usually does. You know that.'

'Not this time. Director Vanag is in Moscow.' Nina had settled herself in the least uncomfortable of the birchwood chairs with a tasselled cushion behind her head. 'Deputy-Director Korotchenko will be in attendance instead.'

'Is Vanag in trouble?'

'Not that I know of, I'm sorry to say. Probably just giving his horrible report and getting his horrible orders. Deputy-Director Korotchenko is bringing Mrs Korotchenko with him.'

'So I should naturally suppose. What of it?'

'You wouldn't say "what of it?" if you'd seen her, *old boy*,' said Nina, using the English words.

'Where have you seen her? How have you found out all this?'

'They were at a picnic we were at last week.' She paused. 'Go on, ask me what she's like.'

'You are the most impossible little saucebox, you know. Oh, very well, what's the woman like?'

'There you go again; that's no way to speak of her. How shall I put it? She's your type.'

'Meaning?'

'Meaning a sulky, bad-tempered look and an enormous bosom.'

'What utter rubbish; that's not my type. Kitty hasn't got a sulky, bad-tempered . . .' Alexander stopped speaking.

His sister laughed in a way that, again, no woman considered beautiful ever does. 'You're wonderful, do you know that? Altogether wonderful.' Looking straight at him while he moved his head to and fro in vexation, she laughed again for some moments. 'Anyway, as well as her being your type, it wouldn't surprise me if you were hers.'

'And what's THAT supposed to mean?'

'Just that the sulky look might be a dissatisfied look and Deputy-Director Korotchenko must be nearly sixty and Mrs Korotchenko can't be much more than thirty-five. I think perhaps I should have said an unsatisfied look or a not-satisfied-enough look, shouldn't I?'

'I really have no idea,' said Alexander, loftily again.

There was a short pause. Nina scratched her neck and stared out of the window. Still staring, she said in a monotone,

'If you like, I'll tell Anatol where you want to eat tonight.'

'Thank you, my dear.'

'It's nothing. Where shall I say you want to eat?'

'What? Oh, in the dining-room.' Alexander sounded mildly surprised.

'Good,' said Nina with an effort, even now keeping her face turned aside; it would not do now to show amusement. 'Did you have a good day?'

'Deadly dull as usual. Nina, I ... did something rather bad this afternoon, coming home from quarters.'

At once she looked him in the eye, all trace of levity gone from her manner. 'What? What did you do?'

'I ... chased a sheep.'

'Oh. That doesn't sound very terrible.'

'I was riding Polly, remember. There are several flocks of sheep in those fields on the far side of the road,' – he pointed approximately – 'and I must have passed them hundreds of times without it ever occurring to me to chase them, but today I did, and one of them ran away from the others and I concentrated on it, and harried it, and almost knocked it over, and then it froze, and it gave such a cry ... Oh, Nina, think how frightened it must have been.'

Alexander was weeping, his hands over his face. First turning her dilated eyes heavenwards and drawing back the corner of her mouth, Nina went to him and put her arm round his shoulders. She said very quietly,

'It'll have forgotten all about it by now, you can be sure of that.'

'How can I be sure? And even if it has, I still did it, didn't I? I was still cruel.'

'Yes, you were. We must be thankful it was no worse. And also you've learned how badly you feel when you've been cruel, and that's bound to help to stop you being it another time.'

'Yes, it's bound to do that. And I should think it probably has forgotten, wouldn't you?'

'Oh, YES,' she said with confidence. 'Now I'd better go and dress, and you'd better start thinking of doing the same. Would you like some orange-juice?'

'What a marvellous idea.' He dried his eyes on a silk handkerchief.

'I'll have some sent up.'

'Nina, there's no doubt you are the nonpareil of sisters.'

He embraced her, able because of his greater height to hold her head against his breast. Unseen by him she pursed her lips. Presently she disengaged herself and left. After a moment's thought he followed her, went to the stairhead and bawled the name 'Brevda' several times. Other voices took it up. After no very long time the sound of running feet became audible. Alexander retreated and stood looking out of the east window with his back to the gallery. The footfalls approached, slowed, shuffled, and an uncertain voice, a man's voice, said behind him,

'You called me, sir?'

'Yes, Brevda, I called you. Would you be good enough to run my bath and then when I'm in it lay out my mess-dress?'

'With great pleasure, your honour.' Brevda spoke readily, perhaps with more than readiness; his master's hardly less usual practice was to converse in unadorned imperatives with manner to match. He never complained or showed the least resentment; to do either would be unproductive at best, true, for Brevda was actually Trooper Brevda, Alexander's batman, on indefinite but all too easily terminable detachment to the parental household in an era of servant shortage. At the same time he had been known to show what looked like a genuine regard, anyway something more than his position required. He stood now in renewed uncertainty, this time wondering whether he was to consider himself dismissed or not. Alexander had still not turned round. A moment or two later he said,

'I think one should take life as it comes, don't you, Brevda, not considering every detail from every possible angle?'

'That would certainly seem to be a cumbersome procedure, sir.'

'It doesn't enhance a pleasure to dwell on it, as far as I can see.'

'My own experience has been along the same lines, sir.'

'It's very important to behave naturally and spontaneously, don't you think?'

'Of the greatest consequence, sir.'

'After all, what are we to do in this world but enjoy ourselves?'

'One might well ask, sir.'

Turning at last, Alexander gave Brevda a keen glance. Brevda, bespectacled, thin, untidy, much scarred by acne, looked

16

steadily back. Then, simultaneously, both smiled. Alexander said briskly,

'Make sure the bath isn't too hot. It's not January.'

'Very good, your honour.'

Three-quarters of an hour later Alexander was on his way to join his father's party. The Guards mess-dress (light-grey jacket with yellow piping and gold-plated bars of rank, matching trousers with a double gold stripe down the outer seam) showed off his handsome appearance to perfection. In the lobby before the drawing-room he paused. Here was the window-pane or panel his mother had referred to, once a small oblong of engraved glass, now a rough triangle of the same with the missing portion inexpertly filled in by a later hand. Part of the east front of the house could be seen depicted, together with some of the trees that had formerly stood near it. An inscription across the top referred to . . . *omas Alexander third L* . . . The very fragmentariness of this text had caught the imagination of the present Alexander, who had built up a mental picture of his namesake that was an only slightly idealized version of himself. Sometimes it occurred to him that, living in the same place and being, he would have said, of a sensitive cast of mind, he might one day attain a special, quasi-telepathic understanding of that distant figure; certainly he often asked himself what 'Alexander' would have felt, thought, done at some local turn of events.

Not so this evening, a warm, still time when colours faded in the ravaged gardens and a tiny breath of cooler air crept across the pond towards the house, one that would in the past have carried with it scents of the rural outdoors, some readily traceable, others strange and puzzling. For a moment Alexander tried to imagine them, to smell them, but even as he did so a delicious, distracting melancholy possessed him; he felt as if he had renounced all ambition, all art, all natural beauty for a doomed love. Peering through the thickening shadows to where the avenue of cypresses had stood, resting his forehead against the window, he whispered, 'I am yours and yours alone, and the world shall end when I so much as permit another to glide into my dreams, my very dear lost one.' He was of course addressing nobody in particular, nobody in existence, though all male persons and all females outside a fairly narrow age-group were unconsideringly excluded from his avowal. The tone of things in general seemed to him gravely lowered when, a moment later, he found he was wondering to quite a degree about Mrs Korotchenko.

2

Mrs Korotchenko had been fairly described by Nina as far as
that description had gone; she, the wife of the Deputy-Director
of Security, was in addition of muscular build, black-haired
with that hair fashionably short and, tonight, clad in a dress of
unprinted muslin so cut as to show off the aforementioned
bosom. She also had on a light, fawn-coloured stole. Her
husband, a thickset, heavily-whiskered fellow in formal olive-
green, stood at her side during introductions in the drawing-
room. The last one in the short line was a dark-complexioned
young man called Theodore Markov, who could not have been
more than thirty but was already going bald at the temples. He
wore a dark-blue linen suit with single-breasted jacket and
narrow trouser-cuffs.

'*Good evening, my dear chap,*' said Theodore Markov in his
melodious voice.

'*Fine to see you, old customer,*' returned Korotchenko, rather
grudgingly taking the other's hand. If he had been surer of his
ground he might not have done so at all, and he would certainly
not have fallen in with the prevailing liberal fad of exchanging
remarks in English by way of salutation. But he was a little
overawed by the rest of the male company, Controller Petrovsky, who was his host, and Lieutenant-Colonel Tabidze, the
military commander of the district. Nor had he been much
comforted by the cool glance Mrs Tabidze had given him on
their being introduced, even though what women thought of
him was of no significance. Altogether the process of settling
down in his new post (he had arrived only the previous month)
had proved to hold its irritations.

In his not-so-distant youth Sergei Petrovsky had often been

19

spoken of as the handsomest man in Moscow, and even today there was a young man's vigour in his bearing and a bloom to his complexion, though his head of tawny hair and neatly-trimmed full beard bore heavy grey streaks. With a smile that showed excellent teeth he said to the newly-arrived Theodore Markov, who had just taken a glass of vodka from a servant's tray,

'Throw that down and have another, my boy. These fiddling little affairs hold no more than a coffee-spoon.'

'Thank you, sir,' said his guest, doing as he was told. 'Your very good health.'

'Fair fortune. Help yourself to the beluga – I really can recommend it – and then come and talk to my daughter. I'm afraid I must insist on that, out of pure self-protection. If I fail to steer an unattached young man in her direction, I never hear the end of it. – Nina, my dear, I believe I told you Mr Markov is a member of our famous Commission.'

Nina had changed into an evening gown of her favourite mauve. It left her arms bare and in so doing exposed a large number of freckles, but there was that in the rest of her appearance or in her demeanour which prevented them from being a blemish. She liked the look of Theodore's mouth and hands and thought his slight baldness only made him seem the more mature and wise.

'Yes, papa,' she said. 'Tell me, Mr Markov, what department do you work in? Or is that a secret?'

Theodore answered her smile with his own. 'Nothing we do is a secret. That's rather the point of us. I'm in the music section.'

'Music?' Nina sounded surprised but quickly corrected herself. 'Oh, I suppose there must be a certain amount.'

'There's a great deal, some of it very interesting, believe me.'

'You don't happen to play the piano by any chance, do you?'

'I don't exactly happen to play the piano by any chance,' said Theodore, smiling again. 'I play intentionally, of set purpose, and rather well. Not very well, just rather well. Well enough for you, Miss Petrovsky, I think I can safely say.'

'Possibly. But this is wonderful. You shall play for us after

dinner and let us hear some of your discoveries. Piano music –
in these parts we're lucky if we have some twice a year.'

'I suggest perhaps your father's permission . . .'

'I don't give permissions,' said Petrovsky. 'I find out what is
to happen and either welcome it heartily, as in this instance, or
submit to it with what grace I can. I may tell you, young
Markov, that your only chance of not finding yourself at that
piano disappeared for ever the moment you revealed you could
play it. I look forward very much to the prospect. – Nina,
darling, are you sure Alexander is to honour us with his
company this evening?'

'I'm sure he said he was going to, papa. That's as much as one
can ever be sure of with him.'

'Do you think I don't know my own son? Not that a father's
experience is needed. The most superficial acquaintance would
suffice. He knows Elizabeth is coming?'

'You don't seem to know that that cuts no ice with him, but
I'm pretty sure he'll turn up this time,' said Nina, momentarily
shifting her glance. 'I've got a feeling he will.'

'It may be useful to you sooner than you think, Markov, to
learn that when my daughter's mouth curls at the corners like
that she has something up her sleeve.'

'Papa! Must I give reasons for everything? Well, you mark
my words: he'll be here any minute now. He's just preparing his
entrance. You'll see.'

'No doubt I shall. Now I'm not sure my presence at this spot
is vitally necessary. Korotchenko there may need a hand – the
gallant colonel has his prejudices, I'm afraid.'

Petrovsky took his leave of the two and went across to where
those just mentioned stood by one of the tall windows that
looked out on the south side of the house. The traces of what
had been inset paintings on the ceiling and walls were too scanty
for even the type of subject to be discernible, though Nina had
once fancied she could see a dog in one of them. Now, against
cinnamon-brown wallpaper arabesqued in gold, there hung un-
distinguished pictures illustrating Russian life and a few frankly
rather gloomy ikons. The furniture, on the other hand, Petrovsky

considered quite good – it was all Karelian except for the horse-hair sofa which his wife had been surprised to pick up locally, and the bookcase of black oak. He was proud of the Kurdistan carpet, the tiger-skin rug from the shore of the Sea of Aral and such pieces as the gold Peter the First clock on the overmantel. Its hands stood at eight minutes to one; they had stood so for an unknowable number of years before it had come into Petrovsky's possession, but he was still proud of it.

The door opened and Alexander strode in. He made straight for the nearest group, which consisted of his mother, Mrs Tabidze, Mrs Korotchenko and Elizabeth, surnamed Cuy, the twenty-year-old girl who had been his dinner-partner a score of times and a spare female disappointed by him almost half as often. Nina watched in fascination as he greeted his mother, Mrs Tabidze and Elizabeth and turned to be introduced to Mrs Korotchenko. Theodore was talking entertainingly enough about his work with the Commission, but Nina could not help turning through a quarter of a circle and uttering a quiet but distinct snigger.

'I seem to have failed to hold your interest,' said her companion amiably.

'I'm sorry, Mr Markov, I hate appearing rude to you, so much so that I'll have to run the risk of speaking rather improperly.'

'That doesn't sound very unsafe to me.'

'Well – are you acquainted with Mrs Korotchenko at all?'

'I've seen her in public two or three times, nothing more.'

'In that case . . . would you agree that she has an exceptional bosom?'

'Well yes, I think I'd have to. A bit too exceptional for my taste.'

'Not for Alexander's. You don't know him well, do you?'

'I've met him twice, and liked him.'

'I'm glad of that. Well, he wasn't going to turn up tonight – he gets silly moods when he goes solitary to try and get attention – and then I mentioned the bosom, which I'd seen on Tuesday, and quite soon after that he said he thought he'd come after all.

But what made me laugh just now was the way he absolutely made up his mind not to goggle at it when he was introduced and then goggled at it. What's he doing now? I daren't look.'

Theodore furtively turned his eyes. 'Goggling at it.'

'Oh, dear God. Is her husband watching?'

'Just a ... No, his back's almost turned and your father's saying something to him. It should be all right if Alexander stops goggling reasonably soon.'

'Good. We don't want Mr Korotchenko challenging him to a duel.'

'He's not the type. Far too cautious.'

'I suppose that helps if you work under someone like Director Vanag.'

'You sound a good deal less than fond of him.'

'He's a pig.'

'What has he done?' asked Theodore, naturally enough, for she had spoken with the heat of personal dislike.

'I don't know. I mean he's done nothing to me. I see as little of him as possible. But anybody who does that job must be a pig.'

He started to say something and checked himself, noticing that Alexander, with Elizabeth Cuy at his side, was on his way to where they stood. Theodore and Nina looked at each other and went on looking, indeed stared hard. She was so sure he was about to take her hands that she drew in her breath and a blush coloured her pale cheeks.

'Can I see you again soon?' he asked indistinctly.

'Of course. Of course.'

Then the other two had come up and there was no further chance of talking privately before dinner. The dining-room, originally the central portion of a hall rising the full height of the house, faced west on to a court bounded by a red-brick wing, a wall of the same material broken by two gateways and, in front, a low stone balustrade. Away from this ran a double line of plane-tree stumps, corresponding to the cypresses on the other side. The fine marble chimney-piece in the room was almost undamaged, and the long table of Crimean walnut was thought to go suitably with it. At the moment the prettily mottled and figured surface of the table was spread with silver plate and cutlery, wine bottles, glasses – three at each place – sweetmeats and bowls full of the roses cut earlier. Brown-clad footmen with white gloves settled the company into their chairs. Petrovsky at the head had Mrs Tabidze and Mrs Korotchenko respectively on his right and left; his wife at the foot repeated the pattern with their husbands. Theodore found himself between Mrs Korotchenko and Nina, an excellent position as it proved, for the senior lady gave all her attention to Petrovsky, while the colonel, on Nina's other side, exchanged a couple of brisk amiabilities with her and began a conversation with his hostess. As he and Nina talked, which they did with some concentration, Theodore glanced over at Alexander a few times. Once he was saying something to the Cuy girl; once he was listening to whatever Mrs Tabidze had to say to him; twice his eye was on Mrs Korotchenko. And once he met Theodore's glance with a look of genial friendliness, as if to encourage him in his attentions to Nina and to wish him well.

A prune soup opened the meal, accompanied by sweet sherry and followed by grilled salmon with radishes and beetroots. The wine was a first-class, long-lived Pouilly Blanc Fumé. The final course consisted of a hot fruit salad, whipped cream and little macaroons; chilled Georgian champagne circulated. Finally chocolates, fudge, sugared almonds, buttered tea, a fine brandy (also from Georgia) and cigars were offered.

Now, with the servants dismissed, Petrovsky rapped for silence and said, 'Let me inform newcomers that the rule of the house requires us, before returning to the drawing-room, to follow the ancient and honourable tradition of spending some minutes in conversation round the table.'

Tabidze, a dark lean man of fifty, very trim in his regimentals, gave a dry chuckle. 'Did I hear something about an ancient and honourable tradition, Sergei? You must be turning conservative in your old age.'

'Oh, I think that's a little unfair, Nicholas. I've never been opposed to traditions as such. It's the unthinking acceptance of them that I deplore.'

'Strange how often it seems to amount to the same thing. Take this land-tenure reform of yours, now. I don't pretend to have gone into the details, but I've grasped the main outline. What you intend is revolutionary. The present system has worked perfectly well for over forty years and you want to turn it upside down.'

'Not at all, I merely want to make it work better. Remember that all I have done – all my advisers and I have done – is frame a set of proposals for submission to the central authority. Who will quite certainly tone them down a great deal at best; we took account of that. I foresee that when the amended version goes into effect, if it ever does, even you, my dear Nicholas, will find very little ground for concern.'

'I hope you're right.' Tabidze inspected a cigar and turned to Korotchenko. 'What is your view of the matter, sir?'

'The view of so recent a newcomer could hardly . . .'

'No, please,' said Petrovsky, 'I want to hear what everybody thinks.'

'I beg your pardon, Controller, I have not yet had time to study the protocol with the closeness required to do it justice.'

Theodore nudged Nina, then looked to his right. Mrs Korotchenko sat facing her front, her attention quite unfixed, as though the talk were being conducted in a language altogether strange to her; perhaps it was, he thought, not yet having heard her speak. In profile her eyelid showed a slight epicanthic fold, suggesting Mongoloid ancestry. Now Alexander spoke, and Theodore listened and watched with the greatest care.

'If you really want to know what everybody thinks, papa, including the young, you shall hear what I think, though I fancy you have a moderate idea already.' Alexander's tone and manner were entirely respectful, neither heavy nor frivolous. 'I can reassure the respected colonel that nothing is going to be turned upside down or even moved more than a couple of millimetres from its present position. – Your account, sir, of my father as nursing revolutionary intentions could not, with deference, be more mistaken; you were unintentionally right when you called him a conservative. But I'd better address him direct. – You dislike and fear change, papa, but you also have a conscience. Something should be done, something is done, something has been done, and everything is as it was before, except that some people feel better about it. Oh yes, you're not the only one; half the men who run this country are of the same stamp. Now I come to think of it, there is one other result of the change that's no change: a lot of those with a grievance will also have the illusion that something has been done, so the rulers are actually safer as well as more comfortable in mind.'

At this point Elizabeth Cuy broke in, a small fair grey-eyed girl whose attractions were perhaps outweighed for Alexander by her direct glance and style. '*Piss off* – how dare you tell your father he's of the same stamp as someone else!' she said with annoyance and amusement mixed. 'Explaining him to himself like that! Accusing him of not being sincere!'

'I meant no impertinence.'

'Yes you did. What you said was impertinent and you meant it.'

'Don't concern yourself, Elizabeth,' said Petrovsky with a smile. 'I took no offence.'

'Well, you should have done, sir, and expressed it too. How else are the young to learn respect?'

'I think the young are pretty satisfactory as they are.'

'Do you really! They appal me, some of them.' Elizabeth glared at Alexander for a moment before unwillingly laughing. 'All right, my great politician, let's hear your scheme for sharing out the land or whatever it is.'

'It's perfectly simple. The land should belong to those who work on it and live on it.'

'I see. So the gardens here should belong to your man Mily and his squad. Who would be quite entitled to keep you and the rest of the family out of them if they felt so inclined.'

'Well . . .'

'Yes, my boy. You say SHOULD. Where does that come from? What right have Mily and the others to those gardens out there?'

'There is such a thing as justice, isn't there?'

'May I answer that, Elizabeth?' It was Colonel Tabidze. 'The

26

answer is no. Justice does not exist. All that exists, all that has ever existed, is a series of more or less unjust actions and events and institutions on the one hand, and the idea of justice on the other. In its name all the great injustices are done. So with enslavements and the idea of freedom, barbarities in the name of progress, lies and ... At least that's how it is and how it's always been with us. Ideas are the curse of the Russian. You can see it in Tolstoy, in Dostoievsky, in Chekhov: a whole class distracted from their duty, their marriages, their work, their pleasures, even their sense of self-preservation – all by ideas. What is to become of us?'

'A good question, Nicholas,' said his large, deep-voiced wife. 'When a Guards colonel is plunged into deep philosophical gloom by a remark made by one of his junior ensigns, instead of telling the young whippersnapper to go to hell, you have every reason to ask what's to become of us. There's only one solution that I can see – Sergei, I'll trouble you for a little more of that sterling brandy.'

There was laughter at that, in which Alexander joined with every sign of spontaneity, Theodore noted. Deputy-Director Korotchenko joined in too after a fashion – a horrible sight, thought Nina. Mrs Korotchenko made no attempt.

3

A little later the party was assembled in the drawing-room, where a still white wine and more tea, together with freshly-cut rye-bread sandwiches, were available. Petrovsky, the Tabidzes and, after some delay, Korotchenko settled down at a card-table for solo whist. Tatiana Petrovsky took out her embroidery, a gros-point chair seat. Her daughter, Elizabeth and Theodore placed themselves near by. Speaking for the first time in his hearing, Mrs Korotchenko said to Alexander,

'It's very hot. I should like some fresh air. Would you come with me for a turn in the gardens? I haven't seen them in the light. I don't want to fall.'

Her voice was harsh and flat, with an idiosyncratic pronunciation of some vowels. Even now she failed to look him in the eye. He noticed that she was thin-faced and thin-lipped, with large ugly ears injudiciously exposed by her short haircut. 'Of course not,' he said. Nina and Elizabeth were watching him. 'I mean of course you don't want to fall. Of course – I'd be delighted to accompany you.'

His brain was operating at several times its usual speed, with two things attaining some prominence: that it was RATHER hot was the most that could fairly be said, and, as he remembered from the small hours of that morning, when he had stumbled out into the open after Mess Night, the moon was almost at the full. But surely . . .

They moved out by the east entrance, went down the steps and reached the nearest lawn. This was not at all well mown, but any sort of serious fall was most unlikely in the intense moonlight. He was considering just how soon and just how to grab her when she grabbed him. The speed and violence of her assault took him quite by surprise. Her open mouth shoved itself at his; her body pushed and wriggled against him; she took hold of him after a fashion calculated to extinguish at once any lingering doubt of her wishes. His arms were round her, or his left arm was.

Taking her mouth away, she said warmly, 'Let me go,' struggling now.

'Let you go? But you – ?'

'Otherwise how can I take my dress off?'

He stepped back. 'But you – '

With her voice muffled by folds of material she said something he failed to catch. As she tugged and thrust at her clothes his lively consternation resolved itself into a daze of excitement. In about the time it would have taken him to untie his stock she had taken off everything but her white silk stockings and her garters, which looked black at the moment but probably were not in fact. Her breasts, on view in full so much more precipitately than almost anyone could have foreseen, charged him with wonder.

'Come on, what are you waiting for?' the lady asked him in a blurred voice. Again he pounced upon her, but again this proved unsatisfactory. 'Never mind about that,' she said, and fumbled with his clothing. A moment later she lay down on the grass. 'Oh do be quick,' she said. 'Hurry up.' Her body weaved slightly and she made sounds like someone in considerable but not extreme pain. When he lay down beside her he got it wrong a third time – 'For the love of God, man, will you do it!' – and was hauled on top of her; her strength was frightening, but not very. The first response she made was so marked that he thought she must have attained her objective; her continuing movements, however, quite soon undeceived him. More than having her in his embrace he clung to her or was enfolded by her. He found that by going all out he could just stay in the game, so to speak. Finally, at about the critical moment for him, she redoubled her exertions and uttered a long, wavering, stifled cry, stifled as he found by her own hand pressed against her mouth – and a good thing too, for the unstifled version would beyond doubt have been heard clearly enough in the house. He felt a little troubled; it had presumably been a cry of pleasure, but he had fancied he heard something else in it, some darker feeling.

He kissed her cheek; by way of return she took his hands and held them to her breasts, then, not roughly, indicated that it was time to move. Still breathing deeply, he started putting his clothes to rights and she picked up hers. His disquiet had passed and he felt only joy and gratitude.

'My darling, that was delightful,' he said, 'and you're very lovely.'

She made no reply.

'When can I see you again?'

'You mean you want to do that with me again? After you've already done it once? What for?' Dressing at top speed, she looked doubtfully at him.

'Well, of course I do. We can take longer next time.'

'Yes, we can,' she said, as if this was an unexpected but, on reflection, valid point.

'When, then?'

'Tuesday afternoon. Two-thirty.'

'I'm on duty at the base then.'

'So you won't be able to come, will you?'

'Oh, I can rearrange it.'

'All right.'

She had finished dressing and moved off briskly at his side, brushing with her hand at the back of her head. It occurred to him against his will that perhaps she kept her hair short so that leaves, twigs, etc. should not get stuck in it whenever she committed adultery on a lawn or other outdoor surface.

'Where shall we meet?'

'Come to our house. It's called *The Old Parsonage* and it's about two miles out of the centre of Northampton just off the road to Wellingborough. Most of the English know it by now; we have plenty of official visitors. Ask for *the Russian policeman* if they don't understand you. Now when we get indoors I'm going to be rather cool to you. My husband will think you've made an approach to me and of course I've rebuffed you.'

'My mother isn't going to like that.'

'Only my husband will see.'

'Very well.' He added, not at all because of what she had just proposed but on general grounds, 'You're a sweet girl. You deserve well of me.'

When he kissed her she failed to respond, but said in her monotonous harsh voice, 'That's extremely kind of you.'

He had by no means settled in his mind that she was a sweet girl; however, she had done as he had wanted, to put it mildly, he had enjoyed himself and, since they had reached the foot of the steps down which they had come an unknown amount of time ago, this must be their private farewell. Ascending, he looked about him at the moonlit gardens, the pond, the faint glimmer of the lake in the distance, and wished with some force that he could have seen the place as it had been in the time of that other Alexander, half a century away. At the top of the steps he looked again, and realized that to anyone standing here what had been going on just now would have been easily visible, and no doubt audible too. Well, time enough to debate the sweetness or otherwise of the girl in question when the next few minutes were safely past.

The re-entry into the drawing-room of the wife of the Deputy-Director and himself came at an unusually lucky moment. The card-players were in a state of some excitement as Mrs Tabidze was about to make good an abundance call; although the stakes were not high (£100 a point) even Korotchenko was too engrossed to do more than glance up briefly. In rather similar fashion, Theodore Markov was entertaining the ladies with a tale about the embezzlements practised by the cashier at his university. Alexander strolled over to the marble-topped table where the wine was, poured himself a glass and nibbled at a chicken sandwich. He would have said that there was no need for him to try to act casually because he felt perfectly casual: it would surely be rather simple-minded to imagine that there had been anything much out of the way in the encounter on the lawn, just a matter of a reasonably personable, normally sexed young buck running into a – well, there must be quite a few women like Mrs Korotchenko round the place and one could hardly expect them to advertise their condition, or rather the downrightness of their nature.

He finished the sandwich, carried his glass of wine across to the card-table, where the players were examining their newly-dealt hands, and looked over his father's shoulder, uncomprehendingly, for he despised the game too much ever to have learned the rules. There was a respectable pile of £100 and £500 coins and £1000 notes in front of Mrs Tabidze. Raising his whiskered face in calculation, Korotchenko gave Alexander a passing look of entire neutrality.

'I'm afraid you gentlemen are in for another thrashing,' said Mrs Tabidze with pretended menace. 'Misère.'

Her husband groaned. 'Shoulder to shoulder, lads.'

Furtively, Alexander took stock of the rest of the party. His mother, gros-point on lap, was talking in low tones to Mrs Korotchenko, who seemed to be actually responding, or at least paying attention, her display of coolness towards him seemingly ended, if it had ever been. The others had momentarily fallen silent; when his eye reached her Elizabeth was already looking at him and within a second Nina was too. Then they looked at each other. Their expressions were alike, though he could not have said what they expressed. In different circumstances he would have gone over and asked them, but not in these. He decided he would have to stick it out where he was, a policy that achieved its end when Nina leaned over and said, 'May we go up, mummy?' – a formula requesting a short leave of absence for the younger guests and members of the household, invariably granted. When the three left, he left with them.

'Did you have a nice walk, Alexander?' asked Elizabeth as soon as the drawing-room door was shut after them.

'Yes, very pleasant, thank you.'

'She didn't seem to think so.'

'Didn't she?' he said lightly, then, having thought about it, repeated with more emphasis, 'Oh, didn't she?' So much for only Korotchenko noticing.

'No, she didn't. But she should have, eh? – There's something funny here, Nina. What do you think?'

'Let's wait till we've got him behind doors upstairs.'

'I find this atmosphere of inquisition quite intolerable,' said Alexander, but relief and triumph together saw to it that he spoke with only a poor show of petulance. 'Theodore, you must protect me.'

'What can I do? What can two of us do against two of them?'

'And such a two. One quiet and deadly, the other brassy and violent.'

'There's gratitude for you,' said Nina.

Theodore nodded gravely. 'You notice they don't dispute the way you described them.'

'You notice something else, Lizzie,' said Nina: 'the younger one objected to the inquisition, but he didn't need to ask what it was going to be about.'

'Highly significant,' said Elizabeth.

By way of the eastern half of the first-floor gallery they had reached Nina's sitting-room, which lay directly opposite Alexander's bedroom with her bedroom opening off it. Objects of various sizes were strewn about: photographs of her parents, of Alexander and of her elder brother Basil (at present serving with the army of occupation in Manchuria), a photograph-album bound in some substance resembling red leather, an ash-wood spinning wheel, an ornamental cage containing a siskin (all the way from home), a full-sized stuffed brown bear, a boruldite quick-kettle and a superb three-inch astroscope. The inevitable music-sounder, instrument and reproducer in one, stood under its hood in the corner. There were also chairs, in or on which they seated themselves, though Nina at once jumped up to hand round cigarettes and tiny silver-rimmed glasses of koumissette. All accepted the first, but Theodore, who disliked sweet drinks, asked for and got soda-water instead of the liqueur.

'Now,' said Elizabeth, with the manner of one who calls a meeting to order, 'what happened out there?'

'In the sense you no doubt mean, very little,' said Alexander equably.

'How much is very little?'

'There was some kind of embrace.'

'Come on, darling, we haven't got all night,' said Nina. 'We're all dying to hear. It won't go any further.'

'All right there was a long, fairly passionate embrace with a certain amount of caressing. Oh, enough to establish that the bosom is real, if you must know.'

Elizabeth shook her shapely blonde head. 'I'm afraid it's still not enough. Not nearly enough.'

'Enough for what?'

'Enough to explain . . . Let me show you.'

She got up, folded her arms and, advancing first one hip, then the other, minced slowly across the room and back, rolling her shoulders and wagging her head to and fro, lips pushed forward, eyebrows raised. Now and then she held up her hands and examined the nails. While she did all this she hummed, whistled, sang wordlessly. Nina huddled herself up in laughter; Theodore smiled in puzzlement.

'What's that supposed to be?' asked Alexander.

'You when you came in from the garden, of course, acting a word like Unconcern or Casualness in a mime. Nobody of your age and experience puts on a show like that just for a couple of kisses and a feel-up. How far did you really get, Alexander?'

'Oh, damn it. Look, if I tell you something, will you promise absolutely not to let it out to anyone? Or refer to it again?'

They all nodded seriously.

'Well, she said she thought I was very handsome. Like . . . don't shoot me . . . like a Greek god. There. It sounds pretty silly and embarrassing when I tell you three, but when she said it I promise you I felt absolutely marvellous. Quite marvellous enough to make me want to strut about with a big grin on my face. That's what I was guarding against. It seems I overdid it a trifle.'

Elizabeth laughed and clapped him on the shoulder. Theodore too seemed quite satisfied. Nina smiled thoughtfully at her brother. After a moment she said,

'If she thinks you're so handsome, why was she annoyed with you? It's harder than ever to see the reason for that.'

'It is odd, isn't it? But are you sure it was annoyance and not tiredness, say, or . . .?'

'Oh yes, quite sure – eh, Nina?'

'Well, it was something all right, but I wouldn't swear it was annoyance. She . . . she was certainly not pleased about something.'

'Something to do with me?'

'Oh yes,' said Nina, 'there was no doubt about that at all.'

'Ah. I suppose it could have been . . . No.'

'Could have been what?' asked Elizabeth.

'It sounds so conceited I can hardly say it, but it's the only explanation that occurs to me. She was disappointed. That I didn't go the whole hog.'

'Why didn't you?'

'Well, she seemed so decided when she stopped me, and I haven't had much to do with females of her age and station. I didn't want to rush my fences. Fancy me getting it wrong – that way round.'

'Did you arrange to see her again?' asked Nina.

'No. She happened to mention where she lived, and I decided I could always find myself in the neighbourhood and drop in one afternoon when the Deputy-Director is snoring his head off in his office. But I didn't say anything about that because I wanted to think things over in a more settled frame of mind.'

Nina put out her cigarette with a decisive twist. 'That was it. She thought that having tried her you came to the conclusion you didn't want her after all. I'm surprised at you, my love. You've probably spoiled your chances there for good.'

'Just as well, probably. It would have been a lot to take on. But it's a pity; I think she's very attractive in an odd way.'

'It's odd all right,' said Elizabeth. 'Tremendous tits and starved-looking face. And that hair-cut, what's the idea of that? If she wants to look boyish that's not the place to start.'

'Did she talk at all?' asked Nina.

'Oh yes, without stopping. Except when I . . . stopped her. All about her house and the visitors they keep having. She's probably shy of anything approaching a throng. Or in awe of that hairy-faced husband of hers.'

'Any children?'

'She didn't mention any, so I rather suppose not.'

'I rather hope not.'

'What makes you say that?'

'I don't know. I'm just glad I'm not her daughter.'

'How funny. I don't go round imagining what it's like to be the son of any chap I meet who happens to be about old enough.'

'Of course you don't.'

'Of course? Is that because I'm a man?'

'No, because you're you.'

'I don't know what you're getting at, but I can tell easily enough that it isn't very friendly.'

Elizabeth had been listening to the latter part of this duologue with some impatience. Now she said, 'Can we please not have a discussion of Alexander?'

'I don't see why you should object if I don't.'

'Who says you object? You adore any and every discussion of you. Some of the rest of us don't share your passionate interest in the topic.'

'If I'm going to allow you to go on coming here, Elizabeth, I must ask you not to dictate the conversation.'

'Alexander!' cried Nina.

'What's the matter? I was only – '

'Have you forgotten already what mummy said to you?'

'When I've just been told I'm in love with myself? Anyone would think – '

'I'm going,' said Elizabeth. She had turned very red.

Nina caught her by the shoulders and remonstrated with her while Alexander said loudly that she could go where she pleased as far as he was concerned. It was soon clear that she would fight her way out of the room if necessary. At this point Nina released her and it was Theodore who barred her way.

'If you go now you'll find it very difficult to come back,' he said quickly. 'And you're going to want to, in spite of how you feel at the moment.'

Within what might have struck some people as quite a short space of time Elizabeth had resumed her normal manner. She even smiled ruefully at Alexander, who patted her on the cheek. Nina took her hand.

'Come with me,' she said. 'Three new frocks await inspection.'

'Three?'

'Three. You remember that woman in Towcester I went to in the spring? Well, it seems her daughter . . .'

The two girls disappeared into the bedroom. The men could hear them opening cupboards and drawers, chattering, giggling, Elizabeth imitating someone, Nina scolding. In silence Theodore brought out a small pipe and started to fill it.

'That was good work,' said Alexander.

'Nothing at all. What is she exactly?'

'She's supposed to be hopelessly in love with me. I can't think why; I've never laid a finger on her.'

'Really? Pretty enough, I should have thought.'

'Yes, but too confoundedly difficult. Imagine what she'd be like with a bit of power over you.'

'M'm.'

Theodore lit his pipe and sat back in his chair. He was staring at the ceiling now, but earlier his eyes had hardly left Alexander for several minutes on end, as Alexander was naturally well aware. After another half-minute Theodore said lightly,

'What really happened out there?'

'What? Oh, just what I said. Do you want details?'

'No, no. Tell the truth – you fucked her, didn't you?'

'No. It looks as though I could have done, but I didn't, like a fool.'

'Very much like a fool. How old are you, Alexander? Nineteen?'

'Twenty-one.'

'Are you? Of course I'm twenty-eight, with that much more

37

experience. But I should have thought anybody not a female or a child could have seen that Mrs Korotchenko was ripe for the plucking.'

'Well, I couldn't, and if that makes me a female or a child that's most unfortunate for me, but I can always call the servants and have you thrown out, but now I look at you I think I could probably manage it myself. Without much effort, in fact.'

'Hold on!' said Theodore as Alexander rose to his feet. 'I was just trying to irritate you into admitting it. Come on, you old reprobate, you fucked her, didn't you? You can tell me. I swear I won't pass it on to anybody.'

'For the very last time, I didn't. And incidentally swear by what?'

'That's a very interesting point, but we haven't time to go into it now. Do you swear you didn't?'

'Well of course I do, by anything you care to name. What's this all about?'

'Your only bad line so far, but we'll let that go too. Do you swear by the honour of your country and of your regiment and of your family?'

'Why not? I so swear.'

Theodore looked hard and very seriously at Alexander. 'My profound congratulations and my heartfelt apologies. I'm truly sorry I had to do this to you.'

'You're mad.'

'You can relax now. Not more than three minutes after you and Mrs Korotchenko had left the drawing-room, your mother asked your sister to fetch her sewing-basket from the room on the other side of the hall. I offered to go myself.'

'Oh dear.'

'I found the basket easily enough, but before I returned to the drawing-room with it I pulled back the curtain and looked out. Pure curiosity.'

'Is that what it's called?'

'I didn't expect to see anything in particular, but I saw ... Well, you know what I saw.'

'Yes.'

'How did you come to be so insanely reckless? The two of you would have been out of sight if you'd walked another twenty or thirty metres. Couldn't you have waited?'

'I could, but she couldn't, evidently. She literally grabbed me and I was quite unprepared. I had no time to think at all.'

'I see. Why do you think she put on that annoyed look afterwards?'

'Well, she told me she was going to do it so that her husband would think I'd made advances to her which she took amiss, but I wonder now if the explanation I invented a moment ago might not be nearer the mark only she was doing it on purpose. In other words, she intended to give the impression that she'd had expectations of me which I'd failed to fulfil. Which in turn would mean she must hate her husband very much. Well, we already have reason to suspect she may not be crazy about him. What are your congratulations for?'

'For the ingenuity with which you disarmed the suspicions of two very inquisitive girls, and the fortitude that made you able to withstand my violent assault on your pride.'

'Thank you. The second was comparatively easy. I wasn't going to throw away at that stage what it had taken me so much trouble to establish. It was just bad luck for me that you looked out of that window when you did.'

'Don't worry, the secret's safe with me.' Theodore relit his pipe. 'Did you in fact arrange to see her again?'

'There's not much point in denying it at this stage.'

'You know, you've surprised me. Not by your sexual adventure but by your conduct since.'

'I've surprised myself rather. But then I have a strain of low cunning which tends to come to my rescue when I really need it.'

Again Theodore stared at his companion. Then he said, 'You're an interesting fellow, Alexander. I'd like to have a real talk with you some time. The trouble is I have nowhere to invite you. My lodgings are vile, there are no restaurants nearer than Oxford . . .'

'I know, I have the same trouble with girls, don't you?'

'Well, it looks as though I might start to, if things go my way.'

'She likes you – I know that look of hers.'

'And you approve?'

'Of course I approve! My little sister and my old friend Theodore – a new friend who seems like an old friend. I've thought of something. Would it appeal to you to come out and dine at my mess one night?' When he saw Theodore hesitate, he went on, 'I can have you fetched and taken back, if that's a problem.'

'Oh ... thank you, for the invitation too – I didn't know civilians were admitted to guest-nights.'

'The regimental mess is pretty well sacrosanct except for an occasional dignitary from London or Moscow, but in the week we eat at the squadron, just half a dozen of us. It might amuse you, the food's not bad and afterwards we can slip away on our own; that's more or less expected. Now next week's orders aren't out yet – would tomorrow night be too soon? I'll get in touch with you at the Commission about the details.'

Soon afterwards Nina and Elizabeth, the latter now in possession of all the relevant facts about the new frocks, returned to the room. Both turned looks of unfocussed but keen suspicion on the two young men. Nina said that they should all return to the drawing-room.

'I should be going altogether,' said Theodore.

'Not before you've played us something,' said Nina.

'Dear God, I thought I'd got out of that.'

'People don't get out of things with Nina,' said her brother.

'It's a family characteristic,' said Elizabeth.

When, at the dinner-table an hour earlier, Mrs Tabidze had called for the brandy-decanter, Alexander had felt very much inclined to pour the whole of its contents over her, with the option of going on to set light to them. It was not that he resented her calling him a young whippersnapper (she was far too old and ugly for him to care one way or the other what she thought of him); the feeling aroused in him, though violent, was much more impersonal than that. The moment came back to him now because the last piece of dialogue had induced the same hostility, even though he had contributed to it himself. What was it that he found so distasteful? Something to do with style, something to do with intention, something to do with being taken outside life and into ... a funny story? A parlour game? But why should that matter? For almost the first time in his life, Alexander sincerely wished he knew more and could think better.

In the drawing-room the card-game had just ended, with Korotchenko and Mrs Tabidze dividing the spoils with winnings of about £10,000 each, enough for a bottle of good-quality spirits and a packet of five cigarettes. Much to Alexander's surprise, his mother and Mrs Korotchenko were in animated conversation; perhaps his extempore patter about shyness in a company of any size had happened to come somewhere near the mark. Nina clapped her hands for silence and announced that Mr Markov would play and sing some of the English songs he had come across in the course of his researches for the Cultural Commission.

Theodore duly offered half a dozen pieces, all short, under two minutes. He showed himself to be possessed of enough, or more than enough, skill and imagination for what he saw as the deceptively simple keyboard writing and also of a pleasant light baritone voice. Quite by chance, the piano had stayed free of damp and so was not grotesquely out of tune. Of those who noticed that it was not in tune (both Korotchenkos being tone-deaf), some, like Nina, thought this was pleasingly congruent with the outlandish material, while others, like Elizabeth, supposed Theodore to be somehow distorting the pitch on purpose for greater effect. All the songs were well received but by common consent the last of the set was best. Although the structure again was simple, two related strains each repeated once, Theodore brought out a blend of vivacity and melancholy in the music that proved, to this Russian audience, recognizable even if unfamiliarly expressed. Cries of approval as well as handclaps followed the final triumphant chord.

'Most enjoyable,' said Mrs Tabidze. 'But could you explain it a little, Mr Markov? I'm afraid my English is far from what it should be. What does it mean, *locked 'em in the Old Kent Road*?'

'Actually it's *knocked 'em*, ma'am, struck them, hit them. The words are obscure, they're largely slang, or more accurately argot. My theory ... but you don't want me to expound my theory at this time of night.'

His hearers assured him that they did.

'The composer and lyric-writer was a certain Albert Chevalier. Now the French community in London was never very large; it was mostly confined to the catering trade. But it seems to have been cohesive, never assimilated by the traditionally xenophobic English. I take this song to be one of defiance, an assertion of French pride and independence in the heart of a foreign land, in the old, historic, quintessentially English road to Kent.'

'But it's an English song,' said Elizabeth.

'It became one. The English always imported or naturalized large parts of their culture, right to the end. During the Patriotic War of 1941–5, when they and the Hitlerites showed great hostility towards one another for a time, a hostility that as you know erupted more than once into armed actions like the bombing of the London docks and the Dieppe raid, the English translated and took over a German song called "Lilli Helene". Musically speaking, too, the song I've just performed could never have been an English product. Not ... not sufficiently direct.'

'Fascinating,' said Nina.

When the guests left, Alexander looked in vain for some signal from Mrs Korotchenko to confirm their arrangement for the following Tuesday, but he already knew enough about women not to be cast down by this omission of hers. He was tired and heavy-eyed and yet had no desire for sleep, or so he told himself. Should he have a last glass of wine? Unable to think of any arguments for or against the proposition he nevertheless returned to the drawing-room, which had the desolate look of all newly-emptied human resorts. While he was gazing inattentively at an opened bottle his father came in.

'Ah, there you are, my boy. Are you away early tomorrow?'

'Not especially, papa.'

'Commissioner Mets is coming to breakfast to discuss general policy. I thought you might care to turn up as well.'

'With anything particular in mind?'

'The Commissioner might be interested to hear your views; you know some of the problems better than I do. It was just a thought.'

'A very nice one. I'd love to come.'

'Excellent. Eight o'clock. Try not to be late. Oh – Alexander . . .'

'Yes, papa?'

'You . . . you and Mrs Korotchenko and your turn in the gardens. I take it you, you DID, eh?'

Alexander had had fully ten seconds' notice of a question on these lines, long enough to think things out as follows. There could be no point in shocking his father, who all the same appeared so far from shocked by the idea that it would be strange if he were to be much shocked by the fact, though on previous form, that of a sort of liberal puritan, some shock, unthickened with reproaches, was to be expected. That left the scales about level; what tipped them was the thought that it was too late at night for another elaborate exercise in dissimulation, especially for such trivial stakes. And there might well come a time when paternal possession of the fact in mind would be vital. Promptly enough to stand to win a couple of extra marks for supposed fearless honesty, he said, 'Yes, I did.'

Petrovsky gave a great laugh. 'I knew it! You young devil!'

'How did you know, papa?'

'Because I know you, that's enough. Fancy that! I tried to get old Tabidze to take a bet, but he wouldn't.'

'What did you say to him? How did you put it?'

'Put it? I just said to him, out of the Korotchenko fellow's hearing of course, I said, "What do you wager there isn't a spot of kissing going on outside at this moment?", and as I say he wouldn't take me. He said, "I wouldn't stake ten pounds against that young spark doing anything in that line you care to name." You see, he knows you too.'

Alexander took his turn to laugh and his father soon joined in. The pair of them went on for some time, like people in a play.

They did a lot of laughing in that house.

4

Shortly before eight o'clock the next morning a large blue motor-car was making its way through the surrounding park by means of a roughly-made road lined with strong young elms. At the sound of its approach the children from the lesser houses, those occupied by the lesser functionaries of the district administration, came running out to watch it pass, as their great-great-grandparents would have done at their age. Its passenger could not but be a person of unusual celebrity.

Commissioner Michael Mets was such a one, though he would have been rather embarrassed at the description. He was forty years old, strong and active, with a sharp nose and alert brown eyes behind spectacles. A brown imitation-leather dispatch-case lay beside him. Actually there was a second passenger: on the folding seat diagonally across from Mets there sat a young soldier in uniform with a pistol at his hip. The weapon was not loaded; the original necessary edict laying down armed escort for all notables had been retained in a period when that escort's most strenuous duty was likely to be the carrying of parcels.

The car swept round a curve to the left, entered the court below the west front of the Controller's residence and pulled up by the steps. Mets got out and ran his eye over the façade, adjusting his short belted jacket and student's cap. There was an inscription below the roof, somewhat defaced but still legible. 'Hora e sempre,' he said aloud. Presumably archaic Italian, meaning 'now and always'. Unless there was an accent on the second word, which would make it 'now is always'. He took a few steps backwards to see better, but was unable to settle the question. Anyway, he ought to have known, just as he ought to have known whether the stylized lions on the roof were of stone or of some synthetic material.

The chauffeur had parked the Rolls out of the sunshine, which was already quite hot, and with the escort at his side came to join Mets outside the front door. The white-haired, brown-liveried butler let them in, showed Mets into the dining-room and led the other two off towards the kitchens. A few minutes later Alexander came hurrying down the stair-case, singing quietly to himself and thinking of Mrs Korotchenko. He thought of her all over again when he noticed the fawn wrap-like object in the hand of a passing housemaid.

'Where did you find that?'

'One of the English gardeners brought it, your honour,' said the girl, startled. 'He said he found it on the lawn.'

'And where are you taking it?'

'To your honoured mother, sir. She may know who it belongs to.'

'Give it to me.'

He half-snatched it, ran back the way he had come and stuffed the offending garment into a drawer among his ties and stocks. God in heaven, he said to himself as he made the out-ward journey a second time, how had the bitch forgotten it, at the time and later? How had she not seen it lying there? – there had been more than enough moonlight. Why had no one else noticed its absence? – women kept a keen eye on one another's clothing. Had she left it on purpose? Why? Such speculations, and where they led, flawed the perfect composure with which he had hoped to meet Commissioner Mets; but in these matters he was his own severest critic by far.

'*How do you do,*' said Mets when they were introduced.

'*It's an honour to make your acquaintance, sir.*' Alexander fired that off readily enough and noted with satisfaction the tiny signs of approval and mild surprise behind the other's glasses.

'This lad knows more about the English than almost anybody outside the Commission,' said Petrovsky.

'And more than a great many people inside it too, I warrant, including myself with my pitiful year of service in the field,'

46

said Mets pleasantly, and went on without pausing, 'This is a confidential meeting, which is why I asked your father if we could have it here rather than in the middle of either of our respective offices. I have some things to say I wouldn't like my staff to hear.'

'I understand, sir.'

'How much do you know about the work we're doing?'

'Only a rough general picture.' By now Alexander had helped himself to liver, fried eggs, and ale and had settled himself at table on his father's left opposite Mets.

'In that case it will probably be quicker if I assume your total ignorance and start from that point, but before I proceed I must do some justice to this appetizing fare. Excuse me.'

And he fell to. Petrovsky looked through a document, no doubt brought by Mets, as he ate; Alexander glanced at a newspaper. Energy production had increased. An under-minister of communications had resigned for reasons of ill-health. The President of Cuba was visiting the President of South Africa. All was quiet throughout the world: nobody was being invaded, massacred, driven into the jungle, harassed by guerillas or terrorists, deported, refused permission to travel or so much as shot at, except in cases involving criminals, and since the introduction of advanced techniques of detection and punishment the number of such persons had been falling daily. Boredom and gloom swept through him like a wave of heat. What was he doing, sitting in this preposterously comfortable and richly-furnished room alongside these two self-important boobies with the supposed object of offering advice on a subject about which he knew little and cared less? He munched his food savagely, as if he were destroying an enemy.

Mets's masticatory procedure was more practical: he cleared his plate with a speed and efficiency that might have been guessed to be characteristic of the way he handled his work. When he had finished he answered a couple of queries of Petrovsky's about the document and then said with his precise articulation,

'Shall I hold forth? I'm sorry, Controller – I'm afraid you're going to be desperately bored by some of this. I'll keep it as short as I can.'

'I find these days I can't hear things too often, Commissioner.'

'So you say. Now the New Cultural Policy for England was first framed nine years ago, though it really started both earlier and later than that. As far back as the first decade of the century it was beginning to be felt, in Moscow and in London, that the denationing programme, though instituted for good and sufficient reasons at the time, was becoming unnecessary and even retrogressive. However, the first practical step, in the shape of the regional reafforestation schemes, was some time coming, and NCPE similarly dragged its feet – well, renationing can't be a quick job. The forestry and rural engineering people, I'm told, have their eyes on 2100 for the complete restoration of the English countryside, and between ourselves I take that as about the target date for English culture too, though officially it's 2060.

'There are of course a number of intermediate objectives, the nearest of which is to be quite soon, on 15 September to be exact, our Festival, which I see you've heard of, Ensign Petrovsky. Perhaps I should explain that it's "our" Festival in two senses. It's a national affair, planned by us of NCPE, but we've decentralized it into the districts, each of which will run its own programme with local material. We in Northampton don't see ours as a grand affair, our resources are limited, but it is a significant event and it will attract notice and interest; above all, we expect to learn from it. The state of our preparedness is ... varied. I should explain that we have six main sections: visual arts, theatre, music, literature, religion, and architecture and interior decoration, the last two are grouped together. Visual arts is really in quite a satisfactory state: we've collected nearly eight hundred paintings and other objects, many of them certified as meritorious, we have framing and mounting facilities and above all we'll be ready in time. Of music there's a positive superfluity: a surprising number of tapes came to light and quite a few of the old discs – yes, after all this time. We even got hold of some sheet music. We'll have to use our own performers, naturally, but that won't matter with the instrumental numbers, the *pop-group-scene* was an international phenomenon anyway, and with at least some of the other songs we have some noteworthy reconstitutions, the work of an outstanding young man in the section called Theodore Markov.'

'As it happens he dined here last night,' said Petrovsky.

'*Well I'm buggered!* What did you make of him?'

'I was very favourably impressed. His erudition is remarkable, and if his colleagues can muster half his interpretative skill you should be happy.'

'I'm delighted to hear you say so,' said Mets as soon as he was satisfied that the last remark was free of irony. 'To resume, opera is beyond our resources here for the moment, but no matter. Visual arts and music, then – adequate. Architecture-and-interior-decoration – impossible. We've nowhere near the money or the personnel. The trouble is, our terms were drawn up by people too far from the reality. Bureaucrats, in fact. The section has done its best to no avail. I'm formally asking permission, Controller, to close it down forthwith, second the appropriate staff to other sections and send the others home.'

'But you're responsible to Moscow, Commissioner, not to the District.'

'We come under you for disciplinary matters, sir. Such a closure could be construed as damaging to the prestige of the units of supervision.'

'Yes, I suppose it could, in theory. And even ten years ago, when I first came here, I should have had to take it into account, but not any more. It doesn't matter now what any of the English think of us.'

'Then may I take it that permission is granted?'

'Yes, yes.'

'Thank you ... Well – two of the remaining three sections, theatre and literature, are making steady progress. I'm just a little worried that steady may not be quite fast enough in the time remaining, since we started so far back. Our expectations weren't high, with the subjects not taught in the schools and so on, but after all they have got thirty-one per cent literacy, and you would have thought that something would have been handed down over the years. Our instructors have had to explain every other word to them. Now that wouldn't be surprising with a play over four centuries old, but with the ...' – for a moment Commissioner Mets turned without effect through his papers – '... the 1950s piece and the comparatively recent literature it seems rather strange. Still, I've every faith in our people, the English have brains and want to learn and we'll do respectably, perhaps much better – good grounds for hope.

'With religion they are few and frail, Controller. When we first appealed for volunteers to put at our disposal whatever documents or other evidence they might possess relating to the liturgy, how it was actually produced and performed, not merely what was said and sung, well, there was a small response to that appeal. I expected it to grow. I was wrong. It died away, to nothing and nobody, literally nobody. And first I should like to know why.'

Silence fell just in time to prevent Alexander from peremptorily asking to be excused and stalking out of the room. As it was he lowered his brows and put a thoughtful, troubled expression on his face. After a few seconds of this he said in a low voice,

'May I make a suggestion, papa?'

'Please do.'

'You must have thought of it yourself, Commissioner, and perhaps rejected it – pre-war influence.' Illogically, but usefully and universally, a pre-war was understood to be a member of the native population born early enough to have acquired a clear and reasonably full impression of what English life had been like in the years before the Pacification.

'Exactly the case,' said Mets with a comfortable smile. 'The youngest pre-wars are now in their early sixties and the group as a whole is of course not large. Are you suggesting that they have enough influence to deter Christians or potential Christians or ex-Christians or simply the inquisitive from responding to our appeals?'

'They certainly have influence on that scale. It should be easy enough to confirm the presumption that it's at work in this case. You see, I don't agree with my father that it doesn't matter what any of them think of us.'

'But for something that happened fifty years ago . . .'

'And for something else that's been going on for fifty years. I was brought up here, Commissioner. These old people would do anything to *put a spoke in our wheel* – frustrate our wishes, papa.'

'Why then,' pursued Mets, 'if this theory of mere obstruction is correct, is there no similar policy of mass avoidance of the theatre and literature projects?'

'I don't know, sir. Perhaps they feel they must concentrate their efforts.'

'Or perhaps . . .' Petrovsky's eyes, a deeper blue than his son's, sometimes, as just then, had a similar trick of turning incurious. 'Perhaps, in a question of religion, religion is involved. Perhaps they're saying to us, "Do as you please with our literature, our theatre, our music – we'll even help you; why not? But our Protestant faith is different; if you won't leave that alone, don't expect us to attend the party." They're a proud people, the English, and they fought and died for their beliefs.'

'Centuries ago,' said Mets quickly, 'when everyone else was doing it too.' Softening his tone, he went on, 'And surely the effect of those fifty years . . .'

'That's not very long in the history of a religion, Commissioner. Even today there are Baptists in Russia.'

'Some, but for different reasons they're in a condition similar to that reached by adherents of the English Church by the time of its suppression. They, the English Christians, were worked on by enlightened forces both without and within. They were in decline both in numbers and in superstitious belief – most of them held scientific or quasi-scientific ideas, even among the clergy, not least the higher clergy, and the remainder were too demoralized not to tolerate them. The suppression merely hastened the inevitable. It doesn't seem to me likely that today – '

Petrovsky had been listening to this rehearsal of the familiar with well-suppressed irritation. Now he broke in, 'My dear fellow, aren't we in danger of believing our own propaganda?'

'Possibly,' said Mets. He was used to such expressions of what he would have called parlour liberalism, not by any means only from the Controller, but had acquired less skill than the latter in dissembling his feelings. He turned almost violently to Alexander. 'What's your view, ensign?'

That officer was in the irksome position of wanting not to agree with his father while disagreeing with Mets and yet not appearing ignorant or indifferent. 'The religious feeling is there,' he improvised feebly, 'but its strength would be hard to estimate. We have nothing else to go by.'

'Thank you,' said Mets. 'Let's return to matters of fact. Here is what I take to be an important one. None of the former clergymen to whom I appealed for assistance to the religion section has answered my letters. Not one. That must be concerted action, for whatever purpose. The second permission I require today is to interview some of them.'

'And apply pressure,' said Petrovsky.

'If necessary. Better I than another.'

'Better you than the other we're both thinking of, certainly. And his deputy, from what I've seen of him. But I have a suggestion, Commissioner. A visit from you, even more a summons from you, would be official and committing. A visit from an individual quite unconnected with you would obviously be neither and might be most valuable.'

'Perhaps.' Mets tried hard to think of another reason for demurring than that he disliked the prospect of yielding up any of his power at all, even temporarily. 'What you suggest is, er, is irregular.'

'Precisely. That's its advantage.'

'Such a visit would have to be soon. Our time's running out.'

'How soon could you do it, Alexander?'

'I'm sorry, I was miles away, trying to think of something a clergyman said to me the other week.' The thoughts, set off by the allusion to Korotchenko a moment before, had in fact been about Mrs Korotchenko, and of an intensity such as to induce their thinker to pull his chair in further under the table. Part of the rest of the morning was thereby predetermined.

'I thought it might be useful if you visited one of these old boys, or more than one, investigated attitudes and reported back to Commissioner Mets.'

'I'd be delighted. As to how soon, today possibly, tomorrow for certain.'

'Splendid, I'm most grateful,' said Mets, all warmth and condescension now that resistance had become vain. He took a list of names and addresses from his dispatch-case and Alexander noted down one he said he had sufficient acquaintance with. Mets expressed gratitude for his contribution.

'May I make a final contribution?' he asked.'Or rather two? The first is just a question. Wouldn't it have been more natural to inaugurate the New Policy with a festival of sport instead of visual arts and the rest? It was far more popular.'

'And infinitely more bloody,' said Mets, gravely shaking his head. 'Faction battles at soccer and race riots at cricket.'

'All the pre-wars I know say that all that is much exaggerated.'

'Well, they would, of course. Anyway, I have no say in the matter.'

'My other contribution is another question. Don't you think your difficulties might be lessened if you left it to the English to organize matters instead of doing so for them? At present they must feel it's our project, not theirs.'

'I sympathize with that, and it is our eventual aim, but at the moment we can't leave it to the English to do anything. We must learn to walk before we can run.'

'How well I know that expression.' Alexander glanced at his father, who to a knowing eye looked faintly uncomfortable. 'Can they not at least be given a plausible illusion that they're in charge? It would make it easier for those who are looking for an excuse to participate.'

'A very fair point,' said Mets, writing on a pad, 'and one I'll bear in mind in the general context. Renewed thanks. *Have a good day.*'

'*I hope we meet again soon, sir. – Cheerio, dad.*'

There was politeness in Mets's rising to his feet and a morsel of real cordiality in his handshake and parting smile. Alexander listened to the silence behind him as he walked down the room and out into the west hall; his father, he knew, was waiting to ask Mets if he didn't think that that was a fine lad. The old idiot! – would he never hit back when baited? But there were more important concerns than fathers ahead, and Alexander forgot his almost before he had shut the dining-room doors after him.

5

A quarter of an hour later Alexander and Polly the mare were moving at a gentle canter past the spot where he had persecuted the sheep, an incident that failed to recur to his mind. He was in a kind of hurry, but his goal would stay till he came; it was a beautiful morning and there was much to look at in the scene about him, if he could only concentrate his attention on it. This proved difficult; somehow it always did; the run of the hoof-beats, the steady leaping motion of the horse under him, the unchanging sunshine were perhaps, in this case, what caused his eyes to lose their focus, so that he gazed rather than looked. Another and habitual distraction stemmed from ignorance. He could particularize no further from grass, flower, bush, tree, tree-stump than he could from sun or sky. Only the grosser objects on view penetrated to him: a stretch of canal with a towing-horse just coming into view round a bend, a great broad road ultimately linking London and Birmingham with lesser roads passing above and below it and elaborate access systems. His eye was caught by a metal sign, flaked and corroded far past legibility but still bearing a trace of blue paint. Horse and mule traffic passed to and fro on the main roadway and, in the distance, the sunlight winked off the metalwork of a motor-car.

Alexander's path took him now between fields of standing grain, wheat on one side, as he could have recognized if he had looked, barley on the other, as he could not. After that came row after row of the green tops of some root vegetable which a man was furthering with a device on the end of a pole, and after that came a house, but for its dilapidated tile roof a nearly cubical object of concrete and two sorts of brick irregularly distributed, as though to insist on its unlikeness to all others whatever. If such had really been the architect's purpose it was at once undone by the next house, and the next, and the next. Soon Alexander was walking his horse between a double row of identical unique dwellings; to them he did pay attention, and of a friendly sort. They showed him the end of his journey was near and, more than that, he knew them to be among the very last houses in the district built before the Pacification. They always put him in mind of that legendary era, and so he looked at them with respect, even a little awe. There was no one to offer him the opinion that they were offensive to the eye and the mind.

The main street of the village was quite different. It had in it many of the things appropriate to such a street in the middle of England: a post office, a grocer's shop, a greengrocer's, a butcher's, a baker's, a barber's, a saddler's, a newsagent's (though the news he supplied came in only two forms, Russian and an English translation), a bank, an eating-house, a small cinema, houses by the dozen. But there was no garage, bookshop, pub or church, nor any building that had formerly served those functions, for the most visible difference between centre and outskirts was that nothing here had stood for more than fifty years. The whole of the original street had been destroyed, some said by fire, in a single day and night, during which period an unknown number of people died, some said Russians as well as English, women as well as men. But it was impossible to say such things with any certainty, because no English survivor had ever been found, nor any English witness; the village had been a Russian military post during the Pacification and its inhabitants evacuated to neighbouring villages. Soon afterwards, in a move possibly related to the events of that day and night, the authorities had officially renamed it New Kettering, but this had never caught on among the English and today even the Russians called the place Henshaw.

The street itself, the road-surface, was remarkably smooth along the middle, owing in great measure to the careful maintenance of the rammed rubble in the various pot-holes. Sickly trees, their lower parts protected by wire guards, stood at twenty-metre intervals along the edges of the gravel footpaths. The buildings, two- or one-storeyed, mostly wooden (there had been plenty of timber then) were the product of English labour under Russian supervision and recalled the domestic designs of neither country. They were narrow from front to back, with few and small windows. That school of architects and furnishers which had ruled, a century earlier, that an object made with nothing but utility in mind must be beautiful might have been strongly impressed by the results of such single-minded rejection of the superfluous. Dark greys and browns predominated, but here and there a shop-sign or a painted doorframe showed a touch of brighter colour.

The people on view at this hour, nearly all of them women, were clothed after much the same style. They had turned out in some numbers, many of them to join the queues outside the greengrocer's (soft fruit on sale) and the butcher's (fresh-meat day). They smiled, greeted one another, gossiped, even laughed. The weather was going to be fine again, husbands and sons would be pleased with their suppers and things in general were no worse than last year, indeed there had been positive improvements, of which the most momentous was the recent introduction of a third fresh-meat day in the week. Some had heard their elders speak of strikes, often adding that whatever else the Russians had done they had certainly put a stop to all that, and the more thoughtful, after an honest attempt to imagine themselves living through a strike, would feel a glow of comfort. Now, as Alexander passed, quite a few of the villagers looked up at him. A middle-aged man touched his hat, although the ordinance requiring this had long lapsed. The glance of all was without fear, without respect, without hostility, all but a pair of obvious pre-wars, husband and wife, who showed a faint, faded contempt as they turned their backs.

None of this was Alexander's concern; he turned his horse and trotted up a short side-street. At its end there was a house slightly larger than the others and standing back from them. He saw easily that it antedated the Pacification; in fact it belonged to a much earlier period, with red-brick walls, a strip of lawn in front, and from gate to front door a short walk between brick pillars and covered by trellis from which white and blue flowers hung down. More flowers, of various colours, grew in beds at the edges of the lawn and under the windows of the house. To the right of the front door a wooden signboard mentioned *J. J. Wright MD* and surgery hours below the equivalent in Cyrillic characters. Alexander gave the mare's reins to a boy of twelve who had followed them from the high street in hopes of a small reward, and plied the brass knocker energetically.

Quite soon a girl of about twenty appeared. She had fair hair bleached in streaks by the sun, bright brown eyes with greenish flecks in them and a pink-and-white complexion. True to Nina's guess, this girl also had a fine pair of breasts. She looked very healthy and wore a blue skirt and white shirt.

'*Darling, how marvellous to see you!*' she said. '*I wasn't expecting –* '

That was as much as she said, because by that point Alexander had hastened across the threshold into the tiny hall, seized her in his arms and begun to kiss her with great intentness, nor did he leave it at that. The series of muffled sounds she made indicated first mild surprise, then more acute surprise, then pleasure and excitement. After a while he released her in part.

'*I love you,*' he said.

'*And I love you.*'

Undressing as they went, they hurried up the wooden staircase and into a low-ceilinged bedroom at the back of the house from which fields of cereal and a large plantation of conifers were to be seen, if one should look. They were out of view from the bed on which, very soon indeed, Alexander closed with the fair-haired girl. Their activities there went on for some time, longer, to go by her responses when they ceased, than she had expected or was used to. At last she said tenderly,

'You went at me as if you were trying to split me in two. What's happened?'

'Nothing, I just thought of you and then I couldn't get you out of my mind. If you hadn't been here I don't know what I'd have done.'

58

'Darling Alexander.'

'My dearest, most beautiful Kitty.'

Russian was very much the preferred medium of exchange between the two speech-communities; it was taught in all schools, and there was no incentive for the units of supervision, except for some of those under Director Vanag, to learn the language of the subject nation. The arrangement suited Alexander perfectly: he had gone to some pains to be able to speak English without accent, or to seem to do so to Russian ears, and he had carefully chosen and mastered some relatively elaborate phrases of salutation and of colloquialism, together with a few useful simplicities like the ones he had spoken and heard just now on arrival, but his vocabulary had remained small and his ability to carry on a conversation smaller still.

For the moment, at least, this was a supportable weakness. Humming to himself, he set about stroking some of the portions of Kitty that he had not bothered with before. He reflected foggily that one great advantage of pretty girls was that they remained positively, actively attractive at all times and at every stage of the game, then, more foggily still, how altogether serviceable it was that what girls, whether pretty or not, most liked receiving exactly matched, coincided with, was no more nor less than what men were most inclined to offer. Kitty gave little groans of contentment. Sweet smells and bird-song drifted in at the open window, where a bumble-bee entered and, after a quick half-circuit of the room, went out again.

'How lucky we are,' said Kitty. 'We might never have met each other. Have you ever thought of that?'

'No,' said Alexander truthfully. He went on, 'And I don't believe it, darling. I think we were intended to meet.'

'You mean by God, or Fate, or . . .?'

'One of those. Something brought me to England and made you cross my path. You remember how we first met?'

'Yes, you picked me up in the street in Northampton.'

'You know, you're very sweet, Kitty love, but you can be frightfully crude sometimes. I did not pick you up. I've told you a hundred times how it was. An important dispatch had to be taken to the Military Secretariat. At the last moment the officer who was supposed to take it went sick and I was sent instead. I was just coming out of the building after delivering it when for no reason at all I looked over my shoulder and saw you crossing the road away from me, and straight away I just knew we were made for each other, so I ran after you and nearly got knocked down by a waggon and said something to you – I can't remember what it was . . .'

'I can. It was, "Would you like to go for a walk?"'

'I dare say it was, that's quite unimportant. And then you told me it was the first time you'd been in that part of Northampton for over a year.'

'Did I?'

'That was later, of course. Well, surely you can see it? I mean, you must agree that what we feel about each other is quite exceptional?'

'Oh yes, I can't imagine many people having such a lovely time as we do or being as happy. And nobody anywhere being happier.'

'Well then, darling Kitty, it would obviously be absurd if something like that could have happened and then never did after all.'

'I can understand it would be a pity, my love. Well yes, I supposed it might be rather absurd too, in a way.'

He pushed the thick fair hair back from her brow and took her face between his hands. 'Let me tell you how I feel – how you make me feel. When I'm with you, even when I'm not but I think of you so hard it's almost as if I can see you, then I feel the blood going through my body with a new life, so that I tingle from head to foot, and I'm so much aware of everything round me that it's as if I'd been half blind and deaf and sort of numb before, and I seem to be within just one second or one metre of understanding the secret of the universe. Everything's incredibly grand and yet completely simple. And then,' he added, determined to go carefully with the next part, 'I wish you could have been . . . kidnapped and taken prisoner by Vanag's men so that I could come riding in to rescue you.'

Rather disappointingly, she seemed not to notice his change of tack there. 'I wish I knew half as much about how I feel as you do about how you feel. I only know I feel wonderful in every way and it's all because of you.'

This was so near to what he would have said himself in her situation that he looked her closely in the eye, but found he was unable to go on doing so; his gaze shifted to her mouth and the thought, all thought, began to slip deliciously away. There was not a great deal about what followed that was the product of intention. The sound of the shutting front door recalled them to the bed where they lay and to each other.

'Daddy,' said Kitty. 'He sometimes comes in for a few minutes in the middle of his rounds.'

'Good, I want a word with him.'

Dr Joseph Wright, a small, pale, bespectacled man with brown hair turning grey, was some years too young to be a true pre-war but, having had both parents killed during the Pacification, he resembled one in many ways. So for his younger daughter to be openly and regularly screwed by a Russian officer, one whom moreover he disliked and despised personally, made him angry. This condition he kept to himself as far as possible; the girl seemed to have no objection to the state of things, and the associated benefits, in the shape of the occasional bottle of cognac or few kilos of fuel, were certainly welcome enough, but it was (or could any day turn out to be) much more important to stay in the general good books of one of the *Shits* – a term in common use even among those many who had no very serious objection to the presence of their masters. Conversely, the meanest understanding could foresee the probable results of trying to cross a Russian officer, especially this Russian officer. And, above all, there was nothing to be done about it, a verdict which sooner or later closed every such inquiry.

When he had politely finished dressing upstairs, Alexander came down and entered the sitting-room at the back of the house. This was cool and rather dark, with trailing plants in baskets and on pedestals and brackets, and more of the same and of other types in a small conservatory at one end. Here a tap dripped slowly into water in a pot or bowl.

'*Good morning, doctor – please don't get up.*' He was unaware of the Englishman's dislike, but always found himself behaving with some circumspection in front of him.

The doctor answered civilly in Russian, which was difficult for him – the civility, not the Russian: nothing annoyed him more than this facile mode of linguistic condescension. Because of this he missed the next remark offered, but pricked up his ears at the one after, a question, banal enough, to be sure, about his practice. As he made some equally tedious reply to this unprecedented show of interest, it occurred to him that the young bastard must want something. What it was remained unuttered till Kitty had come in with a tray of tea and shortbread. Soon after that an evening in March of that year was mentioned. Dr Wright remembered it well as one of an irregular series stretching back over about a year, curious soirées in this house held at the irresistible wish of Ensign Petrovsky, who also provided all the drink, most of the food and two or three of the guests, uncouth brother-officers of his. Wright's part, as well as that of stomaching the occasion, was to provide the remaining guests from among the local populace, a task that called for only modest powers of persuasion with those under about fifty, while those above that age would often surrender principle for unlimited vodka. Well, the wanted something was now discovered: the mounting of a further performance some time soon. What remained mysterious was what was in it all for this particular *Shit*, who could be very readily believed to want to seem interested in England and the English, but who surely had no real interest in these matters, or indeed in anything more external to himself than making an impression. Oh, and sex, of course.

Just when Wright was expecting a date to be suggested, Alexander puzzled him by saying, 'There was an interesting conversation about religion, about the Church of England. One of your friends mentioned a Reverend Mr Glover, I think, who lives in a nearby village.'

'Yes, in Stoke Goldington. Not far.'

'Is the gentleman in good health?'

'Well, he must be nearly eighty, but as far as I know he's well enough.'

'Do you know him, doctor?'

'I've met him occasionally,' said Wright, by now almost shaking with curiosity. 'Not for some years, though.'

'I wonder, if I asked you very charmingly, whether you'd arrange for me to visit him. I mean, get his permission for me to call.'

'His permission? You people can visit anybody you please.'

'This is a matter of some delicacy, my dear doctor. I should like him to express his willingness. If he doesn't, then there's really no point in my calling.'

Wright felt renewed puzzlement. Kitty, the teacup forgotten in her hand, had been showing absorption in this duologue much more obviously than her father. Now she said,

'Darling, what do you want to see an old clergyman for?'

Alexander had foreseen such a question from her without being any the better equipped to tackle it when it came. Alone with her he would have been loftily secretive, but he sensed that her father would somehow puncture anything like that. It seemed best to turn frank instead, though not artlessly so. 'There's somebody called Commissioner Mets,' he said.

'Ah,' said Wright, beginning to understand. 'I've heard of him.'

'Who is he?' asked Kitty.

'A bureaucrat with an unusual job. He's going to give us back our culture.'

'What's our culture?'

'English plays, English paintings, English music,' said Alexander. 'And English religion. That's where I come in. I'm to interview Mr Glover on the Commissioner's behalf, but unofficially.'

'Oh,' said Kitty, now quite lost.

'But you're a ... you're a soldier,' said Wright, not substituting a noun, merely omitting an adjective.

'I shouldn't be acting in that capacity, doctor, just as a sort of free-lance intermediary. The Commissioner seems to think I know more about the English than he does; well, he hasn't been here very long. I said I'd put in a word for him.'

'And you want me to put in a word for you.'

'Yes.'

'And if both these words are heeded, your Commissioner stands a chance of getting old Glover to lend a hand with restoring the English Church.'

'Exactly.'

'I can assure you that any – what was it? – willingness Glover might express to do something, anything you people want would be quite insincere, mere words, mere words.'

'Then tell him,' said Alexander, suddenly tiring of all this patience and simulated modesty, 'that I shall be calling on him tomorrow evening at six o'clock and that he'll make himself available if he knows what's good for him.'

This speech tickled Wright, who had long given up hope of hearing anything straightforward or tolerable from that quarter. 'By all means.'

Alexander thanked him, put on his cap and strode out of the room, followed by Kitty. Not very long afterwards the front door was again heard to shut. The doctor picked up his bag and prepared to leave in his turn.

'Shan't be long, my dear. I wish you wouldn't call that fellow "golubchik" in front of me. I mean, he is helping to hold us all down by force.'

'Sorry, daddy. There doesn't seem to be much force about these days. No need for it.'

'I suppose not. Let's just say that it might have been his grandfather who killed my parents.'

'You don't like him at all, do you?'

'In a sense I can never like any Russian, but your position is quite different; I wouldn't try to change it even if I could. Anything that helps to make life less intolerable is to be seized on. These days.'

6

Alexander's regiment, the 4th Guards, was quartered in what until shortly before the Pacification had been a large private school. This stood in an extensive walled park where several considerable bodies of water and patches of vestigial or immature woodland were to be seen. There was plenty of room for officers, men, animals, equipment and stores in the long, box-shaped main building and the various minor structures, some dating back a couple of centuries, some only a few years old, that surrounded it or lay at a distance down the classically straight drive and across the gentle slopes of grassland where the regiment's horses grazed.

A dozen of them, the property of the regimental head-quarters group, were so occupied near the lodge when Alexander rode in that morning; he recognized the Colonel's elegant grey and the heavily-built sorrel belonging to the commander of the support squadron. Further up the drive, a line of horsemen in battle order was assembled at the start of the obstacle course and being bawled at by a red-faced sergeant: 11 Troop, the command of the most ambitious and unpopular subaltern in the regiment. An echoing fusillade came from the distant red-brick shed that contained the pistol range. Alexander passed close to a section of troopers in the charge of an under-corporal taking their ease, caps off, tunics unbuttoned, chatting, skylarking, sleeping, sudden beneficiaries of one of those mysterious delays that characterize life in all armies in all ages. The under-corporal caught sight of Alexander and struggled to his feet, putting on his cap and drawing his tunic together, managing some sort of salute; Alexander returned it as smartly as one on parade and called a pleasant good morning. Been at the doctor's have we? thought the under-corporal; lucky for us and lucky for your chaps too. He was not especially inquisitive or well-informed, just a soldier on garrison duty abroad in peace-time.

At the gravel-dashed front of the 1920s villa that housed his men, the troop office and the non-security stores, Alexander inquired of his sergeant whether there was anything to report. There was not; there never was. Then, having handed the mare over to his orderly, he went on foot to the main house, informed his squadron commander of his return to duty and asked if there were any special orders. There were none; there never were any. The rest of the morning passed inspecting the men's quarters, visiting the horse-lines, completing forms for the commissary, drinking tea and gossiping with the sergeant and one of the corporals, and finally doing something that was out of the ordinary and yet routine, making the monthly check of the security stores. Accompanied by the sergeant, a burly Latvian called Ulmanis, he again went to the main house, picked up from the orderly room an authorization signed and dated by the adjutant and made his way to the reinforced door to the basement lift. Here a sergeant of Field Security and a sentry were stationed side by side. The sentry covered the arrivals with his pistol while the Security sergeant examined first Alexander's identity-card, then the authorization. At his nod, the sentry lowered his firearm, Alexander and Ulmanis turned their backs and the Security man pressed a row of numbered buttons in a sequence that was changed daily. The door slid aside. In the armoury it took the two visitors twenty minutes to establish that everything in the racks appertaining to the troop concerned, 8 Troop, was as it should have been. It was; it always was. As soon as the inspection was completed, Alexander followed standing orders by returning the authorization to its source.

At 1430 hours Sergeant Ulmanis paraded the troop and reported all present and correct to Alexander. They numbered just twenty: one officer, one sergeant, one artificer-sergeant, four corporals, four under-corporals and nine troopers, the ninth being Alexander's orderly, who was told off to remain in the office. The orders to mount, to proceed to the right and to march were successively given and obeyed. In their rough dark-grey undress uniforms and dull-yellow cross-belts 8 Troop were not a showy sight, but a trained eye would have noted the relaxed carriage of the riders and the fit condition of their mounts. Such an eye, or its owner, might also have noted the unusual composition of the small force: apart from those of the headquarters group, every riding-horse had attached to it a pack-horse, in each case a Cleveland cross-thoroughbred put back to a Welsh cob, specially trained to carry a heavy load across rough ground. Their burdens today were not quite what they would have been in action, but they were of identical weight and distribution. Breast-girths and cruppers kept the packs in place even at full gallop.

The party moved at a walk out of the main gateway, along the road and down a series of lanes for some kilometres; an unfamiliar stretch of terrain was required for the intended exercise, one not used in the same way before. Eventually Alexander, in the lead, reached a high point, raised his hand to signal a halt and passed the word for sub-section leaders. The eight NCOs dismounted and came forward.

'You see that church?'

'Yes, sir.' 'Yes, your honour.' They saw it.

'Good. Remember, anybody caught using a road goes straight on register. Sub-sections to the right extend in open order and await my signal. Double time.'

Very soon afterwards eight pairs of guardsmen were strung out twenty-five metres apart along the top of a grassy slope. Alexander, at the extreme right of the line, blew a loud blast on his whistle and they were away downhill at the gallop, the pack-horses not trailing the riding-horses but, as they had been schooled to, moving up level on the left-hand side for an improved field of view. It might have been thought that a glance at the map would have justified a couple of minutes' delay, and certainly it might have been hoped (at least by the senior officers concerned) that a glance and more than a glance would precede any such move in a real engagement, but excitable, highly-competitive young men, confident of their proficiency and eager to show it off, are not famous for looking at maps at the outset of a steeplechase. But, again, this steeplechase was still a useful activity, fostering that sine qua non for any sort of cavalryman, eye for ground, as well as the peculiar capacities required for piloting two horses at once.

The slope was gentle and became gentler, perfect for a vigorous gallop, but Alexander pulled back behind the two pairs on the right flank, Sub-Section A and Sub-Section B, recognizable by their chestnut horses as much as by their position. When a troop of this category was carrying out the present exercise, it fell to the troop officer to keep an eye on the performance of the sub-sections on this side, so far as he could, while the artificer-sergeant covered the centre and the troop sergeant the left. His real reason for staying in the rear, however, was not this. A single, unencumbered horse and a rider of his own inadequate abilities and excellent sense of direction were bound to beat any pair to the objective, a victory that even he (as some might put it) would find hollow. So, denied what he would have really liked, a fair or less unfair overall race, he prepared as always to devise a series of small races in which he would try, successfully for the most part, to beat a selected pair to some minor landmark a couple of hundred metres ahead, then hang back again to handicap himself for the next round with a different pair. It was hard to distinguish this pattern of behaviour from that of a conscientious officer watching his men closely but without interference or fuss; none of Alexander's men had ever managed to. In the same sort of way, his simple love of playing soldiers made him take those men out of camp whenever possible and meant that he was good at devising tests of a skill, initiative and endurance – games, in fact. As a result, 8 Troop's physical fitness, state of training and general morale were unsurpassed in the regiment, even by the showpiece 1 Troop; it would be strange if they had not valued their officer for those benefits. The army, with all its outlets for childish interests, its elevation of them into rules of behaviour, had been an excellent choice of career for Alexander Petrovsky.

The ground became level, then rose to a crest. The whole

troop was spread out on the further slope in brilliant sunshine, making towards a long plantation of poplars, the sub-sections on the left keeping a straight path with their pack-horses already dropping back into line behind the ridden horses for the passage through the wood, those on the right swinging out to round its corner. From the crest to that corner it was something over three hundred metres. Alexander pushed his blunts into Polly's sides and made off at top speed on a transverse course towards a point to the right of the wood which, he estimated, would just allow him room to overtake the sub-sections moving that way. The going was ideal here, short turf, level surface, dry but not baked hard; he was soon coming up fast. As their paths converged, he saw the corporal of S-S A glance over his shoulder, grin at him, turn to his left and shout something to his partner, who grinned too and nodded vigorously. A bare ten metres short of the invisible winning-post Alexander considered he was in front by a head and slowed to a canter.

The wood was evidently thicker than had appeared from the top of the slope, and those who had elected to go through it instead of making the detour had lost ground; at any rate the field was now well scattered, from front to rear as well as laterally. Along the foot of the hill ran a road with thick hedges both sides. As Alexander approached, he saw the four grey horses belonging to S-S D – the under-corporal's rangy gelding was unmistakable – jump the nearer hedge beautifully, almost together, then be pulled to a halt before the much higher further one. Perhaps the NCO would defy the rules and move along the road in search of a gap or a part low enough to be safely jumped; no, without hesitation he and his mate drew their sabres, leaped to the ground and began slashing away at the obstacle. (They were called sabres out of piety; they were more like heavy knives, part of the men's stock of tools and other devices designed to help them in a most important aspect of their function in combat, the speedy crossing of rough terrain.)

The two had made a sufficient gap and were remounted and through it and away before Alexander reached the spot. It was time to put on the pace again, but that would not be easy in the bushy stretch in front of him; there would be no more races for a spell. After a few minutes' frustrating work he found his way clearing and soon reached the edge of a field of wheat. S-S D or another had been through it fifty metres or more to his left, but despite the consequent loss of time he followed in their track so as to limit the damage done to crops to what was strictly necessary. There were horsemen ahead of him now, two groups crossing a strip of pasture where cows drew together in alarm. He followed at a full gallop, came to a hedge as high as any he remembered having jumped, sat tight in the saddle, pressed his knees in and pushed his hands and heels down and landed awkwardly but safely in a vacant space with buildings on two sides, turned a corner through a gateway and found himself in a farmyard among rearing mules, fluttering chickens and swearing English; somebody snatched a child out of his path. Then he was through and in the open again.

The church was four hundred metres away at the top of a steep slope up which S-S A – as it proved to be – was struggling; no others were to be seen. This race was too easy: Alexander dismounted at the foot of the steeple, complimented Polly on her speed and agility and was perched on a gravestone smoking a cigarette when the two men and their four horses came clattering into the churchyard. All showed signs of exertion, but of some complacency too, the men with broad smiles, the horses hardly blowing, shaking their heads about.

'Best of a bad lot for once,' said Alexander airily.

The corporal, a tall melancholy-looking lad by the name of Lyubimov, gave a chuckle; he had dismounted and run up his stirrups and was loosening his charges' girths. 'For once, your honour? This makes the third time out of four that Lomov and I have nearly strolled in ahead of you and that cart-horse of yours.'

'Of course, we know that Polly has a great burden to bear,' said little Lomov, accurately gauging his officer's mood.

'Fortunately for you I choose to ignore that, Lomov. As for you, Lyubimov, you may well be right with your statistics, which seem to be unimpressive in any case. Only three times out of four? Surely, as befits its seniority, Sub-Section A must come first every time. And where's S-S B, which I remind you is part of your command, Corporal Lyubimov? Oh well, let's ignore that too. And now, to stop you standing there with your palms itching and your tongues hanging out, let me recognize the only motive that has made you exert yourselves and your wretched hacks this afternoon and satisfy your greed.' Alexander took out his wallet. 'For you, Lyubimov, a munificent £10,000' – the two notes were accepted with a bow – 'and £5,000 for Lomov as befits his even lowlier station. And well done, the pair of you. Good work.' It would have taken two much less elated soldiers than these to find anything wrong with the way some of the foregoing had been said.

Presently there were men and horses everywhere. Warsky, the artificer-sergeant, arrived last. He reported that he had seen S-S E using a road. The sub-section corporal contended that he had merely crossed one at an angle. At this trivial dissension all Alexander's good-humour departed. He announced snappishly that he would decide the matter at troop office the following morning, warned Ulmanis to make ready to move off in ten minutes and strolled over to the church door. Here a bilingual notice told of hours of business; the present moment lay within them. He could not remember having been this way before and had no idea of the nature of the business conducted, meat-or vegetable-market, communal eating-rooms, laundry or, as was most common, administrative offices. No signboard was to be seen: the old English hostility to strangers, he thought to himself, still going after all these years. Out of curiosity he decided to take a quick peep inside; he might even be able to get a drink.

He pushed at the heavy door and immediately heard an organ quietly playing a scale, a voice raised in exhortatory style and the murmur of a sizeable assembly. It was not what he had expected. In the small vestibule inside there stood a table with four or five identical books on it. He glanced at one and read without comprehension the words *The Book of Common Prayer*. Advancing further into the building he saw that the organ, elevated above the inner doorway, was being tested or altered or was perhaps still under construction. The voice he had heard was finishing a short speech about the necessity of consulting its owner on certain points, and the assembly, now seen to be after all not large, was very active, though what it was doing was not at once clear to Alexander, nor did he come to understand those doings in more than outline in the short time he stayed. He had evidently entered during an imposed silence, or comparative silence, which abruptly ended in an uproar of hammering, sawing and the whining of old-fashioned drills as he moved into the middle of things. Everywhere there were metre-square copies of the same photograph; it showed a large interior, but he had still not identified this when the man who had spoken, a Russian, clearly a supervisor of some sort, noticed the uniform, it seemed with no great relish, and hurried over. His companion, white-haired, round-backed, clearly a pre-war, gave a sideways look and turned away.

'Is there anything wrong, sir?' asked the supervisor. He was about fifty, pale, wearing a grey overall.

'Not as far as I know. What's going on here?'

'Going on, sir? Why, we're beginning to put the things into place. You should have seen it when we started. Those stairs up to the *pulpit – this would be easier in English, sir, if you –* '

'*Easy for you not same as* . . .' Alexander reflected belatedly that here was a person of no account, and started again, 'It might well be for you, but it certainly wouldn't be for me. Now you haven't told me the purpose of all this.'

The man gave a frown of exasperating puzzlement. 'The purpose? We're restoring the church, sir. That's to say, we're putting it back like it used to be, before it was an iron-mongery. So that when – '

'Yes yes, of course, but . . . what are those men there doing?'

'They're building the, the places for the choir to be, sir.'

'Just so. And that basin there?'

'That's the font, sir.' Just in time to save his front teeth, the supervisor went on, 'For the holy water, sir.'

'Good,' said Alexander, sounding relieved that these important details had not been overlooked. 'And this, I take it, is how it was originally.'

'Correct, your honour. In 1983, as you see. It had been out of use for some years before then, but not yet deconsecrated.'

'No.' How strange it looked, as if it had been the product of a different civilization, showing nothing at all that could be paralleled in the surviving theatres or other public halls of those times. Even those features with an identifiable function, like the rows of benches where the audience must have sat, seemed almost perversely odd in their design. Perhaps that design could be traced to the Eastern origins of Christianity, but if so all the other progeny of that stock, if any, must have died out. As this one had. Once, as a small boy, Alexander had been taken into a church in Sevastopol, and he thought he remembered now that he had experienced the very same sense of the alien, almost the inhuman. And yet there had been something about what had been here, and in innumerable other such places, that men had been ready to die for – long ago, as Mets had said. Whatever it had been, it must have changed remarkably over the years.

It seemed time to be off, but just then a bald-headed fellow in an apron came bustling up to the supervisor. He said in some agitation and with a strong English accent,

'Sir, sir, there's a crowd of soldiers outside. I think you'd better – '

'It's all right, my good man,' said Alexander blandly. 'They're my chaps.'

At the door he found to his mild surprise that he had taken his cap off; he could not remember having done so. On his reappearance Ulmanis called to the men to tighten girths and be ready to march, and Warsky gently shooed away the small crowd of children who had gathered to sit in the saddles and to beg £10 pieces. Alexander announced a tactical exercise for the return journey, naming a map-reference as assembly-point; no prizes were offered for first arrival there. Within a minute the churchyard was empty and the sound of hooves had faded. Suddenly the note of a bell came from the steeple, was repeated three or four times and then ceased, and the children on their way home wondered what it was.

7

When his day's work was done, Ensign Petrovsky walked slowly across the park to 'B' Squadron mess. This was a small farmhouse built about the middle of the nineteenth century. On the ground floor there was a dining-room just big enough for the seven officers and up to three guests, a comfortable, low-ceilinged ante-room with a small bar in one corner, and an extensive kitchen and attachments. The upper floors provided good accommodation for the squadron commander, Major Yakir, and for his second-in-command, and accommodation for five subalterns. As one who slept out of mess except when too drunk or lazy or cross with his family or disinclined to face the weather to ride home, Alexander had the worst bedroom, according to him at his own wish, but in fact the major had so ruled without consulting him.

This evening, as on all such evenings, his standard-dress uniform, the military equivalent of a lounge suit, had been laid out on his cot by a brother-officer's batman in return for money. He showered in the tiny second-floor bathroom, put on the uniform and went down to the ante-room, feeling, after his varied and strenuous day, as well physically as he had ever felt in his life. His mental and emotional states were hardly if at all more complicated: Theodore Markov was coming over that evening – was due shortly, in fact – and he knew he would be able to think of plenty of things to say to him.

A pleasant breeze was fluttering the blue-and-white gingham curtains of the ante-room. As Alexander came in, a handsome dark-haired young man of about his own age looked up from the long chintz-covered sofa that faced the window, his expression changing from a sullen gloom to a rather rigid cheerfulness. There was an empty glass on the arm of the sofa beside him.

'*Good evening, Victor, how are you making, old chap?*'

'*Hällo* – would you very kindly get me a vodka? I'll pay you for it. The major kicked up a bit of a fuss about my mess bill last month.'

'Kind words of good advice would be wasted on you, would they?'

'Completely, I'm afraid.'

'Then I'll save my breath.' Alexander turned to the under-corporal mess waiter. 'A vodka and a beer.' Tonight was not an occasion for drinking deep. When the time came he signed the chit, carried a glass of dill-flavoured Ochotnitscha across to the other officer and took a thirsty pull at his own lager. This resembled only very generally the sometime product of the Northampton brewery whence it came, a famous drink made to a Danish formula under Danish direction and enjoyed all over what had been the kingdom. 'We'll call that six hundred *quid*.'

'I'll give it to you tomorrow; I seem to have left my cash upstairs. And it'll be easier to settle up all at once.'

'What? Oh, you mean you'd like another one.'

'For the time being, yes.'

'Is this just on general principles, or has something out of the ordinary come up?'

'Both, really,' said Victor, at once reverting to his gloomy manner. 'All days stink, but today stank specially.'

'I thought all days did that too.'

'That pig Ryumin – he told me this morning that if I didn't pull myself together, as he chose to call it, he'd apply for a posting. I'd been giving him more or less a free hand with the troop, I thought that's what somebody in his position would like, after all he's been a sergeant longer than I've been commissioned, and now he says the troop is the worst mounted in the regiment and it's all my fault. And before he'd finished one of my corporals came into the office and he didn't stop.'

'That was very wrong of him.'

'It was all very wrong of him. Dear God, perhaps it wasn't,

perhaps he was quite right. I can't wait to get away from this vile country.'

'Are you joking? It's a beautiful country. Just look out of the window.'

'Everybody's miserable.'

'Nonsense, that's just how you're feeling yourself at the moment. When you're in the right mood you'll see there's nothing wrong with the place at all.'

'Alexander, not everything done and said is because of someone's mood. Sergeants don't have moods.'

'Of course they don't; what do you think makes them into sergeants? With us, you'll find moods are about as good a way of looking at things as any. You've finished that one too, I see. Why not have another? On me this time. – Ah, Boris, you've turned up at exactly the right moment as usual. What can I get you to drink?'

The newcomer was thirty years old, with close-cropped hair and a face that would have served unimprovably as the model for the Russian entry in some illustrated catalogue of racial types. Each epaulette of his standard-dress jacket, which was of inferior cut and material to those of the other two, bore a pair of nickel bars enclosing a rhomb, for this was the lieutenant-commissary of the squadron. He answered Alexander's question in a deep, deliberate voice, and hesitantly. 'It's most kind of you, but do you think you should? The major doesn't approve of treating.'

'Oh, he doesn't really mind as long as it isn't flaunted in front of him. Come on.'

'Oh, very well. I beg your pardon, Alexander, I mean of course thank you very much. I'll have a beer.'

'Two beers, corporal, and one Ochotnitscha. Large. – Actually this is early for you, isn't it, Boris?'

'I suppose it is, yes.'

'It shouldn't be. What I mean by that is that you ought to give yourself more time off; I've told you before.'

'I'm grateful that you bother about me, but this is just when I can't, with George on leave.' The commissary referred to the second-in-command.

'No, you can't. I think everybody else I know could quite easily. It's a good job the army's too stupid to realize what you're worth, or you'd shoot up to colonel-general and we'd never see you again.'

Boris sent Alexander a devoted look that made Victor want to kick them both. The trouble was that Alexander would kick back painfully and Boris would not kick at all, would do nothing except look noble and guileless. Luckily there was no time for these feelings to rankle very much, because just then one of the camp guard brought a guest to the front door of the mess building.

In a moment Theodore had come into the ante-room, trying with fair success to hide his feelings of constraint. By nature he was quite at ease in most social encounters, but he had discovered early that the Commission aroused little in the way of amiability or respect among the civilians of the administration, and had not yet had enough experience of the military to know whether they were any better disposed. As it soon turned out, none of the three officers to whom Alexander introduced him – the third had followed him in almost directly – had as much as heard of his and his superiors' business. That third, in his mid-twenties and already running to fat, made a rather disagreeable impression with his loose mouth and habit of twisting it in a smile or sneer for no perceptible reason. He was called Leo, Alexander alleged, adding that it was all first names in the mess, except of course for the major, and shortly afterwards that, with one man on leave and another serving as officer of the day, the company was now complete, except again for the major. Neither of these additions proved fully accurate, for when Major Yakir in due course arrived he had with him another civilian whose name, first or last, Theodore for one never learned. Host and guest were remarkably similar to look at, both short and stout, both all but bald, both heavily moustached, guest however blemished on the right cheek by a purple birthmark that host lacked. Neither seemed to have much to say to the four younger men.

At dinner, Theodore was placed between Alexander and the ensign called Victor. Asked how he had made the journey from

Northampton, he answered truthfully enough (though perhaps in needless detail) that he had come on one of the power-assisted bicycles scantily available to members of the Commission for recreational purposes. A discussion of fuel policies and prospects naturally followed. Alexander committed himself to the opinion that the new synthetics were proving ruinously expensive to produce, that Moscow was at its wits' end and that mechanical transport would soon run down, perhaps even by the end of the decade, and Victor agreed with him. All this was said quite roundly and openly, as was natural, even to be expected; nobody thought anything of such talk these days. Actually it might have been that Victor did not so much agree as find it convenient to behave in one way or another while he drank. On his other side, Leo seemed to be thinking along these lines, to judge by the contemptuous glances he sent his colleague's way, unless these were in some way mechanical. Boris the commissary, on Major Yakir's left, said little and drank less; the major was silent, nodding now and then at what his guest, inaudibly to the others, was saying. When the mess waiters had taken away the dishes, Leo said in a loud teasing voice,

'Does anybody fancy a small portion of gambling tonight?'

It was instantly clear to Theodore that this remark was not to be taken at its face value and that its true meaning must at all costs be kept from the major. A glance at Alexander showed him to favour saying nothing. Victor spoke after a short silence.

'All right, I'll give you a game if no one else will.'

'Are you sure you really feel like a flutter?'

'Absolutely.'

'Very well, on your own head be it. Alexander, are you going to take a hand?'

'No thank you, Leo, I have my guest to consider.'

'He's more than welcome to join in.'

'I couldn't allow it, he has an appalling head for cards.'

'I suppose we must let him off, then. But you're with us, Boris?'

'I'm sorry, I have some things to clear up before the morning.'

'You always have some confounded excuse. I reckon you're afraid. Of losing your money.'

'You know it isn't that,' said Boris in a hurt voice.

'Of course it isn't,' said Victor indignantly. 'The thing is that they don't gamble in Kursk, and what they don't do in Kursk must never be done anywhere. That's it, isn't it, Boris?'

For a moment Boris's heavy features showed him to be on the edge of changing his mind. Then he shook his head energetically. 'No, I must go and work.'

'Spoil-sport,' said Victor. 'Well, it's just you and me then, Leo.'

The major looked up at that point and said, 'You may take tea,' evidently a form of words permitting junior officers to leave the table.

'Thank you, sir. Good night, sir.'

Leo, Victor and Boris rose, clicked their heels and departed. Theodore had started to follow their example, but Alexander put a hand on his arm, saying they had some wine to finish. After a minute or two Major Yakir and his companion also left and Alexander dismissed the remaining waiter.

'Well?' asked Theodore.

'When it's really dark, Victor and Leo will go outside and shoot at each other with old-fashioned revolvers.'

'Shoot at . . . At what range?'

'Oh; thirty metres? Twenty metres? It's not certain death at any one time – you don't show yourself, not deliberately at least: you call out and the other man fires at your voice. But they'll go on till somebody's killed, one of them or a passer-by.'

'Where do they do this? The sound of the – '

'Silencers. I went with them once; I thought it was a joke. It was no joke. There were four of us, me and those two and the other subaltern, the one that's on duty. The first time I shouted I was standing at the corner of a building in deep shadow. One bullet hit the wall beside me and a splinter cut my cheek and I heard another go past about shoulder-high and less than a metre away. I started running and I didn't stop till I was back in the mess. If that's cowardice then I'm a coward.'

Theodore shook his head. 'Only a fool goes looking for danger.'

'You may be wondering why they don't kill somebody every night if the shots they got off at me were average. I was so naïve I hadn't realized that when they put you on your honour to keep stock-still after you've shouted you aren't meant to take it too literally. But when I found out my mistake I didn't try it again. I'm worried about Boris. He's just the sort to take it literally for however long is sufficient. Of course they may never talk him into it, his training and temperament are dead against anything of the sort, but he has this obsession about being smart and dashing which Victor works away on. Victor – he'll be out there soon, blazing away. At least Leo's sober. Which is worse, I suppose.'

'Why don't you tell your major?'

'They put me on my honour for that as well, before they explained the game. Some game!'

'Anonymously?'

'They'd still know it was me. I'm worried about the major too, in a different way. You don't know him, but he has plenty to say for himself as a rule, and he seems to like all of us, even Leo. Well, you saw him keeping his mouth tight shut, and I don't know whether you noticed the look he gave me when he said good night, but it wasn't friendly, whatever else it was.'

'Perhaps he resented having to put up with that guest of his.'

'Poor Major Yakir,' said Alexander. 'He's always having to return hospitality he never wanted in the first place.'

Just as he finished speaking the door opened abruptly and the man with the birthmark came in and walked straight across the room to where he had been sitting at table. As he moved he spoke in a monotonous voice and with a perceptible accent, Theodore thought Czech or Polish. 'I am sorry to come bursting in on you like this, gentlemen, but I foolishly left my spectacle-case behind, at least I think I did. Ah yes, here it is under the table by my chair. What a relief. And now I apologize for this intrusion and I leave you in peace and again I wish you good night.'

'Good night, sir.'

The door shut with some emphasis.

'Do you think he heard anything?' asked Theodore.

'What if he did? Let him fuck his mother.'

'By all means, but I'm afraid that wouldn't be the end of him.'

'What?' said Alexander rather crossly.

Without answering, Theodore got to his feet, overturned the chair lately occupied by the man in question and began closely examining its legs and the underside of its seat.

'How romantic.' Alexander sounded amused now. 'Enemy agents planting concealed microphones. Or is it time-bombs? It really takes me back. Admit it, Theodore: you made the last part of your journey here by parachute.'

'It's no joke, I'm afraid. There is a risk that Vanag's men are taking an interest in me, a slight one, but it's there. Well, this thing's clean.'

'What about the table?'

'He didn't touch the table, I was watching. I'd better check the floor.' And Theodore went down on his hands and knees and peered at the rug.

Alexander sniggered. 'I'm sorry, I just can't take this seriously. Hidden microphones in a – '

'Can you suggest what he was doing if he wasn't planting something?'

'Fetching his spectacle-case.'

'*Don't talk balls*.' Apparently the rug was clean too.

'All right, fetching something else that wasn't his spectacle-case.'

'Why do you say that?' asked Theodore, frowning and staring.

'It's the only other possibility.'

'But what could he have been fetching?'

'I don't know. That's your department. Why might Vanag's men be interested in you?'

'Last night a girl in my section was arrested. I know her because she's in my section. Nothing more. What she's sup-

posed to have done, whether she did it, even who arrested her –
very likely the ordinary civilian police, not the Directorate at all
– everything else: no information. But there is that possibility.
Nothing more than that.[2]

'I see.'

Theodore produced his pipe and looked at it without friendliness. 'I must give this up; it's much too expensive. Are you the
junior officer here?'

'Yes, to Victor by six weeks,[2] said Alexander in a serious,
literal-minded tone, one he maintained when answering subsequent questions. His manner was that of a witness intent on
establishing the truth and altogether without parti pris. If he
suspected that some of the information he gave was already
known, he betrayed no sign.

'But you have men under your command?'

'Yes, so have we all except Boris. A Guards squadron is in
effect a double squadron, with four troops. 5 Troop is the
senior; Leo's lot. That's a rifle troop, though what they carry
isn't exactly rifles. 6 and 7 are the same.'

'Which is yours?'

'8. 8 is a cannon troop; there's one in every squadron. But
what we . . . have isn't exactly cannon.[2]

'What, then?' asked Theodore, pressing down the tobacco in
his pipe.

'Projectile-launchers, eight of them, designed to operate
singly or in pairs. They can destroy any visible man-made
object, and quite selectively too, with the improved sonar sight.[2]

'My dear Alexander, should you be telling me this?'

'Oh yes. If there were such a person as somebody wondering
whether it might be a good idea to fight us or neutralize us,
which I'm sure there isn't, it would be very useful to us for him
to know the fire-power he'd be facing. It's official policy not to
be excessively discreet in these matters.'

'What if I were such a person? Mightn't I try to steal one or
more of your contrivances?'

'If you succeeded, which would be very unlikely indeed, you
would still be unable to load, aim and fire it, because you

haven't had the necessary special training, which is extremely hard to come by. You couldn't even arm one of our projectiles.'

'That's a relief. The whole thing is a responsibility, though, and you the junior officer. Was it because of . . .?' said Theodore, and stopped.

Alexander laughed heartily. 'My father's position? Well, in a way, though it's complicated. There may be a shake-up soon, if Victor finally decides to get himself posted home.'

'Is it as easy as that? A home posting on demand?'

'After two years, yes, virtually. I'll be eligible myself in a couple of months. But then I have a home posting already: England is my home.'

'Then you've no desire at all to go back.'

'For me it wouldn't be back, Theodore. I've spent no more than a quarter of my life in Russia, and most of that was either as a young child or on visits that were too short for me to settle down. You don't settle down anywhere when you're being trained. I'm a stranger there; I have no responsibilities there.'

'You speak as if you have responsibilities here, or . . .'

'I consider I have. All of us have, by virtue of the position we hold in this country.'

'You consider in other words that you owe the English something. I wonder how much, and how far you'd go to see that that debt was repaid.'

'It's not easy to be definite about the first part; you can't measure an obligation. But perhaps what I say about the rest of it will be enough. I'd go as far as might prove necessary.'

Theodore struggled to control his breathing. A delicious excitement, compounded of joy and fear, possessed him. In one sense this was the highest point of his life so far; in another, he would have given everything good that might happen to him in the future not to be where he now was. The heat had gone; very soon it would be quite dark and, presumably, Leo and Victor would go out and start their shooting. But they were a long way from Theodore's mind; he stared at the patched yellowish table-cloth, the wine-bottle with its would-be elegant label, his glass, empty, Alexander's glass, still a quarter full, the purple arc

83

where the base of Victor's unsteadily-held glass had rested. These sights had a portentous quality, as if something – an explosion, an earthquake – were about to change them altogether, or more like the furnishings of a dream, which themselves carry such significance. It was half a minute before Theodore realized that he was waiting for some sound – a footfall, the striking of a clock – to mark the stillness. This idea seemed to him absurd, puffed-up; he started to speak at once.

'You remember when we were talking last night and I was trying to get you to admit you'd fucked Mrs Korotchenko, and I made you swear by the honour of . . .'

'Of my country and my regiment and my family. So?'

'You swore falsely then. But over the question of being put on your honour not to tell your major about these shooting affairs – well, you haven't. You implied that you'd like to, but couldn't think of a way of doing it that didn't point to you. Do you really expect me to believe that? Somebody with your low cunning, as you called it? No, you've kept quiet because you'd given your word of honour.'

'What of it?' said Alexander irritably.

'Just, how do you resolve the contradiction? Not caring about the honour of your country and the others but very tender about your own.'

'Of course, you're an intellectual, aren't you, Theodore? I keep forgetting. It takes one of your sort to see a contradiction in what an ordinary person would regard as a simple difference. Swearing falsely by my country's honour doesn't hurt my country; it doesn't even get to hear about it. I benefit to the extent that I encourage belief in my assertion and no one suffers. But if I'm on my honour not to tell what I know and then I tell, people suffer – from severe disciplinary action – and at best I suffer loss of esteem. Which is different, you see.'

'Yes, I do see.' Theodore had been listening so attentively that his pipe had gone out; he relit it. 'I see that it's very plausible. Till I remember another difference, between the chance of losing my bars of rank and the no less likely chance, in the end, of losing half my head. Then I see there's an inconsistency somewhere after all.'

'Are you saying I ought to go to the major in spite of everything?'

'No, I'm saying that for you to be put on your honour overrides everything. So I don't think you were quite honest with me when you said just now that it was because you were naïve that you stood still after calling out to Leo and the others. It was really because you'd been put on your honour not to move.' Busy with his pipe, he missed the oblique look and very slight smile that Alexander gave. 'And you withdrew at that point because you'd have had to go on standing still the next time and the next, if there'd been a next. Very sensible behaviour.'

'Oh, rubbish, man. Listen, I've just thought of something you said last night. After you'd had me up before your court of inquiry about Mrs Korotchenko you congratulated me for something like steadiness under fire – thank you very much – and also apologized for having had to do it. I forgot to ask you what the devil you meant by that.'

'You'll soon see. Now, Ensign Petrovsky, I put you on your honour not to tell anybody what I'm going to tell you. I know already, having carefully tested you, that you're very resistant to ordinary interrogation, no one of course being in the least resistant to extraordinary interrogation. All I ask is your word not to say anything voluntarily.'

'You have it. You also have my congratulations, not for steadiness under fire but for making me believe in that arrested girl for nearly a minute.'

'No longer? Now let me begin with a question. You said a moment ago that to repay the English what you feel you owe them you would go as far as might be necessary. If killing became necessary, would you lend your hand to that?'

'Yes,' said Alexander without hesitation.

'Including your friends here? Including the major? Including your men?'

This time it took a little longer. 'Yes.'

'Very good. I now invite you to . . . What was that?'

'I didn't hear anything.'

'It probably wasn't anything. I'm sorry, Alexander, but I have an aversion to going into these matters except in private; it's become second nature. Is there anywhere else we could go? Your bedroom?'

'My bedroom is overcrowded with just me in it. We could ... Ah, I know the very place.'

'Before we go, could I possibly have a drink? A serious drink? I can't think why, but I suddenly feel like one.'

The ante-room was deserted. Alexander poured two glasses of Johnnie Walker Black Label and made out the chit. He stood facing Theodore, who winked and said resonantly,

'Welcome to the Northampton Music Society!'

'Success to all its concerts!'

They drained their glasses and, as if drilled beforehand, looked at each other, hesitated briefly and threw them into the empty hearth. They then embraced.

'Ought we to have done that?' asked Theodore, nodding at the scattered fragments. 'Your servants aren't going to have much fun clearing it up.'

'Oh, they have a couple of English chaps in for all that kind of thing,' said Alexander, picking up a pair of cushions from the sofa. 'Come along – let's have the rest of your story.'

'Where are we going?'

'Outside. Where else?'

'I've just thought we stand a chance of getting shot if we go out there.'

'Not near the mess. If they're going to shoot anybody on the whole they'd be quite satisfied if it wasn't Major Yakir having an outdoor pee.'

In the open the air was still and pleasantly warm and carried a faint odour of dry vegetation. The moon shone brightly and up and down the park windows were lit up, many of them uncurtained and shining out on to the near by grass. Three uniformed figures were running down the steps of the main house, their footfalls on the stone just audible at this distance. Alexander led the way to a small Doric temple built nearly two centuries earlier and closely copied from a Hellenistic original at Pergamum in Asia Minor. The designer had made two visits there to ensure the accuracy of his reproduction.

'What is this?' asked Theodore as they passed between the central columns of the portico.

'Some kind of summer-house, I imagine. It's certainly the place to come on hot days.'

Indeed, pleasant warmth almost at once gave place to pleasant coolness. A couple of metres inside the temple proper the floor rose in a high step, high enough to provide, with the necessary aid of a cushion, an unluxurious seat. The two were in shadow here, but strips of moonlit pavement lay all about them. What they would have called weeds, what others would once have called camomile and pimpernel, grew in the spaces between the stones.

'From what you were saying to your father,' began Theodore, 'I gather you want England to be given back to the English in one piece, so to speak, without any phases or probationary periods or conditions; is that correct?'

'Yes – unless it's done like that it'll never be done at all.'

'Good, that's the essential first step. So they must be put in full political control at a stroke. And someone must put them there. Someone must take the power away from where it is now and give it to the English. And whoever does that must be Russian – the English can't come to power by themselves; they'll follow, but at the beginning they can't lead. It was with this in mind that Group 31 was founded in Moscow four years ago. Its first task was to get as many of its men as possible into the Cultural Commission and to try to win over the remainder. This has been spectacularly successful. Today two-thirds of the personnel are either of us or actively on our side, including all the section heads and deputies, and the remainder, including Commissioner Mets, are not expected to give any trouble.'

'Are you saying that the whole Commission and the whole of the New Cultural Policy for England are nothing but a front for a revolutionary movement?' Alexander sounded sceptical.

'Certainly not, it's all quite genuine. The two go together.

We'll go on with our work after we've put the English in control.'

'If they want you to.'

'I'm sure they will. They must. If I may continue, we've infiltrated all the departments of the administration. The civilian police have been particularly responsive – they're underpaid, they get no privileges and of course they hate Director Vanag – and their support will make our job almost easy. They'll simply arrest everybody on the other side who matters.'

'What would you bet that Vanag's men haven't got your side infiltrated to hell?'

'I thought it was your side too, Alexander.'

'I'm sorry: our side. I have to ask these . . .'

'No, no, you're absolutely right to be cautious. Anything's possible, but the tentative view of our leadership is that no infiltration has been suffered as yet. All right, you can't prove a negative; even so, there is one striking and suggestive fact. What does a wise man do when he's moving about among his enemies? He keeps looking over his shoulder to see if he's being followed. Well, we've been looking over our shoulders, and there's nobody there. Not one of us has noticed the slightest sign of unwonted interest in him, as it might be hearing by chance that somebody has been round the place asking questions. And we think we know the reason. Naturally we've been keeping a close watch on certain of Vanag's men and listening to what they say in the *pubs*. The position seems to be that they're so disaffected that if they should notice anything of what's going on they wouldn't follow it up and they wouldn't pass the information to their superiors, who would only use it to advance themselves. Something of the sort may already have . . .'

He stopped speaking as a sudden uproar broke out in one of the buildings further down towards the road. What sounded very much like female voices rose in protest, in mutual hostility, in fury; male ones remonstrated, tried to pacify, tried to quieten. Shrieks followed, then a bump as something fell and a crash as something broke. Men began to shout.

'Are they allowed to bring women in?' asked Theodore.

'Certainly not, but nothing's done about enforcing that rule unless something like this happens, a case of the old army don't-let-me-catch-you understanding. But now I'm afraid the guard'll have to intervene.'

The noise continued, though not so loud or so near that it would have hindered their conversation, had they wanted to resume it; instead, both watched intently. The resemblance between what they saw and a stage performance was increased by their view of it framed between two of the pillars of the temple and by the intensity of the moonlight, which seemed to have grown since they had come out of doors. Behind the upstairs windows gesticulating human figures, some of them partly nude, came into view, milled about or grappled with one another, and vanished. Once, the shape of a man moved rapidly backwards across the entire breadth of the visible space, no doubt as the result of some blow. Sound effects included the smashing of glass, twice repeated, and a periodic thumping like the driving-in of nails with a heavy mallet. Little groups of men from other buildings were strolling over for a closer view, and there was something of an audience when four of the guard arrived under an NCO and shortly afterwards dragged off three women, all by now weeping loudly. The NCO stayed a moment to bawl promises of retribution at the occupants of the offending house, and then he too was gone.

'What will happen to those girls?'

Alexander made a disdainful noise. 'Girls? They'll be thrown out of the main gate when the guard have finished with them.'

'That seems a bit harsh.'

'Not a bit of it; they're lucky it's a fine night.'

'How will they get home?'

'They'll probably pick up a horse-bus. Why all the concern? They're animals. How do I know? Because those fellows down there are no better and no worse than my fellows, and any female who'll fuck any of my fellows has got to be an animal – anyway I hope she is for her sake. You were saying, about the ... revolution.' He brought the word out with an air of surprise.

'Yes.' It took Theodore nearly half a minute to collect his thoughts. 'Well . . . on the night of 21st September, the last night of the Festival of Culture, when there'll be celebrations and attention will generally be distracted, we strike. We seize the broadcasting station, the post office, the administration buildings and the other nerve centres. And we arrest Vanag and all his staff and other prominent figures, including I'm afraid your father, but he'll be well treated and very soon confined only to his house and its grounds, which is no extreme hardship.'

'No great matter if it were. Meanwhile I'm subduing the rest of the regiment single-handed. Lucky you happened to find me, isn't it?'

'We had and have something up our sleeves for the whole regiment, including you. Just before we move a fake message from London reaches your colonel telling him to confine all troops to quarters. At the same time we cut his communications with Northampton. Then at H-Hour two of us release TK into the park.'

'Almighty God! How did you get hold of that? And the impellor?'

'From Moscow,' said Theodore lightly. 'We're constantly in receipt of deliveries of cultural equipment and stores.'

'You know, Theodore, if the 4th were the only troops in England the thing might conceivably work.'

'I'm sorry, I'm so taken up with our local movement I forgot to tell you. We here are just part of an organization that covers the whole country, the whole EDR. Surely you knew at least that the Festival was a national affair.'

'No, I didn't know. I didn't know anything about any of it. And if there'd been the slightest whisper in the regiment I'd have heard.'

'The Guards' morale is known to be high. And in rural districts like this one the military are isolated, impossible to mix with on any scale. It was decided that outside the larger towns, where circumstances are different, the safe course was to leave them alone and then neutralize them.'

'With certain exceptions.'

'You're special, Alexander, you must admit. Son of the Controller, lover of the Deputy-Director's wife – when are you seeing her again, by the way?'

'Tomorrow afternoon.'

'We'll come back to her in a minute – and now somebody with the means of blowing up half England. We have to have you.'

'What would you like me to blow up?'

'One can't say yet. You must just be ready, prepared. You'll be able to lay hands on some of those projectiles?'

'With everybody else knocked unconscious for twelve hours I should be able to manage it, yes.'

'What chance have they got of reaching their insufflators in time?'

'None whatsoever. One whiff and you collapse, so suddenly that there's often a high casualty-rate from men injuring themselves as they fall. Anyway, that's what the manual says.'

'Excellent.'

After a brief pause, Alexander said, 'Of course, fighting off the entire Russian army and air force the next day will stretch me somewhat.'

'There I go again. I should have said much earlier that there's to be a change of government in Moscow timed to coincide with all this.'

'A coup in Moscow? *Sweet Jesus!* We'll be having the Martians in next.'

'A change of government is how it was described to me. The new leaders will be favourable to an autonomous, neutralized England. That's all I know.'

There was a longer pause. Alexander could be heard rubbing his cheek or jaw. In the distance a pane of glass broke suddenly and violently.

'Our friends. At least they're presumably still alive as I speak. Well, Theodore, I think this scheme has some very interesting possibilities.'

'Then you're still with us now you know more about us?'

'Yes,' said Alexander's voice firmly out of the darkness.

As when he was relighting his pipe, Theodore did not see his co-conspirator's expression. This time it was accompanied by a slight lift of the shoulders.

8

The Old Parsonage turned out to be a rather large, squareish building painted pink. In front of it ran a plank fence on which someone of no great talent had recently drawn in chalk an erect penis with testicles appended. Alexander, riding through the gateway, considered that some generous neighbour, rather than the lady of the house herself, was most likely responsible, but that the second hypothesis could not be dismissed with any confidence. On the far side of the fence, out of sight from the road, there was an untidy lawn that had evergreen bushes on it. Untying the couple of metres of head-collar rope he fastened Polly to the gate and began a cautious advance, his eyes open for alternative escape-routes as if he expected to meet a Cambodian suicide squad rather than a presumably unarmed female.

The front door was ajar. He hesitated and pressed the bell beside it, which he heard ringing both then and on a second and a third try, but nobody came, so he pushed the door. A short passage manifested itself with a tiled floor of chequered pattern, rooms on each side behind glass doors, more passage beyond at right-angles and the foot of a staircase. Continuing to advance cautiously, he found a dining-room to the left, a drawing-room to the right and nobody in either. When he reached the right-angle he thought, he was almost certain, that there was a person on the landing or half-landing of the staircase, but his direct look a second later showed nobody. On the left-hand side of the house, behind the dining-room, he noticed another door that was not quite shut. It proved to give into a kitchen in which there was somebody: Mrs Korotchenko, leaning naked against the wall that faced him.

Alexander was not the kind of man to linger (or muddle his brains) over such a sight, his advance now was precipitate and he closed with her fervently. Not long afterwards he muttered,

'Let's go upstairs.'

'No. Here.'

'Come on, darling, don't be silly, it's so much more comfortable.'

'Here, I tell you!'

Resolutely but not violently he caught her round the waist and tried to pull her away from the wall; in response she lifted her hands above her head and gripped what he saw to be the roller of a roller towel against which, rather than against the wall itself, she was in point of fact leaning. So supported she was in an excellent position to fend him off with her powerful legs and he soon gave up his attempt. Now he did look at her with some curiosity and she returned his look with her eyes and nostrils dilated and her lips drawn back.

'For the love of God,' she said through her teeth, and reached out for him. At this stage he remembered how the night before last she had shown herself to be no friend of amorous delay, and in the very least time possible set about answering her appeal. Once or twice he found her mouth with his own but each time she lifted it out of reach. She had evidently kept hold of the towel-roller and quite soon took him unawares with the strength of her arms and shoulders. By then his own strength was under severe test; however, it remained equal to all the demands made of it, even at the end when, except for the relief provided by her leaning posture, her entire weight was upon him. Her strange cry sounded, in its unmuffled form (given close to his ear, too) not liable to wake the dead but bidding fair to bring round anyone in the house who might have been merely dozing. This time the note of helplessness or hopelessness seemed plain to Alexander; another quality, perhaps more than one, still eluded him.

As silence abruptly fell he thought, he was again almost certain, that he heard a noise behind him, a slight cough or perhaps a snigger. He looked over his shoulder as smartly as he could, but saw nobody.

'What was that?' he asked.

'What was what?' Her tone was incurious.

He shook his head and said nothing. After a moment she moved unsteadily to one side and half-lay in a sprawl across the top of a line of cupboards running towards the door. This stood open; he could not remember whether or not he had shut it and dismissed the matter from his mind when Mrs Korotchenko put his hands against her as she had done before.

'That was wonderful, darling,' he said, and he was not exaggerating, though he would have been describing his own feelings more accurately by calling what had happened so odd as to be hard to believe already. He gazed into her face, but could find no emotions there, only signs of her physical state. Her glance met his briefly and moved on as if he had been a stranger whose eye she had caught in a public place. 'Shall we go upstairs now?'

'What for?'

'It's more comfortable. As I said.'

'Yes, but why do you want to go there now? All right,' she went on before he could answer, perhaps remembering their conversation in his father's garden, and lowered her bare feet to the floor.

'What about your clothes?'

'What clothes?' It was true that there were none of hers to be seen.

'The ones you . . . were wearing before I arrived.'

'What? My clothes are upstairs,' she said, starting for the door, her arms hanging by her sides.

'There's nobody about, is there? Servants or anything? I could have sworn I saw someone.'

'You're mistaken, there's nobody but ourselves.'

They went out and down the passage to the foot of the stairs. As they began to climb he slipped his arm round her waist; she looked down over her shoulder to see just what constituted this outré gesture, scratching her stomach meanwhile. The room they went to was at the far end of the upstairs passage, narrow from side to side but with a high sloping ceiling. There was not a great deal of light in it because the windows were small and half-covered with squares of heavy brocade that must have been cut from some much larger piece, and the dull crimson wallpaper and sepia rugs made it seem darker. The pictures provided no cheer either, water-colour or crayon landscapes and figure-paintings all by the same prodigiously untalented hand, the drawing inept beyond compare, the uneven colours overflowing or falling short of their boundaries. Other objects showed translated versions of the same truly childish incapacity: a bulging earthenware mug, a piece of dirty knitting with a forsaken look to it, and out-of-focus photograph of a girl aged about ten, a book-cover of some artificial material on which the lettering was badly spaced and aligned. Nevertheless it proclaimed clearly enough that the book inside the cover was 'Anna Karenina', by Count Leo Tolstoy, and if Alexander had been interested he could have established with great ease that this was indeed so, and further that the pages were creased and occasionally spotted with food and drink up to about the middle of Part One, after which they were quite smooth and clean. But of course he was not in the least interested in that, nor in the pictures nor in any inanimate object in the room other than the bed. Its dimensions and surroundings proclaimed it not to be the marital bed in style or fact, but it would serve well enough.

He pulled off the counterpane, a cheap bought article, and quickly undressed while Mrs Korotchenko watched him from a stool set before a large mirror decorated with picture postcards secured by the frame and with more crayon. As he looked about he became aware that, although he could see articles of clothing here and there around the room, her clothes, in the sense he had meant just now, were still missing. No doubt she went naked indoors at all reasonable times. When he finally sat himself down on the bed and asked her to join him there, he half-expected her to prescribe some unusual alternative place or activity, or at least to ask him what he wanted her to do that for, but she came over at once and in silence. Even so, when he embarked on the activity he had had in mind, which was simply and obviously (for the moment, at any rate) the detailed exploration of what he had so far been able only to glimpse in large outline, her response was not warm, nor even very friendly. She was submitting with a fairly good grace to perversities like being kissed and gently caressed when any normal woman would naturally have preferred to be wriggling about on the sod or dangling from a wall. Her body was so interesting to Alexander that at first he could ignore her indifference, but after a time what he would have called his self-respect began to suffer a little. Asking her her name seemed a good move, especially since he had never been told what it was.

She answered up in full like a child. 'Sonia Korotchenko.'

'Mine's Alexander,' he said out of politeness, for he quite thought she knew this.

'Oh yes? Alexander what?'

'My surname happens to be the same as my parents'.'

'What's that?'

'Petrovsky. Your hosts of the night before last.'

'Oh, I never notice the names of the people my husband takes me out to.'

'What happens when you return hospitality?' It took them off the track but was too striking to let go.

'We don't, because my husband's too mean,' she said like someone mentioning a sick man's infirmity. 'If he has to give people drinks he takes them to the club.' In the same breath she asked, 'Have you had a lot of girls?'

'I suppose you could say that. But none of them were as sweet as you, Sonia.'

'Do you like young girls?'

'Not particularly,' he said, adding after only a small interval, 'They're so immature, most of them. I'd much rather have a – '

'How old was the youngest you've had?'

'Thirteen, I think; I started quite young. How beautiful you are. You've got the loveliest – '

'Have you ever had two girls at once?'

'Two girls at ... I see what you mean. No, I haven't. It's having one person for your very own that really matters, isn't it? Unless you – '

'Would you like to try it?'

These all seemed to him to be perfectly proper questions, but he had no desire whatever to go into them now. He said with more gentleness than he felt, 'But darling, what business is it of yours, eh? Why do you want to know?'

'I'm sure you would. Have you ever fucked a man? You must have done.'

'No I haven't – men don't attract me in the least,' said Alexander truthfully and angrily. Part of the anger was real, based on the thwarting of his conversational wishes, but more of it was assumed, based on his sudden perception that something more and other than displeasure was called for here. What she wanted, and would get, was a great show, a theatrical simulation, of disgust and disapproval. Taking her by the shoulders and glaring hard into her face, he went on in an unnaturally deep, expressive voice, 'How dare you talk to me in this way! Here I am being as pleasant and loving to you as any man could be, and this is the thanks I get – to be asked the most intimate questions, have foul insinuations made and finally stand accused of unnatural practices with my own sex! And this after I've lowered myself to indulge your shameless, debauched fancies! It's monstrous, obscene! You're a vile, wicked woman, a whore and a degenerate!'

Long before the end she had begun to stir and twist in his grip, to breathe like someone suffering acutely from cold, to stretch out towards him. As he watched, her eyes dulled, her thin mouth slackened and her whole face grew lumpish and lubberly, an expression quite different from the one she had shown him in the kitchen. But he was not going to pause over the possible meaning of this, and certainly not to need urging on a third time, and very soon he had her snarling and howling away in his arms. When they had finished she fell asleep at once, still in his arms. She was not a quiet sleeper, giving little moans or groans as she exhaled, but Alexander was content. He stroked her cropped hair, which perhaps unexpectedly had not long been washed, and allowed his mind to rove.

Ever since his schooldays one of his favourite books had been

Esmé Latour-Ordzhonikid Ze's 'Some Thoughts and Sayings'. He still knew large parts of the section on Love almost by heart.

It is the most vulgar of errors to suppose that when a passion comes upon us quickly it serves notice by doing so that it cannot stay. Is an instant, instinctive loathing sooner relinquished than a reasoned antipathy?

The mystics tell us that the love of God is infinitely strange, sometimes cruel, frightening, even outrageous ... We must not forget that it was He who taught us how to love our own kind.

Those who contend that we cannot love more than one person at once would surely not deny that we can fear two or more persons at once, admire them, hate them, wish to protect them. A store of feeling is not a larder or a bank.

'Love is a game with [only] one rule: that the fact of its being a game must never be acknowledged in word or deed, and as rarely as possible in thought,' said Archilochus, and men reviled him for his wisdom.

True passion always takes us by surprise, even throws us into disarray. Angels arrive unexpectedly; no-one was ever amazed to see a tax-gatherer.

He whose wish to love is unreserved, free from all thought of self and with no eye for the future – him the fay grants his wish.

To love is to become again as a child and to have a child's immunity conferred on one. Even attorneys acknowledge an age of responsibility.

These were some of the maxims that, verbatim here and there, floated through Alexander's head as he lay in the narrow bed with his arms round Mrs Korotchenko. His posture happened to be one he could sustain for a relatively long time without discomfort, a rare accident for one so situated. It may have contributed a good deal to his present feelings, which combined well-being and amiability at a pitch that seemed to him new, or partly new, or relatively new. He believed that he had had a kind of prevision of Mrs Korotchenko as he stood in the lobby at home immediately before their first meeting. Preternatural events of that sort were often associated with important emotional experiences, as Latour-Ordzhonikidze had remarked (under Ghosts, not Love). He was grateful to have been given the chance of pleasuring her, or if not that of satisfying her, or at least of doing what she had wanted him to do. And he was grateful to her in a different way: however a good fuck might be defined (and after half a dozen years of extensive and varied experiences he was still not quite sure) she was one all right. Suddenly he found his thoughts had drifted to Kitty. Of course he loved her too, but not quite in the same sense: more impulsively, less variously, less remarkably. It had something to do with their respective ages. He would learn from the older woman and teach the younger, so improving his capacity for love in an altogether licit fashion: Latour-Ordzhonikidze had made an observation on this head, though Alexander could not recall the exact text.

Time passed. He dozed off. When he woke up Mrs Korotchenko was awake too and looking at him expectantly.

'How long have we got?' he asked.

'My husband' – she pronounced the words with sardonic emphasis – 'won't be here till after six o'clock.'

'I must be away before then in any case. Do I gather you're not as fond of him as you might be?'

'I hate him, but he doesn't know I do, I make sure of that. I'd do anything to make a fool of him, humiliate him. Anything.'

'Such as making him think you'd wanted me to make love to you and I hadn't obliged?'

'I don't know what you're talking about.'

'No, naturally not. Why do you hate him? Why did you marry him?'

'I married him because I thought he was one kind of man and I hate him because I found out he's really another.'

'What kind is that?'

'Which one?'

'I don't care, whichever you like. All right, the kind he is.'

'An ordinary man.'

'I see,' said Alexander, seeing only that he had asked about the wrong kind of the two and not pursuing the matter, since he had no curiosity about her idea of an extraordinary man. 'How would you like to make a fool of him? In what connection?'

'His work, his job. It would have to be that, it's the only thing in his life.'

'I suppose he talks about it all the time,' he said guilelessly.

'Not a word, he's as close as any oyster. So he doesn't talk about anything. As you may have noticed.'

'M'm. Er, you mean showing him up as incompetent, something like that?'

'Yes, no good at dealing with the English resistance, say.'

He was completely unprepared and his face must have given him away, or given something away, if she had not as she spoke shut both eyes, one of which she was now rubbing. 'What English resistance? I didn't know . . .'

'There must be one. I certainly don't know anything, but there can't not be one, and probably with a lot of Russians in it. People like you.'

'Me? Why me?'

'Young. Impulsive, not afraid of a few risks.' She opened her eyes; their Asiatic quality seemed accentuated. 'Chivalrous. You must be in it.'

'I've just never heard of there being anything to be in.'

'I'd join it myself if I got the chance. Fight the lot of them in any way I could. I wouldn't mind dying.'

There was not much to be said to that, not that he could think of anyhow. What he did finally say was, 'I'll think about that idea. Of showing your husband up. See if I can concoct a scheme.'

Later, as he was finishing getting dressed (she made no move to do so), he took her stole out of his haversack and handed it to her. 'I'm afraid it's a little crumpled.'

'Thank you.' She seemed embarrassed.

'Why did you leave it there?'

'I must have forgotten it.'

'No. You have just missed your second chance to ask where it was found, which if you really had forgotten it you'd have wanted to know. You left it there in the garden on purpose and I want to know why. By good luck I stopped it being taken to my mother; if it had been I'd have some very awkward explaining to do. And suppose she'd noticed you weren't wearing it when you came indoors. Suppose your husband had; a fine thing that would have been.'

'He never notices anything about me.'

'He'd notice something about you if he came walking into this room now. And about me too – the fact that I'm here. How do I know you haven't arranged it as an amusement for yourself?'

'I wouldn't do a thing like that. Do you think I'm mad?'

'I don't know what you are, Sonia, but if you tell me why you left that stole behind I may have something to go by.'

'It was a sort of joke,' she said in her lifeless way.

'Joke! On who? On me, I suppose.'

'Well, on ... on everything, really. I was just stirring things up, on a small scale. I knew nothing serious could happen. But of course I shouldn't have done it; I see that now; I'm sorry.'

Alexander recognized his cue. 'I'm glad to hear it. So you should be; it was a piece of absolutely disgraceful behaviour. You're a naughty girl, Sonia.'

What followed held more than one surprise. She smiled slightly, something he had expected her never to do at all, and a touch of animation was in her voice when she said, 'Do you think perhaps I deserve to be punished for it? There's still time.'

9

At about the time Alexander was leaving the Korotchenko residence Theodore Markov was riding his power-assisted bicycle up the drive of a large house on the other side of Northampton. Several other such machines stood near the portico, as did two motor-cars: he recognized those of Controller Petrovsky and Commissioner Mets. There were also a number of horse-carriages of various kinds. Theodore dismounted and moved to the side of the building, where a path lined with flowering shrubs took him into a large open garden. Here some dozens of people were sitting or standing in groups round two all-weather tennis-courts, on each of which play was going forward. White-coated servants moved about with trays of wine, soft drinks, fruit, cakes and cold meat pasties; more substantial refreshments were being prepared in a marquee. Beyond the courts, where four English ball-boys darted to and fro at need, a woodwind orchestra occupied a small bandstand and played waltzes and galops from a century and a half before, while two or three couples danced on the surrounding paved space. Everything was supposed to be done in style, for this was one of the regular summer parties given by Igor Swianiewicz, victualler-general to the units of supervision.

And everything, from a sufficient distance, looked as if it had been done in style, looked right; to everyone there everything was right. No one thought, no one saw that the clothes the guests wore were badly cut from poor materials, badly made up, ill-fitting, unbecoming, that the women's coiffures were messy and the men's fingernails dirty, that the surfaces of the courts were uneven and inadequately raked, that the servants' white coats were not very white, that the glasses and plates they carried had not been properly washed, or that the pavement where the couples danced needed sweeping. No one thought, no one perceived with other senses that the wine was thin, the soft drinks full of preservative and the cakes stodgy, or that the orchestra's playing was ragged and lifeless. No one thought any of that because no one had ever known any different.

In Theodore's eyes it was certainly grand enough, to an intimidating degree in fact, and he looked round with some eagerness in search of a friendly or even a known face. It was Nina he had come to see, must find before long in order to exploit the stroke of luck by which they had both been invited here at this stage, when for him to have asked her out might have seemed forward. There was no sign of her between the back of the house and the tennis-courts – or rather there was, in the shape of her parents in conversation with Colonel and Mrs Tabidze and Commissioner Mets. First taking a glass of wine from a proffered tray, he went up and paid his respects, in silence for the time being because the colonel was evidently in the middle of advancing some strongly-held view of his.

'Where shall we date its death?' he was saying in a not very interrogative tone. 'The year 2000? 2020? – before that, surely. It doesn't affect the point: as an active force, as something to be reckoned with, Marxism has ceased to exist. Its followers have died or fallen into cynicism or impotence. And what has replaced it? Ah, good evening, my dear boy.'

'Good evening, sir,' said Theodore, and exchanged greetings with the others, including Mrs Petrovsky, who thanked him for his thank-you note after her dinner-party. When this was over he said, 'Please don't allow me to interrupt you, colonel.'

'Oh, a smart young fellow like you doesn't want to hear an old buffer's maunderings,' said Tabidze.

'The voice of wisdom,' said his wife. 'Heed it.'

'I promise you I'm most interested,' said Theodore with sincerity.

'Very well, you bring it on yourself . . . Where was I?'

'What has replaced Marxism.' Petrovsky's face showed a great deal of eager expectancy.

'Indeed. What has replaced it is nothing, nothingness. No theory of social democracy, or liberalism, anything like that, nor even a non-political code of decency or compassion. And when the computer revolution broke down the idea of progress or just betterment in general broke down too. Christianity had gone long since and none of the new religions and cults took hold. And as for being Russian ... No belief, no confidence, no guides to behaviour. All our books are lies. So what do we live by? Self-interest isn't enough for most people, there are too many activities it doesn't enter into. Sensual enjoyment – even more limited. So we act; we choose a part not too incongruous with our age and station and play it out to the best of our ability and energy. We can't keep it up all the time, but it's there when we need it, and being Russian is a great help.'

'You were saying just now that being Russian was no good or had disappeared or something,' said Mrs Tabidze.

'No no, my love, that was the idea of being Russian as a system of conduct. I mean the fact of being Russian as an aid to play-acting. The essence of the Russian character, in fact as well as in fiction, has always been theatricality. Of course, some of us have more trouble than others with the part available to us. I'm one of the lucky ones – my part's the honest soldier: loyal, hard-working, a father to his men, strict but fair, all that, and devoted to some mysterious relic called the honour of the regiment.'

'I'm sure you really are every one of those things, Nicholas,' said Petrovsky earnestly.

'Thank you, my dear Sergei, I have to say I hope you're right because it would be out of character to say that the question is of the most perfect indifference to me, and also untrue, because obviously the game must be played to the full.'

'How is it you're playing a part?' asked Mrs Tabidze. 'If you really work hard, and I know you do, you're not pretending to be hard-working, you are hard-working.'

'What I say to myself about everything I do is quite different from what a real honest soldier would say to himself.'

105

'I've never heard such rubbish, my dear. However great the difference, it could make no difference.'

'But how does all this philosophizing fit the part?' Petrovsky went on evincing curiosity while he beckoned to a waiter. 'An honest soldier surely confines himself to honest soldiering.'

'That's all you know about honest soldiers, Sergei. Cultivation of unexpected interests is de rigueur for the type. My squadron commander in India was an authority on the fauna of Lake Balkhash.'

'That's not quite the same thing, is it?'

'No, but it's almost the same sort of thing.'

As he spoke Tabidze helped himself to a glass of wine, his fourth since arriving forty minutes before; it was another hot day and he had been thirsty. What with his hard head and the weakness of the drink its only effect was to introduce a certain relish into his tone. If he took much more that evening he would be troubled the next day not with a hangover but with taking off the resulting added weight. Not even his wife fully appreciated the savage self-discipline by which he kept his figure. She knew he kept his grey hair dyed black. This and the dieting she put down to harmless vanity, wrongly: they were necessary effects of his determination to retain the semblance of the particular variety of honest soldier he had chosen thirty years before in preference to, among others, the tubby, grizzled and usually less intelligent type to be seen in others' messes everywhere.

'I wonder how you'd apply your theory to other members of this company,' said Petrovsky with a reflective air. 'What part am I playing, for instance? Don't spare me, now.'

'Spare you? You're the all-round liberal, unreservedly tolerant, not least of what others condemn, in favour of equal treatment for unequals, exercising no authority over his children, the master who's patient but firm, but more patient than firm, where I'm strict but fair, but more strict than fair. The character's greatest fear is to be caught disapproving of something.'

When, on his way home at the end of the evening, Theodore went over this moment in his mind, it struck him that what

Tabidze had been doing was trying to impress the others with how unlike an honest soldier he was while asserting the opposite; nothing more than that. But at the time his feeling about what had just been said was that he had never heard an utterance more delicately poised between compliment and insult. He held his breath as Petrovsky's interested smile grew fixed on his handsome face. It was a relief when Mets spoke up in his clear tones.

'That's good but rather obvious, colonel, if I may say so. What about my part? I can't wait to hear what it is.'

'I don't think I know you well enough, Commissioner. Well enough, that is, to see if there's anything beyond the obvious administrator-with-imagination. I mean of course anything in the way of a further part, not anything more in your actual self.'

'You mean it's possible to play more than one part?'

'Oh, it's usual. Singletons like my soldier and the Controller's liberal aren't all that common.'

'Stop this nonsense, Nicholas; you don't even believe it yourself.'

'Sometimes I don't, my dear, and sometimes I do.'

'Sometimes I do too – I mean at this moment,' said Petrovsky.

He nodded in the direction of Theodore, who after standing stock-still for an instant was hurrying over to where Nina was approaching with Elizabeth Cuy at her side. Both girls wore tennis outfits and carried rackets.

'What do you see in that, Sergei?'

'Nobody in that youngster's position, nobody as bright as he, is really as smitten as that at the sight of a girl he knows so little, even a girl as attractive as my daughter. So smitten, I mean, that he really forgets the existence of his elders and supposed betters and goes rushing off without a word. Not really. Do they? So as well as the conscientious researcher we seem to have the romantic lover – I don't of course mean' – he turned to Mets – 'that he isn't in fact a conscientious researcher.'

'No no, Controller, point taken.' Mets looked at the ground

107

and went on, 'There must be cases where parts are taken.'

In fact Theodore had briefly weighed the advisability of interrupting an animated conversation among important persons and decided against it; it was his bad luck that nobody had noticed the little bow and wave he had given between laying eyes on Nina and moving away. Now he stood in front of her and looked at her. She was wearing her satin-weave waistcoat over a white blouse with mauve edging and the white culottes then in favour for sports. He noticed the freckles at the base of her neck. After some hesitation they shook hands, awkwardly, as if repairing a quarrel. Neither spoke. Elizabeth began patting herself lightly on the arms and thighs.

'I seem to have gone invisible,' she said. 'I hope it won't get any worse.'

'I'm so sorry, Elizabeth; I was coming to you.'

'Of course, in your own good time.'

'Why aren't you dressed for tennis?' Nina sounded accusing.

'Well, there wouldn't be much point in that, I can't play it. You see, it's never really caught on in Russia,' Theodore found himself explaining, 'and since I've been over here there doesn't seem to have been time to learn. Anyway, I . . .'

'Merciful God, it's not a crime not to play tennis,' said Elizabeth. She looked as though she had caught the sun a little. 'No need to cite extenuating circumstances.'

'I was only –'

'I think I'll go and try and fix up a four for us; there's –'

'No, stay,' said Nina, this time with excessive urgency, then at a more natural level, 'let's go and sit down.'

'I'm sorry, I can't stand any more of this.' Elizabeth was now equally agitated. 'Why two grown-up people have to gape and roll their eyes and babble nonsense at each other just because they want to, I suppose I'd better say have sex with each other I simply . . . If anybody wants me I'll be by the further court.'

Theodore looked troubled. 'I hope it was nothing I said or did.'

'No. You'll have to bear with her. She took a bad tumble

over Alexander about a year ago – she was very serious about him, still is, but of course as far as he was concerned she was just another girl. Not even that in a way. He doesn't like girls to scold him and make fun of him, give him any sort of opposition. I can never understand why she can't see that if she's really after him she's going about things completely the wrong way. He wants to be told that he's wonderful, not that he's wrapped up in himself. I can't understand it, she's usually so bright about things like that. But she won't discuss it. Anyway, she's dead against . . .' Nina stopped.

'Strong emotion in others.'

'Yes.'

'I see. Alexander told me he's tried to persuade her to have an affair with him but she'd turned him down. About a year ago.'

'You don't want to believe everything he says,' said Nina, more easily now that the talk had shifted from strong emotions.

'I can assure you I'm very far from doing that, but I believe him in this case because to a small degree it shows him in a disadvantageous light.'

'Or alternatively in an engagingly frank and humble light. It's always one light or another with him, you'll find.'

'Obviously you know him very well.'

Theodore had not changed his view of the truth of the statement under discussion. He had already noticed that Alexander talked for effect sometimes, but he was confident of being able to identify these occasions accurately enough, more so at least than Nina, whose manner at their previous meeting, as now, had suggested an unrancorous envy of her brother's sexual success. This envy might lead her, he judged, to take the less favourable view in questions relating to that success. What was much more interesting was how on earth she came to have anything to be envious about. With the amiability driven from her face by tension she was as beautiful as most men would require. She sensed the direction of his thoughts and said quickly,

'Is he coming this evening, do you know? You've seen him since I have.'

'No, I don't know,' he answered untruthfully but usefully for smothering the digression. 'Aren't you going to play tennis?'

'We can't yet. I mean the older ones have to play first, the important ones, that is.'

'Good. You'll tell me when you want to play?'

'Yes, but I don't really want to play,' she said.

They had strayed away from the marquee and the courts and there was nobody near them. This time he did take her hands and kissed them and let them go. Presently he said,

'I'm excited, aren't you?'

'Yes, but very certain as well. Confident. Till a few seconds ago I thought I never could be.'

'And happy.'

'Yes.'

Later Nina and Elizabeth played tennis and lost almost every point that involved Nina, who also kept forgetting things like her turn to serve and thereby annoying Elizabeth. Later still the two girls and Theodore and another young man who had attached himself to Elizabeth went up for their five minutes with Igor Swianiewicz. He was said to be the richest man in the district; he was known for a fact to have made his fortune by selling supplies illegally. But he was generous – as well as giving what were thought to be good parties he reputedly allowed the mothers of his illegitimate children to buy from him at a reduced rate – and after all somebody had to run a system of that kind, as even Director Vanag would have agreed. There was also the consideration that virtually every Russian household had had unofficial dealings with him. He spent the first part of the allotted five minutes describing the house he was having built in Cornwall, the second part asking his listeners riddles with obscene but otherwise impenetrably mysterious answers, and the third part telling them that a dozen English ought to be shot every day to teach the others a bit of respect.

When that was finished, they went into the marquee for supper. The noise was like that of a mob perpetually on the point of breaking through a line of police. Great wafts of stale sweat relieved with dense cigar-smoke drifted through the sticky air. It was not easy to find four places close together; a waiter came to the rescue by grabbing an unconscious woman under the armpits and hauling her out. The heels of her shoes made an excited whining sound on the canvas floor. At the other end of the tent, a very fat man who had climbed up on a table at once fell off it again on to a large tray of empty bottles and dirty glasses just then being carried past by another waiter. Two younger and less fat men, each with his hands at the other's throat, went out of sight under the same table and those near them moved their legs aside as they continued without pause to eat, drink, smoke and bawl anecdote, assertion or invective. The main dish, narrowly preceded by a cold nettle soup with capers in it, was beef stroganoff served complete with knife and fork on the plate; the texture of Theodore's portion, if nobody else's, was such that it might well have included a stray tennis-ball sliced up along with the meat. There was wine on the table and vodka and brandy were swigged, in many cases straight from the bottle. Bowls of tired fruit and cups of coffee arrived after another short interval, not because the English waiters were efficient in the ordinary sense but because they wanted to pack up and go home; no doubt this threw some light on Igor Swianiewicz's corrective proposal.

'It was stuffy in there,' said Nina when they had finished and emerged.

'Yes,' agreed Theodore. 'Noisy too.'

They left the brilliantly illuminated area near the house and moved into summer twilight as far as the deserted bandstand. Here they halted; if they had gone much further they would have started to come upon the fornicating couples that littered those parts of the garden. Soon they were comfortably settled on the dry grass.

'When we met before,' began Theodore in that agreeable voice of his, 'you said something that made me think you were very strongly opposed to Director Vanag. Was I right? Why do you dislike him so much?'

'He's a tyrant.'

'And you hate tyranny. What would you do to fight it?'

'I don't know, I haven't thought about it. What can I do?'

He started to tell her. In a little while he was saying,

'I'm not a romantic revolutionary in the way that Alexander half is, even though he's a soldier. I know wounds hurt and cold freezes the blood and prison eats away the mind and soul. But against this enemy . . .' He fell silent.

'What did you say?' After several seconds, Nina went on, 'Alexander? Do you mean he's part of this?'

'He's about to – '

'But he can't be!' she said violently. 'He's quite unsuitable. You can't rely on him. He'd give you away if it suited him. He'd tell everything if he thought it would help him to get hold of a woman.'

At this last remark he shook his head in a troubled way. 'Admittedly you do know him better than anybody else does in one sense, but . . .'

'As you were saying earlier.'

'But there are other sides to him. He has qualities you don't know about that make him absolutely – '

'He has one quality that you can't know about or you'd never have gone near him: everything he does depends entirely on his own will, on whether it suits him to do it. If he keeps a promise it's because he wants you to see how he . . . You're not listening.'

'My dear Nina, I recognize what you're describing – there is an impetuosity there which could be dangerous, it needs watching, but it's potentially very valuable to us. If Alexander can be induced to identify himself with the revolution, to embrace it completely, and you can help to make that happen – then I promise you we'll have a weapon that Vanag himself ought to be afraid of. And I didn't walk into this business yesterday afternoon; I've spent years preparing for it, and I have been trained. That doesn't make me infallible, but I might be right, mightn't I?'

'Yes,' said Nina. In the half-minute since she had last spoken, her look of distress and disquiet had altogether disappeared, and when she spoke again it was almost abstractedly. 'I suppose it can't be done peacefully, the revolution I mean.'

'No, I was just coming to that. If I thought reform would come in twenty years, in thirty, fifty years, I swear I'd work for that. But it won't. You can't reform a monolith, you can only knock it over. We're going to use force, and that means locking people up, and if they resist they'll be compelled, and if they won't be compelled, if they shoot, we'll shoot back. A terrible thing to do, so terrible that only one cause in the world can justify it. Our cause. Freedom. Freedom for Russian and English together.'

They had both got up as he spoke and now stood facing each other in the darkness; clouds had covered the moon. Slowly he put his arms round her and kissed her on the lips.

She said hesitantly, 'I think this must be . . .' and could not go on.

'It is,' he said.

10

'But what does a Guards officer want with an ancient clergy-man?'

'According to him it isn't in his capacity as a Guards officer but to oblige Commissioner Mets.'

'So you said earlier. I meant, what does the particular kind of barbarian that officers their Guards want with me?'

'I'm sorry, sir – what this one wants, I think, is to impress this chap Mets with his powers of diplomacy and his knowledge of the English. He rather plumes himself on that, I'm not sure why.'

'How? Impress his friend how?'

'By persuading you to do what Mets wants and take a hand in this festival I mentioned.'

'Take a hand in what?'

'In the festival of English art and –'

'Yes, yes, yes. If that's the case his knowledge of the English is in some disarray.'

Dr Joseph Wright wanted to say that not all the English were the same, but held his peace. On their brief reacquaintance he had not found the Reverend Simon Glover the easiest of men, though no less easy than most nearly blind, rather deaf, rheumatic and very old men must tend to be. This one, clearly robust and handsome in former times, with an aggressive high nose, was housed and looked after by his granddaughter and her husband, the manager of a village eating-house and so quite prosperous by local standards. Their cottage was comfortably furnished: the chair Glover sat in, and nowadays rarely left by choice except to go to bed, was too well made not to have dated from before the Pacification. He wore carefully-pressed grey flannel trousers, a check shirt with open neck – no clerical collar, not for fifty years – and a navy-blue cardigan his grand-daughter had knitted. His expression was of slight but settled contempt for something outside his immediate surroundings.

'*What are you going to say to this fellow?*' Wright pitched his voice well up.

'*That depends rather on what he says to me.*'

'*I meant,*' said Wright, summoning his charity, '*I take it you will turn down his suggestion.*'

'*Well, I'd better hear what it is precisely, but yes, I can certainly see no reason for accepting any such proposal at the moment. That's to say while it remains no more than a proposal. If he applies pressure I shall obviously have to think again.*'

'*To be fair, they don't really behave like that these days, Mr Glover.*'

'*Can you see them refraining if they want something badly enough? I may be very important; that's one of the things we don't know. I can't imagine why I should be, but that's always the way where they're concerned. You can't tell what they'll be up to next because they can't either. You can see it in their faces – anxious, desperately puzzled, like children suddenly made to take part in some adult activity. I remember . . .*'

The old man fell silent, tightening and relaxing his clasped fingers. He had not seen in any detail the face of a Russian or of anybody else for several years; nevertheless, what he had said did not sound like the product of fancy. The doctor looked at his watch.

'*He's late.*'

'*He'll probably not come at all. Are you sure you understood him correctly?*'

'*Oh yes, sir, he was quite specific.*'

'*It seems slightly odd that he should go to all this trouble to win a good opinion that can't be much use to him.*'

It seemed something of the kind to Alexander himself, now entering the village. With Theodore's revolution so much in his thoughts, or rather in his day-dreamings as yet, standing well with Commissioner Mets seemed even less important than it had at first. But he could not get out of this evening's visit; to say that he had changed his mind, simply not done what he had undertaken to do, was unthinkable. His mistake had been in agreeing to see Mets in the first place; he might have foreseen that his father's silly paternal pride would light on some ridiculous chore that all the same could not be refused – indeed, must even so be prosecuted as vigorously as possible.

He found the cottage without trouble. It stood nearly opposite the village church, from which came the music of a synth-accordion and voices raised in song and raucous laughter. As he drew level the heavy door swung open and the racket was intensified. Two middle-aged men lurched out, talking loudly, drunk at half-past six. When they saw the Russian uniform they quietened down and straightened themselves and one of them hastily shut the door, an unnecessary switch to decorum, for the days were past when a member of the units of supervision would have been likely to correct English misbehaviour with riding-whip or pistol-butt. These two must have learned their lesson thoroughly in youth.

A dark-haired young woman answered Alexander's knock. She was pleasant enough to look at but not such as to arouse his desire, or no more than any other undeformed female of her age would have done, which was just as well in the circumstances. A boy of five or six had his hand in hers. After greeting them pleasantly in Russian Alexander picked the child up – he at least showed no mistrust – and set him in the mare's saddle. A short game ensued, evidently acceptable to both him and his mother. By the time it was over a man who was evidently his father had appeared. He took the reins and led Polly away round the side of the cottage. Alexander was shown into a long narrow room that ran from front to rear and had a window-bay at its far end. As he entered, two men who had been sitting in this space got to their feet without alacrity and faced him. He recognized Dr Wright with an irritation he strove to conceal; what lay ahead was going to be hard enough without such a presence on his flank, so to speak. He wished them good evening, again in Russian, a choice which surprised Wright and almost roused a flicker of respect in him.

'Do please sit down,' went on Alexander. 'It's good of you to be at home, Mr Glover. Now this won't take long.'

'What does he say?' asked Glover.

'Just politenesses. – You'd better speak up, and go slow too; his Russian isn't much good.'

'Very well. – Dr Wright will have told you why I am here, sir. May I ask how you feel about taking part in the festival he will also have spoken of?'

'The same way as I feel about everything you people … demand of me.' Glover's accent was thick and his delivery halting. 'If I can resist you I will.'

'I'm sorry to hear that, sir. I agree we are in a position to demand this. But there's more to the case than our demanding and your complying, or, possibly, not complying. What we demand is also what will benefit your fellow-countrymen in an important way, and you are one of the very few in a position to bring it to them.'

'What do you know of this "it" that I can bring my fellow-countrymen?'

'At first hand, nothing, of course, but am I wrong in thinking it important?'

'You have no … you don't know what importance is. Or truth. You Russians simply have an uneasy … feeling about having taken our culture and our religion away from us.'

'Perhaps you mean an uneasy conscience. That would be an excellent description.'

'Why stop there? Why not set about giving us back our history? To take away our books was a crime as great as taking away our churches. Until the year before you came we were still free. We … *we chose our rulers and dismissed them if they were unsatisfactory, within some limits we could say and write what we pleased, the courts were fair, we could come and go … And we had fought for our freedom, again and again. The knowledge of that you had to take away, because our national pride was rooted in it. It won't be very long now before nobody*

117

knows how we stood alone against Hitler, how but for us and the Americans your own precious country would have been defeated. You yourself don't know the bare fact that we and our allies invaded Western Europe in 1944 – I do, because my father was there, at a place called Arnhem. You don't even know how we fought you. You think it was all over in three days, you poor ignorant illiterate incurious nitwit . . .'

The old man said a good deal more to the same effect. Alexander listened respectfully, or with a show of respect. His English was good enough for him to be able to follow the general drift and he was familiar with the material, especially the part about the 1944 'invasion', the usual pre-war term and a surprisingly grandiose one, given the English tendency to understatement, for a raid on a single port. Like the rest of the stuff – the talk of choosing between one or other set of nominees of the boss, freedom of the press when the boss owned the press, unhindered access to any slum or ethnic ghetto – it was a comforting myth, important to a proud nation that had held India and large parts of Africa before being chased out by the indignant inhabitants. (Not that those inhabitants were much better off today, if the truth were known.)

The myth apparently meant a good deal to Glover, who was crying as he finished his tirade. Wright went across and laid a hand on his shoulder. He said quietly to Alexander,

'I think you'd better go now, don't you? You won't shake him.'

'We shall see.'

'Why are you doing this?' asked Wright abruptly.

'No good reason. My father suggested it and I couldn't think how to get out of it.'

'I suppose that might even be true.'

Alexander made no reply. He started thinking hard. After a couple of minutes he raised his voice. 'What about your duty as a Christian, Mr Glover?'

'*My what?*'

'*Duty as a Christian, sir,*' said Wright.

'What do you know of that, *you atheistical swine?*'

'As before, nothing, but you must know more than a little.'

'My duty as a Christian is a matter for my own conscience.'

'In that case let's save ourselves some time. This is a very attractive cottage and your granddaughter – yes? – is a delightful young lady. It would be terrible if a party of drunken soldiers broke in and wrecked the place and raped her. And her husband might get badly hurt if he tried to intervene, or if they thought he was going to. Even the boy – fine little chap, isn't he? – well, you know what brutes those Russian rankers are; some of them aren't even Russian, they're Tartars, Uzbeks – Asiatics. No one would be safe from them. Except you, Mr Glover. They'd have too much respect to lay a finger on you. Apart from making certain you saw everything of course. Now if – '

'Oh, dear God.'

'And you could fix that up easily enough, couldn't you?'

'What do you think, doctor?'

'I think you could and would, out of spite at being crossed in a matter you admit is of no concern to you.'

'Good. If you think that, so will others.' Alexander spoke up again. 'I couldn't arrange that, Mr Glover, even if I wanted to. Suppose for the moment it none the less took place. Somebody would be able to identify those soldiers – wearing civilian clothes would do no more than delay things slightly. Every Russian in the district would be paraded and the culprits picked out and sent to die in the Arctic. But it would never come to such a pass. If I were to give my men an order like that they'd simply not carry it out, quite confident I'd never dare charge them with disobedience. They know all this. The English don't, and wouldn't be inclined to believe it if they were told. So when your friends hear indirectly that you've been threatened with the rape of your granddaughter and sundry other dire things, they'll understand why you've agreed to cooperate with Commissioner Mets and they won't do what you're so afraid of and . . . *send you to Coventry*. Yes, I've learned a little about pre-wars over the years. I was brought up here, you know. Perhaps Dr Wright told you that.'

Glover had put his hands over his face. He said something in a pathetic whimpering tone to Wright, who looked consideringly over at Alexander. Finally he spoke, but his voice was hard and cold.

'He says it's worse being lonely when you're eighty and it's harder to be brave too.'

'I believe him. I don't quite see why you're talking to me in that strain, doctor. Mr Glover is in my debt. He can now do his duty without fear.' When Wright said nothing to that, Alexander went on more loudly, 'Am I to take it, sir, that Commissioner Mets is welcome to call?'

Wright turned to relay this but Glover was already nodding his head. Alexander got up and adjusted the hang of his tunic.

'So you've got what you wanted,' said Wright, not quite so coldly as before.

'It seems so. And what I wanted is in the general interest. For once. Is Kitty at home?'

'I hope she is. She's meant to be cooking the dinner.'

'I'll call on her. I won't stay.'

'I'll be along in an hour. Why aren't you at the grand levée given by that thieving grocer of yours?'

'It's not my sort of party.'

'Really, I should have thought that that was just what it was.'

'Off my home territory it's hard for me to shine as I like to do with all those important people there. I might look in late when most of them will have gone.'

Wright laughed without merriment. 'You're a fraud, Petrovsky, but quite a clever fraud.'

'I call that handsome of you, doctor. And I might surprise you one day about the fraud part.'

'Everything's possible.'

Alexander nodded, clicked his heels and called, 'Good night, Mr Glover.'

After a long pause the old man said, 'Good night. Thank you.'

A little later, in Wright's house, in the sitting-room next to the conservatory, Alexander and Kitty were vigorously kissing and caressing each other.

'*Oh darling, you make me so happy*,' she said.

'*I love you.*'

'*And I love you*, but it'll have to wait a minute or two – I've got to take the bean salad off the stove and dress it while it's still warm.'

A little later yet they were lying side by side in the bed upstairs.

'What are you thinking about?' said Alexander.

'Just wondering what's going to happen to us. I mean will you be coming to see me like this in a year's time, or in ten years' time, or what? Will we be married? I'm not asking you to, just wondering what you think will happen.'

'Darling, I couldn't marry you – I can't marry you. The law won't have it.'

'They might change the law. Things are getting easier.'

'Yes. Well, if they ever do change the law, of course we'll get married,' said Alexander, who never minded making this sort of promise, or indeed any other. He added deftly, 'That's if you still want to.'

'Oh, of course I will, of course I will. Where would we live?'

'In a grand house somewhere.'

'Where?'

'I don't know,' he said rather irritably; this sort of imagining bored him. 'Where would you like it to be?'

'Don't laugh, dearest, but where I'd really like it to be is Moscow.'

He stared at her in unaffected surprise.

'I know it could never happen,' she went on wistfully, 'but I keep imagining it. The Kremlin and the Kitai Gorod and Red Square and Lenin's tomb and the Praise of the Holy Virgin church. There's not a day goes by but I think of it all and wish I were there.'

'Why? From your point of view it's a foreign place at the other end of Europe where you've never been.'

'That's just it, it's so remote and mysterious and romantic. The great city in the snow. The last citadel on the road to Asia. After all it is the centre of the world.'

11

Though closed down, like all other public meeting-places, at the time of the Pacification, the theatre had never been converted into another use. Only three years previous to that event, it had been partly rebuilt and completely reseated to accommodate nearly four hundred people, its lighting system modernized and an apron stage installed. The structure was sound and dry. All this had meant that the theatre-section official in charge of premises had had to do little more than give the place a thorough springclean and replace the movables that had been confiscated or looted. By the time Alexander saw it, rehearsals were in their third week.

He went into the auditorium, where there was a faint, pleasant smell of the twentieth century. On the stage were two middle-aged men with an academic air to them, a third, younger man and a girl in her middle twenties with a book in her hand listening to some point one or other of the men was making to her. Alexander looked round casually and without result for Theodore and then less casually at the girl. She was what Nina would have called his type except that her expression was not so much sulky or bad-tempered as reserved and watchful, which made little difference to him; she was also rather tall, rather snub-nosed and very dark-haired. He moved right to the front of the house and cleared his throat in the hope of catching her attention, but failed to do so for the moment and settled himself on an aisle seat. Of the couple of dozen other people scattered about, none took notice of him, no doubt because he was wearing civilian clothes. The deliberations on the stage were suspended, the girl walked into the wings, emerged again almost at once and read from her book:

> '*Gallop apace, you fiery footed steeds,*
> *Towards Phoebus' lodging: such waggoner*
> *As Phaeton would whip you to the west,*
> *And bring in cloudy night immediately.*
> *Spread thy close curtain, love-performing night,*
> *That runaway's eyes may wink, and Romeo*
> *Leap to these arms, untalked of and unseen!*'

That on '*waggoner*' she dropped her voice, linked '*in*' with '*cloudy*' rather than with '*bring*', stressed '*close*' and showed misunderstanding in several other places made as little difference to him as the nuances of her expression; he listened with only half an ear, no more than was needed to assure himself that her voice was suitable for a young female, and concentrated his attention on how she looked and behaved. After speaking for a couple of minutes she stopped and glanced expectantly at the men. One of the academics said with warm approval in his voice and manner,

'That's very good, Sarah. Remember not to attach too much importance to individual words – it's the overall effect that matters.'

'I see, sir. I'm still not quite clear about Phoebus and Phaeton. What are my feelings towards them?' The girl's Russian was excellent.

'I think you regard them with great respect,' said the other academic. 'You're rather proud to be a fellow-citizen and neighbour of two such distinguished figures.'

At this point an inconspicuous door beside the stage opened and Theodore descended a short flight of stairs into the auditorium. Beside him was a big man of about forty with a closely-trimmed black beard and large, very dark eyes that fastened directly on whatever they looked at. Alexander knew him by sight as Aram Sevadjian, holder of some senior post in the Commission, in fact, as it very soon transpired, head of its theatre section. Led by him the three settled themselves at the end of a row near the back, where they conversed in suitable undertones. On stage an older woman had joined the girl.

'What do you think of our play?' asked Sevadjian.

'I haven't been here long,' said Alexander, 'but it seems promising.'

'I'm glad you think that. We've had a lot of trouble with it, you know. I suggested we might try another by the same author; it seems there's one about a Danish aristocrat who goes mad and thinks he sees a ghost which tells him to murder his uncle. More straightforward than this, I'd have thought, but the director, that young fellow there, he assures me there's no time to make a fresh start now, it's this or nothing. Well . . . It's so hard to understand the characters and to make out what one's meant to think of them. A young man meets a girl at a party and feels her up in public, in front of her parents, in fact. We all know such things happen, but then instead of having an affair with her he marries her, and after only one night together he suicides when he thinks she's dead – very flimsy, that part – and she suicides when she finds him dead, and the author makes no attempt at all to explain why; I mean they're not insane or anything like that. I expect I'm trying to take it too literally, and that part's meant to be a symbol of a couple completely going off each other when they've been powerfully attracted only a few days before, but one can't tell the audience that. Still, there's a certain amount of violence which we can play up, and the costumes and sets are going to be spectacular; I'm sure the thing will go down well enough. It's the occasion that matters. Well, you didn't come here to listen to me chattering about an old play. Allow me to welcome you to Group 31, Mr Petrovsky.'

'Thank you, Mr Sevadjian, but is it wise to do so in a place like this?'

'The answer to your commendably cautious question is Yes. One couldn't say the same for the dressing-rooms and offices. The reasoning of the Directorate is almost pitifully transparent: what audiences do is listen, not talk. All the same, I suggest we pay attention to events on stage from time to time.'

They watched while the girl read aloud, stumbling frequently,

> *'Hath Romeo slain himself? Say thou but "ay"*
> *And that bare vowel "ay" shall poison more*
> *Than the death-darting eye of cockatrice.*
> *I am not I if there be such an "ay",*
> *Or those eyes shut that make thee answer "ay".'*

Sevadjian chuckled appreciatively. 'I must say the comic parts still have their charm. Now to business. Our committee has discussed your access to Mrs Korotchenko. Members were very dubious till I pointed out that, even assuming Theodore here is under suspicion, up to the time she, er, made her approach to you the only contact you and he had had was at the races, at a game of croquet and at a dinner-party, with others present at all times on all three occasions. So unless the enemy has enough dedicated women to fuck everybody who gets within twenty metres of any of our workers, her motives would seem to have been innocent, if that isn't too strange a word. We therefore proceed. Your instructions are to strike for nothing less than a list of all the undercover agents of the Directorate in the district, but you must continue not to reveal in any way whatever that you work for any kind of resistance movement, even a one-man one – it was felt that the risk of an anonymous tip-off was too great.'

'Why? Why would she do that?'

'A dozen reasons. To protect herself. To dispose of you when a successor appears. To get her own back after a quarrel. Or some other motive that's unpredictable. She's an impetuous lady. I can't for a moment imagine how you're going to persuade her to get you that list without telling her something, but perhaps you can.'

'I can indeed. A reason tailor-made for her psychology.'

'I'm quite happy to leave you to handle it in your own way. When are you seeing her again?'

'Not for ten days. She wouldn't say why but she was quite firm.'

'How annoying of her.'

'It'll be worse than annoying if she keeps us waiting another couple of weeks after that.'

'There'd still be time. You must exercise your powers of fascination,' said Sevadjian, and turned towards the stage.

> '*O serpent heart* [read the girl], *hid with a flowering face!*
> *Did ever dragon keep so fair a cave?*
> *Beautiful tyrant! fiend angelical!*
> *Dove-feathered raven! wolvish-ravening lamb!*
> *Despised substance of divinest show!*
> *Just opposite to what thou justly seem'st.*
> *A damned saint, an honourable villain!*'

Sevadjian, who had been listening closely, frowned, sighed, and shook his dark head. 'The text must be corrupt – surely it's *a damned villain, an honourable saint,*' he muttered, making nine syllables of it, as the girl had done. Then he turned to Alexander again. 'Your father is greatly respected in the district. From my small personal knowledge he seems at any rate a humane man. How do you see him?'

'He's so humane – '

'Lower your voice.'

'I'm sorry. He's so humane he'd protect the rights of a mad dog. He has it both ways in perpetuity: tilting at the system while getting all he can out of it and working to keep it in being, sympathizing with the English and having Director Vanag to dinner. I despise him.'

'Am I to gather from that that you would have no objection to personally arresting your father when the time comes? It was felt that here would be a certain symbolic value.'

'I'd sooner shoot him, I think.' Alexander blurted this out, stopped, and went on in a normal tone, 'I'm quite prepared to arrest him, yes.'

'We intend to keep our operation as bloodless as possible.' With these words there came an abrupt change in Sevadjian's manner, which had been severely practical with an occasional jocoseness. Now, he turned in his seat so as to face Alexander squarely and fixed his remarkable eyes on him. 'I wonder if you feel as I and some others do about our movement, a sense of inestimable privilege at being able to take part in a great histori-

126

cal transfiguration; I hope you feel that. And it's more than taking part, it's directing, shaping, building. When we have finished our work, the world will never be the same again. In the end our names will be forgotten, but we'll have left our mark on events for as long as human society lasts. Our monument will be in men's minds. By liberating others we'll have liberated ourselves and all who come after us. I imagine the same thoughts, the same consciousness of purpose, uplifted our great predecessors in Petrograd as the autumn of 1917 advanced. Our task is to restore that revolution. And we shan't fail.'

What most struck Alexander about this speech was not so much its entire conviction nor even its top-speed, word-perfect delivery as its low volume and the almost total lack of gestures accompanying it. To anyone more than a couple of metres away and not directly in his line of sight Sevadjian might have seemed to be further expounding, not uncritically, the plot of the play in rehearsal. For some reason this increased the difficulty of devising an answer to what he had said. Alexander could find no words that were quite free of the risk of sounding frivolous and contented himself with nodding earnestly.

For the first time, he started to believe that what he had taken for an amusing fantasy was going to be tried and might succeed. And if it did succeed and he had had no part in it, then from being an officer in the Guards he would presumably become some sort of prisoner, even though not for long, perhaps. On the other hand, he was pretty certain to have a far worse time if he joined in and it failed. But in that event would he not be considered to have joined in already? It would do him no good to plead that he had not actually done anything yet, and advanced techniques of interrogation left no chance whatever of his name not becoming immediately known to the Directorate. If only he had considered earlier, not whether or not the confounded scheme would succeed, but that it was becoming more and more certain to be tried!

The sensible course was to return to quarters, change into standard dress and pay a call on Vanag – returned from

Moscow the previous day. It was also out of the question. Alexander affirmed to himself that he was proof against all moral compunction; what he could not abide was being seen to be the sort of person who did that sort of thing. And how desirable, how necessary, how *bloody marvellous* to be the hero of a successful revolution! Because on the strength of that list and those projectiles . . .

Sevadjian wished him luck, shook hands and was gone. Speaking for the first time since the moment of his arrival – he was good at staying silent – Theodore said,

'Isn't he magnificent?'

'Most impressive. Is he the leader?'

'The cell leader. The identity of the leader of the whole movement is known only to two other people.'

'I can see the point of that, but it must raise certain – '

'Alexander, I want to come to talk to your father about something, something quite different obviously, but I'd like you to be about the place too. When would be a good time?'

'Friday is his open-house evening. If you want a long chat with him you'd do better to wait till next week. I can be there almost any night.'

'Friday will do nicely. Thank you for not asking questions. I hope you won't mind if I ask you one. Did you mean what you said about your father, that you were prepared to shoot him?'

'I said I thought so. I still think so, but I can't really imagine what it would feel like to be actually about to do it.'

Without further inquiry Theodore removed himself, mentioning a pile of work at the Commission. Alexander, left hand in pocket as traditionally allowed off-duty Guards officers, strolled down to his earlier position near the stage, on which a break had just been called and mugs of tea were being handed round. This time the young actress did catch his eye, long enough for him to give her a nod of greeting but no longer. He waited to see if she would turn towards the others, from whom she was standing a little apart; when she did not, he moved. Almost at once he was introducing himself as a newly-appointed member of the Commission.

'My name is Sarah Harland,' she said in an inexpressive tone, quite different from the one she had used when speaking her lines. 'What can I do for you?'

'I thought you might do me the honour of letting me take you out to lunch. I'm afraid there's nowhere very – '

'Why should I?'

'No important reason. I got interested in the play, and we could – '

'No you didn't, Russian; all you had any time for was whatever the boss was telling you.'

'You were watching me, then.'

'I was watching the audience – an actress always does that in rehearsals. No, you're not interested in the play, you're not even interested in me; all you want is to get me on my back as fast as possible. You *Shits* are all the same.'

She was not speaking inexpressively now. Seen close to she looked sprightly and rather formidable, Alexander thought, with something very attractive about the way she moved her lips and something even more attractive about the development of her figure. Carefully underplaying the honest bewilderment, he said after a pause,

'What can I do to convince you that at least I'm interested in you? – never mind the play.'

'I haven't the faintest idea.'

Sarah Harland turned her back and went and accepted more tea while he grinned a little to himself. Even during their short conversation she had invisibly led them away from the main body, now augmented by a young actor and an old actor, and had kept her voice down. So all he had to do was the only thing open to him to do and watch more of the play, watch an hour of it, watch till the rehearsal was over, watch on a future occasion, but anyway introduce a long enough pause, whether of minutes or days, for Miss (or Mrs) Harland to feel able to satisfy some mysterious power that she was not making herself cheap. Then would come lunch and then, after minutes or days, but inevitably from the moment just now when she had spoken her first words to him, bed. Once, when he was sixteen, he had known a

129

girl from a remote country district who pulled his hand away the first few times he laid it on her breast and again when he thrust it up her skirt; the same trait on a different scale. When one looked at it in a certain way, it was quite remarkable how little there was to understand about women.

12

'You know, Brevda, when you come to think about it, life is hell.'

'It notoriously has its negative aspects, sir.'

'There seems no rest from having to decide what one ought to do in a given situation.'

'The necessity of moral choice can be most onerous, sir.'

'Self-interest just isn't a sufficient guide to behaviour, is it?'

'Sadly deficient in many respects, sir.'

'After all, there is such a thing as right and wrong.'

'Bravely spoken, sir.'

Having paced the length of the gallery a couple of times engaged in this style of talk, master and man halted at the east window of the house. It was Friday evening about six-thirty. In the afternoon there had been a heaviness of the air that had seemed to threaten thunder, but this had passed and the sun sparkled brightly on the dark waters of the pond below them. Alexander's mind was blank; he could not now remember why he had started this conversation, nor had he any idea what to say next. In an effort to shake off inertia he turned abruptly on Brevda, saying almost at random,

'Have you got me some fresh cigarettes?'

'No, sir, I – '

'Why not?'

'Well, I have to go in tomorrow, sir, and you still have about ten, and you never smoke more than about two or three in a – '

'Tonight might be just the night I want twenty. Simply because you lead such a wretchedly repetitive mean little life you needn't suppose others do the same. In future see I have a full packet at all times. I'm sick of the sight of you – be off and draw my bath.'

'Yes, sir.'

'Brevda.'

'Sir?'

Alexander stared at his valet for a long time, blinking and slowly opening and shutting his mouth. Then he said, 'Sorry. It's ... the heat,' this in such a way as to leave no doubt that, whatever it was, it was not that. 'Well, am I forgiven?'

'Of course, your honour.'

Half an hour later Alexander was in his bedroom putting on his mess-dress. By now he seemed in the best of spirits; he was whistling a song of the regiment, fresh in his mind after hearing the band practising it in preparation for the next morning's ceremonial parade. The vodka bottle still stood on the writing-table, but its level had not changed for over a week. In the same kind of way he had given notice of his intention to turn up this evening and had spent the last half hour quietly reading when he could have been lying face down on his bed. These improvements originated not in any self-reformatory efforts but in the completeness with which his energies were now absorbed: any time left over from work and sex was used up by the revolution and there was none to spare for drink, plaguing the household or behaving like someone in a nineteenth-century Russian novel. As a result he was nearer to being contented, even happy, than he had been for years; it was true that his second visit to the rehearsals of the English play, paid the morning after the first one, had been productive only of irritation, but a kind of semi-discreditable relief had soon followed. His obvious response to the setback must be complete inactivity for as long as possible, not a daunting prospect to one already so extended. In fact, he had since realized, his original approach to Sarah Harland had been in pursuance of that earlier and comparatively juvenile policy of his that dictated instant pursuit of any attractive female – earlier than his association with Mrs Korotchenko, the most unjuvenile passage, it seemed to him, of his career to date.

132

His comb struck a tangle of hair at the crown of his head, spun out of his hand and skidded across the top of the dressing-table to vanish between it and the wall. Cursing loudly in English, he used excessive force to make an aperture for his arm. His groping fingers soon found the comb, but they had already found something else as well, something that felt like a crumpled piece of card. It proved to be a treasure he had thought for a year or two to be lost – he had had no cause to look behind the dressing-table in that time, and no more had any servant: the ancient photograph, taken seven metres below where he stood, that had told him of the cypress avenue, the yew hedge, the statues of nymphs and hunters, the little stone lions once to be seen from his window. Whether because of the lapse of time, or the renewed effect of the old flatlook process, or most likely the experience he had gained in the interval, the sight affected him strongly.

In a few seconds his manner lost all its new firmness and sobriety and his eyes grew unfixed. He imagined, or tried to imagine, the scene in the photograph not as it was, not empty, not strange and sad, but enlivened by some of the people who had known it just as it was then, at the very moment the camera had recorded it, the men in tweed suits, striped shirts and the ties of their school, university or regiment, the women wearing elaborate dresses of light coloured silk and fine silk stockings, with much jewellery. At this hour, perhaps, they would have been eating gherkin sandwiches and drinking gin, Scotch whisky, port, champagne, out of crystal goblets.

What had they thought was awaiting them? – for Alexander had always fancied, had taken it for granted, that the picture commemorated a vanished world not by chance but by design, that it dated from the last months or days of that world and had been pushed under the gallery floor for him to find, or more strictly for him to take possession of some years after a workman replacing rotten boards had found it. What had they said to one another, those men and women of the final stage of capitalism? Had they talked of the starving pensioners in their tiny unheated rooms, of the dying children turned away from

133

hospitals because their parents could not afford to rent a bed for them, of the immigrants cowering at the backs of their shops while the racist mobs looted and burned and the police stood by or joined in the rapine, of the groups of workers hastily assembling and training for the supreme struggle? (Hardly of the last-mentioned, which could be assumed to have taken place in secret, though details of this and of all the other matters were lacking.) Or had that conversation of long ago revolved round traditional interests, fox-hunting, pheasant-shooting, cricket, the London theatre, adultery? He had no idea whatever of the answers to any of these questions, just hoped very much that some sort of Yes could be attached to the last one because that made the participants more admirable, more aristocratic, more English. And surely that other Alexander would have enjoyed his hold on the life he had always known until the instant when it was forcibly taken from him.

At the thought of his namesake and predecessor, Alexander Petrovsky raised his head and lost some of his dreamy look. After a pause he stepped across to the bookcase, took out the purple-bound volume, opened it at an acute angle and popped his finger inside. Then he read aloud, in a high, slow, monotonous voice, the passage that either chance or a prodigiously close knowledge of the lay-out had put in his way.

> 'Freckled hands reach out to clasp in love,
> The mouth drools that would kiss, the straining eyes
> Hold sweet images of what never was;
> Ah, shut them with a blow, strike aside
> The hands, silence the mouth for ever
> Before it calls for reason, faith, justice,
> And the hangmen come.'

This time the reader shut the book without a sound and replaced it gently on the shelf. After standing a minute in thought, evidently unpleasing thought, he gave a long sigh, checked his appearance in the wardrobe mirror and marched out, straightening his mess-jacket.

Downstairs, in the drawing-room, in the east hall, by the east front, the first guests were assembling. Three long tables formed an open square on the paved space between the entrance staircases and the edge of the pond. There were dishes of ham, smoked goose, cold mutton, cold chicken, cold sliced beetroot, marrow, red cabbage, watercress and endive, bowls of date chutney and pickled mushrooms and onions, and plates of thick white bread and butter. Peaches, gooseberries, loganberries and cream and junket were also offered, together with several varieties of cake. Bowls of a transparent plastic meant to resemble glass contained a cold punch of Krasnodar Riesling with lemon-juice and sugar-syrup and a slight stiffening of vodka. Vodka itself was to be had for the asking, and of course there would be plenty of asking.

These informal receptions of the Controller's, held on the second and fourth Friday of every month from March to October, were highly valued throughout the units of supervision, not for the generous hospitality alone, though this was indeed a factor, nor so much for ordinary social reasons as for the opportunity, provided almost nowhere else, of running into colleagues, opposite numbers, persons normally inaccessible for reasons of rank or protocol and, in these unceremonious circumstances, settling in a couple of minutes difficulties that weeks of official exchange might have failed to solve.

The difficulty which now occupied the Controller and his wife had been doing so on and off for nearly ten years and was certainly not going to be settled in a couple of minutes. Even so, the urgency in Tatiana Petrovsky's tone and manner suggested that she had by no means given up hope of one day carrying her point. She and her husband were standing some distance round the curve of the pond, away from the sprinkling of guests; it was years since, in furtherance of informality, Petrovsky had left off the practice of having individuals presented on arrival at the fortnightly receptions.

'You must speak to him,' she said, not being a believer in originality for its own sake.

'I can hardly speak to him this minute, my love.'

'That's precisely what you can do, Sergei. He's just arrived,

135

he's on his own, he'll be sober and above all he'll be unprepared. That's your only chance of getting him to listen to you. If you signal your intention by telling him you want to have a chat with him, or ... however you put it, by the time you see him he'll have worked out which attitude to use to keep you at a distance, cold or humble or ... You know how he is.'

'Yes, I think I do. What do you want to me to say?'

'Dear God, what I've just been telling you, that she's a notoriously disreputable creature, also that one of her young men committed suicide and she was suspected of murdering another, or at least accidentally killing him, but she was never charged, nobody was, that she –'

'All allegation. Rumour.'

'What else would you expect? One's friends and their friends aren't on oath, but why should they lie, and tell the same lie? That woman is a pervert. She likes ... Well, Agatha Tabidze wouldn't specify, and we've been friends for ten years. Surely that suggests something.'

'Indeed it does, like everything else you say about her – that the lady must be irresistible to any young man of spirit. Oh, I don't welcome it, of course, but ...'

'But what?'

Sergei Petrovsky's handsome bearded face showed a refined discomfort, an awareness of duty left undone coupled with mild, regretful cynicism about the real value of that duty. His attire was similarly diversified: austerely-cut suit of dark-grey flannel or an approximation to it, bright-coloured striped waistcoat with copper buttons in student style and cream shirt with open collar, bureaucratic necktie thrown aside. Beside him, round-shouldered and not tall, in finely-woven azure cotton with lilac ribbons, Tatiana was to the casual eye a much less impressive figure. A second glance might have noted determination in her gaze and in the set of her mouth, and strong will or at least obstinacy in the prominent bar of frontal bone above her eyes, a characteristic inherited by her sons but not her daughter, and one who had noted so much might very likely have gone on to feel a certain sympathy for a man whose wife knew so precisely and so certainly how he ought to behave on any occasion and was so fully prepared to make him a present of that knowledge at any time. Only a close and attentive friend of the family, perhaps, Agatha Tabidze or another, was in a position to observe how unimpressively, how lamely Sergei answered Tatiana's scoldings and urgings and how serenely he did or went on doing just as he pleased, which in practice usually meant not doing something that would incur hostility.

'But what can I do?' he answered her now. 'What should I do? And what makes you so sure there's an affair going on? I'm not aware of any evidence of it.'

'My darling, you wouldn't be aware of any evidence if you saw them in bed together, but if you want to hear I'll tell you what makes me so sure. Two things at least. The way she behaved that night when they'd come back indoors. Not a word out of her all evening and then all of a sudden interested in everything. Like a drug-addict in a last-century movie, before and after taking a dose. He carried it off very well. But then he's grown so secretive, that's the other thing. Oh, he has his silly fits but until this started, one way or another I always knew what he was up to. He senses I'd disapprove more strongly than I usually do. His manner's altogether different.'

'Young men may have all manner of reasons for being secretive.' Petrovsky spoke very gently, or at least in a very propitiatory way. 'And why do you disapprove? Having moral attitudes these days seems rather ... pointless.'

'These days there's more point then ever before. But no need to take things as far as morality – surely you can see other grounds for disapproving, practical ones. Suppose her husband finds out; have you thought what damage he might do? And what she might do? At least you should warn him.'

'I'm sure he's taken all that into consideration, my love.'

'Are you really? When was he last seen taking into consideration anything that might hinder him from doing whatever he wanted to do?'

Still gently, Petrovsky said, 'We've come as far as morality now all right, haven't we? Moral disapproval of someone doing as he pleases, of that in itself. I'm afraid I've never been able to summon up very strong feelings along those lines.[2]

'Yes, Sergei, that is your serious misfortune, and others'. All human beings, especially those with good looks or some other advantage over their fellows, need strong opposition when young, that in itself. If it isn't forthcoming, their characters suffer. They become egotistical, impossible to deflect from any course of action they may have set themselves, and yet erratic, given to abrupt, entire changes of direction for no external cause. I can't imagine why it's always supposed to be the over-indulgent mother who spoils her son when the father is obviously so much more important in teaching him how to behave. It must be more difficult for a father to take in the fact that his son is growing up, that he isn't still the little boy whose activities are too harmless and unimportant to have a strict watch kept on them. And of course being tolerant is so much less trouble. At the time. But just wait. Our son is now a very dangerous person – to himself. I hope for all our sakes, Sergei, that you're a less liberal administrator than you are a father.'

When he judged she had finished, he said in the same tone as before, 'Goodness, I could tell there was a good deal of moral disapproval about. What I hadn't realized was how much of it was reserved for me.'

As they stared at each other, the lines of bitterness and accusation round her mouth and eyes began to fade a little, but there was still an edge to her voice when she said, 'We all need opposition from time to time, including you, dearest Sergei,' thinking to herself as so often before that this time there was a chance he might actually do something about the matter in hand.

'I'll speak to him. If he knows we know, at least it'll make it easier for him to come to us in a crisis.'

'Don't let him get away with denying it.[2]

'I think you can trust me not to do that,' he said, sounding less than bland for the first time.

Already wondering whether she thought so too, she looked over his shoulder and at once her manner changed slightly but perceptibly. A small figure, no more than a metre and a half high but finely proportioned, had just emerged from the house and now stood for a moment surveying the assembled company before starting to walk down the steps.

Petrovsky glanced briefly at his wife and followed her gaze. Without conscious thought the two moved nearer each other as if the better to resist some form of physical attack. For the new arrival was Director Vanag, who had never been known for certain to do anything whatever in his official capacity except go to his office in Northampton Town Hall five and a half days a week, but who was always brought to mind (though less often mentioned) when someone was recalled to Moscow and never heard of again, or when someone else met an unnatural death in the district. Earlier that very week, the drowned body of a clerk in the administrative department concerned with housing had been pulled out of the river Nene, a man of unblemished public and private life, a man with no visible enemies. He had suffered a blow on the head, perhaps in falling, perhaps not. It was inferred as a matter of course that Vanag had been responsible, the victim's strongly-presumed innocence being taken by some as positive confirmation, on the argument that indiscriminate 'demonstrations', as such acts had become known, were more efficacious than selective ones. According to a simpler and more fashionable view, Vanag was too lazy or incompetent to track down any real undesirables there might have been and ordered the occasional random murder purely as evidence of zeal. Whatever the truth of that, nobody was amused, and the need to stand well with the Director was so thoroughly understood that nobody, except perhaps Alexander, seriously blamed the Petrovskys for inviting him to their parties.

Now he paused again, standing on the bottom step, and again looked about him. As always he was unaccompanied; at no social gathering had he ever been seen with a companion of either sex and, although he was universally believed to be under strong guard night and day, any guards were never identifiable as such. He seemed just on the point of resuming his progress when he caught sight of his hosts and raised his hand to them. It was a curious gesture, prolonged until what had looked like a greeting became something not far from a warning; then he moved off and was lost to sight among his taller fellow-guests. The Petrovskys looked at each other once more, this time in a way that showed deep intimacy and mutual trust, he conveying a mild request for moral support against any difficulties that might ensue, she warmly promising it. They were about to join a nearby group when Alexander, Nina and Theodore came up to them. The latter pair were holding hands and had an air of great seriousness and suppressed excitement and a little discomfort.

'These two have something to say to you, papa.' Alexander too seemed ill at ease, but amused at the same time. 'For some reason they want me to be present when they say it, though I can't see what business it is of mine.'

'Have I your permission to speak, sir?' asked Theodore.

'To speak? Why, certainly.'

'Nina and I are in love with each other, I have asked her to be my wife and, subject to your approval, sir, she has accepted. So I now formally request your daughter's hand in marriage.'

'I see. Well . . . of course. A splendid idea. I formally . . . award you her hand. A splendid idea. My congratulations to you both. We must arrange a party. An engagement party.'

Alexander and his mother added their congratulations. Petrovsky stepped forward, his arms held out, but Theodore checked him for the moment, took Nina's hand and put on her fourth finger a ring that featured a large purple zircon or other imitation gem set in a platinum claw. When he had kissed her there were sundry embraces, followed by some discussion of dates. After that Petrovsky said there were other family matters to be discussed with Alexander, and the engaged couple withdrew.

'Your father looked thoroughly mystified,' said Theodore with a chuckle.

'Oh, wasn't he sweet? Just managing to prevent himself from asking why on earth you needed permission to marry a female indisputably of age. But he came through like a born admini-

140

strator. I was proud of him. You two should get on like a house on fire.'

'There was something else he'd have liked to ask, or rather get confirmed – that we're sleeping together.'

'Oh, yes. I'm glad he didn't, aren't you? We'd have had to say No, and he'd either have been hurt at our lying to him or been terribly shocked at our unprogressiveness.'

'I know, but really I think it would be hard to find anybody much who'd understand that we both simply would much rather not until we're married. Perhaps your mother would.'

'I doubt it. She's very moral but her ideas are rather fixed. And of course someone like Elizabeth would just think we were mad. That reminds me: she says she'll join the . . . music society. She'll do anything within reason that isn't either dangerous or disgusting. By disgusting she means sleeping with Vanag's men to get information out of them.'

'Very sensible. I'm so happy I'm going to do something that isn't sensible at all and may be both dangerous and disgusting.'

'Oh, darling, he knows I hate him.'

'He must know everybody hates him . . . *Good evening, sir – I trust I find you in good health.*'

'I beg your pardon, I so rarely have need for that language. Nevertheless good evening, Miss Petrovsky, Mr Markov.' Director Vanag spoke in a high tenor, almost an alto. He wore one of the badgeless uniforms, very dark blue and buttoned to the neck, in which he was always seen, this version being of distinctly superior cloth to that of his everyday dress. Theodore's greeting might not have been to his taste, but he had responded to it with what in almost anyone else would have been taken as a pleasant, even attractive smile. The glance of his large, clear grey eyes had similar connections with friendliness and candour. In repose his face, almost unlined and of a healthy complexion, had a wistful, unworldly look. His crisp, sandy hair, cut short and parted on the right, lifted a little in the faint evening breeze. His teeth were small and regular. He was forty-five and looked thirty-five.

'You must congratulate us, Director,' Theodore went on. 'Miss Petrovsky and I have just become engaged to be married.'

'Indeed? What a splendid concept. I do very heartily congratulate you.'

'We can take it that you approve, then, can we, sir?'

'Approve?' Vanag gave a merry laugh of pure amusement. 'Of course I approve, but what possible difference could it make whether I did or not? The view of a humble pen-pusher can hardly be of much interest to anyone. Well now, this chance encounter is very timely, Mr Markov. I was thinking to myself just the other day that my ignorance of the activities of your Commission was quite shameful. You can enlighten me. Perhaps you'd be good enough to give me a short account of them.'

Theodore set himself to do so and the talk flowed with some freedom. After a couple of minutes Alexander joined the group, but seemed to have nothing to contribute. He soon began making small impatient movements which the other two men paid no attention to.

'It's an impressive undertaking,' said Vanag in tones of great interest and also of finality. 'More ambitious than I'd realized.'

'It's the least we can do, after the way we treated them in the past.'

'I'm sorry, I'm afraid I don't quite . . .'

'The denationing programme was nothing but an act of savagery.'

'With respect, Mr Markov, if it was that it was also something more: it was the means of breaking the English will to resist, and that had to be done.'

'It broke everything English. The scale of the thing was altogether wrong. After all, organized resistance collapsed on the third day.' Theodore was trying hard to speak calmly and civilly. 'Isn't that true, sir?'

'Perfectly true. Hostilities didn't cease immediately, however.'

'There were isolated pockets of resistance, according to the official history of the operation.'

'Just so. I take your point, Mr Markov, and if your feelings about these events cause you to approach your work with heightened enthusiasm, so much the better for everybody concerned. I've enjoyed our chat. Now I fear I must leave you. Miss Petrovsky; gentlemen.'

And with a gracious inclination of the head Director Vanag turned away and took a proffered glass of the freshly-squeezed lemonade that was always available to him wherever he went and whatever the hour.

'Strange, isn't it?' said Nina a moment later. 'If you didn't know – '

But Alexander interrupted her. 'Forgive me, darling, I must just have one minute with your fiancé. Men's talk. Then I'll get you a lovely drink.'

As soon as they were alone, Theodore said, 'What on earth's the matter? You look – '

'My parents know about me and Mrs Korotchenko.'

'Are they here tonight, the Korotchenkos?'

'I haven't seen them.'

'Let's hope . . . Sorry, go on.'

'Well, I was all surprise and indignation but my mother just went on saying she knew – she's always much tougher than my father over things like this, over most things, in fact. They were trying to warn me off, saying she's mad and bad, but that's no news, though they had plenty of documentation, I must admit. At any rate, they know.'

'How?'

Alexander drew in his breath and shook his head. 'That's just it. My mother was quite firm that it was nothing but her observation of me and Mrs K on the evening in question, but she may have some source she didn't want to mention.'

'Who could it be?'

'I can't imagine. It's depressing. Perhaps I could . . . No. Let's think. Not Korotchenko or they'd have mentioned it, and so would he, presumably. They'd have mentioned the Tabidzes too. Or would they? Who else is there? Think.'

'Look, will your parents keep quiet?'

'My mother will. My father . . . well, yes, probably. I'll take a chance on it, anyway.'

'You must. The great thing is that Korotchenko clearly doesn't know. That list of their agents is important to us.'

'All right.'

'When is it, next Thursday? *The best of luck, my dear fellow.*'

Before the night was out Theodore Markov had another conversation that was later to seem important to him, even though this later one lasted only half a minute. The sturdy figure of Commissioner Mets had approached him and Nina rather abruptly.

'How did it go?' Mets had known about the impending engagement.

'Oh, very well, thank you, sir. The old boy was rather taken aback but he soon rallied.'

'Good. I saw you having a word with the big boss. Vanag.'

'Yes, sir. Just briefly.'

'What do you think of him?' asked Mets in a loud expressionless voice.

'We had met once before. He was most polite.'

'Good. He didn't make any interesting remarks, I suppose, about any of us? I mean he's a bit of a joker in his way.'

'Is he? No, the conversation was general.'

'I see. He can be quite a joker, you know. Well . . . good night.'

'Your boss might have congratulated me or something,' said Nina as soon as it was opportune.

'I think he must have been drunk.'

'Probably. He looked to me as if he was frightened.'

Time was advancing. No food remained on the tables; a large part of it had been eaten by the guests, the rest smuggled out of sight by the waiters for selling to the English gardeners, grooms and lower house-servants for a few hundred pounds a time. The punch had all been drunk, and the company, now somewhat reduced in both numbers and condition, was regaling itself on inferior white wine, rye beer and various spirits. As the light began to fail there was a general move indoors, partly because the breeze had freshened, partly because a good deal of noise was now coming from an impromptu male-voice choir and, round the miniature temple, a remote kind of prayer-meeting with the principal role being taken at the moment by a naked man flourishing a bottle of vodka, during the day a senior official in the department of communications.

A visitor who knew the house as it normally was would have noted certain arrangements made for the occasion. The standard of behaviour expected tonight was far higher than that at, say, Igor Swianiewicz's parties, which were as different as they could possibly have been from the present gathering. Otherwise the outer doors would have been barred and heavy furniture run up against them, to be removed only when the last departure was reliably reported. As it was there was free access to east and west halls, in which hard chairs and folding tables were set, and only the more expensive appointments had been locked away. All internal doors except those of the downstairs lavatories, where the floors were covered with sheets of waterproof material, had of course been securely blocked.

The more sober spirits were grouped at the western end. It was here that, about eleven o'clock, Mrs Tabidze yielded to persistent requests and began telling fortunes with a pack of playing-cards. She stipulated that she would not choose her clients – individuals must suggest themselves, thereby nettling Alexander, who felt that this undemanding way of holding the stage would be unacceptably degraded if one were seen to bid for it. Nina had no such inhibitions. Ignoring Theodore's mild dissuasion she went forward and sat at the small baize-covered table on the other side of which Agatha Tabidze was putting out the cards face down in heaps of half a dozen and turning them over apparently at random. Nina's virtues were rehearsed, then some of her accomplishments, like making a good lemon soufflé; this part was light and facetious in tone. Her engagement was treated rather more sedately, with a few minor facts revealed which it seemed she had not thought at all generally known. Finally – it was soon clear that the fortunes told were to be of no great comprehensiveness – Mrs Tabidze drew a fresh card and said in a gentle voice,

'And what is to come will be good. Soon there will be a time of trial, not of your making, for between the two of you there will never be any serious difficulty, yet none the less it will be a troublesome time. But it will pass, and you will be together, and you will be happy.'

There was shouting and applause from the couple of dozen in the west hall. Nina jumped to her feet and embraced Mrs Tabidze, then, streaming with tears and grinning broadly, ran to Theodore's arms. Petrovsky made a confused reannouncement of what had just been made public and the company cheered, renewed their applause and proposed and drank toasts. One of the drinkers, a burly bearded man in a short bottle-green jacket and white trousers, immediately afterwards clapped his hand across his mouth and made off towards the lavatories at a lurching trot. Then things quietened down for a time. Successively, two middle-aged ladies, each the wife of an official, were taken at a smart pace through their pasts, presents and futures. General attention wandered; after emotional farewells, or in one case after being hauled upright and supported from either side, several people left. When the second lady had been dismissed there was a pause, and the entertainment, already languishing, seemed about to cease altogether. At last Commissioner Mets put up his hand and was accepted.

The fortune-teller had run into a small difficulty in that her acquaintance with her new customer was recent and slight, though it certainly included the fact that he held an important and therefore sensitive post; banter, the obvious recourse, would not do here. Hesitantly at first, consulting the cards a great deal, she told the Commissioner that he was a man of wide knowledge, refined taste and steady judgement, that he showed total dedication to his job but was always extending his horizons in new directions, and other things no self-respecting bureaucrat could demur at. When the talk turned to the inevitable difficulties along the way and the patience that would in time resolve them, someone gave a great yawn, but the next moment Mrs Tabidze turned up a card, looked at Mets and gave a sharp exclamation of surprise. She was not hesitating now; it was just that the words would not come.

'Those difficulties we were speaking of,' she said. 'Are some of them . . . is one of them exceptionally severe?'

'Yes,' said Mets in a neutral tone, sitting forward in his chair with his hands pressed together.

'In fact, would a stronger word be more appropriate? Quandary? Dilemma? Crisis?'

'Yes. Well, in a way, in a manner of speaking.'

'And has it presented itself recently? Very recently?'

'Somewhat recently.'

Mrs Tabidze turned up another card and stared at it for some time in silence. Without lifting her eyes she said slowly, 'Then I have to tell you that within a comparatively short time, certainly no more than four weeks, the situation will have resolved itself in your favour. You will have achieved success.'

'How satisfactory. Thank you. Thank you very much.'

'I've never known her to behave like that before,' said Tatiana Petrovsky to her husband. 'It's as if she really had seen something in those cards.'

'Oh, old Agatha's a marvellous actress.'

'I don't think it's that, or not only that. There's something funny going on here.'

Alexander had had a poor evening: no real chance to show off, irritating conversation with parents, and now boredom with no end in sight. He was weighing the merits of getting sonorously drunk against those of denouncing the company as rotten with credulity and superstition before storming off to bed (quicker, for one thing) when Sonia Korotchenko passed him on her way to the vacant chair at the baize-topped table. He made no sound but gave a start that scraped his foot on the stone floor. If asked at any previous stage, he would have stated with total confidence that she had not turned up at the party. Where was her husband? Not in sight, or not completely or identifiably; a pair of trousered legs and the crook of an elbow on the far side of a nearby pillar might quite well have been his.

Several voices asked more or less loudly who that woman was, meaning the one now seeking (with some determination, to judge by the set of her bare shoulders) to have her fortune told.

For a moment Alexander considered withdrawing as quietly as he could. It was impossible, no, but it was most unlikely, that she should not know he was there, far from impossible that within a minute she would tell of or otherwise reveal, as it might be by diving at his genitals, something he would on the whole prefer should remain undivulged, and quite certain that parts at least of this risk would be removed if he should prove not to be there after all. And yet – the limelight was always the limelight, whatever colours it showed one in, and the sort of things she did were apt to lose heavily in the telling. He was finally decided to stay by Mrs Tabidze's expression of restrained disquiet coupled with having heard from his parents something of what she knew about the lady in the low-cut muslin dress – the same, he was nearly sure, that she had twitched so unreluctantly over her head on her previous visit to the house. It could well be her only garment if when at home she went about naked all the time instead of just when receiving visitors.

After thoroughly shuffling and cutting the pack Mrs Tabidze put it out as before and glanced at the top card on each heap. Alexander could see her chewing at her lips and hid a grin. After a false start she said rather hoarsely,

'When you were very young you made a long journey. You and your mother and father came from – '

'I don't want to hear about the past. I know about the past.' Mrs Korotchenko sounded as if her mouth and lips were dry. 'Tell me about the future.'

'Very well . . . You will have a long and happy married life. You will continue to be a source of strength and comfort to your husband. Over the years, you – '

'That's the sort of thing that happens to a lot of people. Isn't anything going to happen to me that never happens to anybody else? And shall I never do anything? Surely I shall do something, however trivial, that nobody else has ever done?'

148

The wooden phraseology, the loud, grating, uninflected voice seemed to add to the impression made on the audience. Unbelievably, they fell silent, except for the continued frenzied coughing of a hugely fat, pop-eyed old character whose frilled shirt lay open to the navel. The cards clicked loudly in Mrs Tabidze's hands. Coming to the last one of a heap, she sat still for a moment and turned it over. What she saw, or the interpretation she put on the sight, made her spring to her feet and grunt with an astonishment much more acute than that shown over Mets's fortune a few minutes earlier. In years of acquaintance Alexander had never known her behave so excitedly before. Mrs Tabidze looked up, became aware she was standing and sat down again in some confusion.

'I could have sworn I'd ...' She paused and collected herself, blinking rapidly. 'Forgive me, all of you – the cards spring their surprises on occasion. Now ... my dear, I have good news for you. Soon, you will perform an act of great virtue, of great courage and humanity, an act for which your name will live in praise. And this will be soon. Within four weeks. No, sooner than that,' she added, looking momentarily troubled again, but went on with all her usual firmness, 'The performance is at an end. Thank you for your attention.'

Mrs Korotchenko rose almost as quickly as Mrs Tabidze had done and, looking to neither right nor left, marched away and into the spacious corridor that ran the breadth of the house. When, after leaving it long enough not to court suspicion, he followed in her track, it appeared that he had also left it long enough for her to disappear. She was not to be found in the east hall nor anywhere within sight in the garden. On his return he saw that the chair beside the pillar was empty, and so he never knew whether its occupant had been Korotchenko or another.

13

The original (or perhaps just the former) picture of the male parts on the Korotchenkos' fence had been blotted out with some dark paint or stain and another, executed with rather more dash, laid on top. As he approached the house on foot, having left Polly at the stables on the Northampton road, Alexander wondered whether there were not dozens, even hundreds of such drawings sited there one under the other, the work of successive afternoon-visitors regularly blotted out at the husband's decree or the wife's whim, yet in a sense still there. Alexander half-remembered a Latour-Ordzhonikidze aphorism according to which each of our lovers adds something to us which no subsequent experience can efface. He wondered what Mrs Korotchenko was going to turn out to have added to him.

· No new information on this point was immediately available. As on his previous visit, the door was not shut, his ring at the bell went unanswered. Inside, he moved a few paces along the tiled floor in the passage, looked through the glass door to his right and saw nobody, looked to his left and saw somebody, the same somebody as had been leaning against a wall before. This time she was sitting at a dining-table instead but of course was naked again or (her brief appearance at the fortune-telling hardly seemed to count) still. He hurried into the room and stood before her, aware after brief but quite intense experience that to seize her was no good till she had indicated exactly how she wanted to be seized. In a voice like that of one about to fall into a coma she told him to sit down, indicating a chair placed side-on to the table, on which, he saw as he complied, there stood a plate bearing a cracker spread with pink paste, a small glass of what was probably vodka, a packet of Fribourg and

Treyer's Virginia No. 1 cigarettes and a gold metamatch. Even for cigarettes, these he knew were expensive, over £20,000 for twenty, or a full day's wage for a skilled worker. It was no wonder that people rarely –

His thoughts shifted (not to anything in particular, just away) when, necessary preliminaries completed, she lowered herself wheezing and whinnying astride him. At the point when, given another few seconds, his thoughts would have begun to re-assemble, starting off with some sort of recognition of the fact that so far all seemed strangely straightforward, she reached to her side, picked up the cracker and proceeded to cram it into his mouth. No gourmet had ever concentrated harder on the act of eating than Alexander now; though the flow of his saliva was feeble he got it all down in the end, even contriving to notice that the paste was fish, probably salmon. The vodka followed, every drop, with her holding the glass to his lips and hanging on to the back of his head with the other hand. By some miracle, or series of them, he succeeded in not coughing. Then she opened the packet and took out a cigarette, an operation that cost her some time and trouble. This was nothing, however, to the prob-lem of getting the thing lit. She conveyed it to his mouth quite readily, pushing the heel of her hand against his cheek and turning her wrist till her fingers brought the tip within his reach; the real teaser came when she set about bringing fire to the other end. She made a platform against her bosom with her two hands, but it was only firm relative to herself; their mutual position was still very much that of two people on the deck of a small craft in a short sea. He would have accepted a brief inter-val at rest, but he could tell that that would not have suited the lady's sense of style. Finally she pressed her forearm against his shoulder-blade and brought it up to a point where by turning his head at right angles he could get to the flame of the meta-match. Even now, not content with merely letting him puff away, she rested her hand on his jaw and took the cigarette into and out of his mouth. Three times he drew in smoke, not daring to inhale; the fourth time, guessing what was required of him, he pulled her hand aside and blew a jet into her face. At once

151

her eyes shut tight, her mouth opened further and she gave that cry of hers. In it he heard clearly, so clearly that he wondered for a moment how he could ever have missed it, the accent of loathing, of shame, of grief at having done what she had done but, after successfully carrying out the equivalent of a break-neck gallop down a mountainside with stirrups up, he was too pleased with himself to bother about things like that.

Mrs Korotchenko detached from her palm and let fall to the floor what was left of the cigarette, crushed in her grip a minute earlier. When she had briefly held his hands to her breasts, she got up and adopted what could not have been a very comfort-able position on the table, stretched out on her back with legs dangling and toes brushing the floor. Alexander attempted no conversation; he knew that to her he was no longer there, had indeed only been in existence for a few minutes in the last couple of weeks. Well, after no very long time he would be reborn. Meanwhile there was only one thing to do; the chair had a satisfactory high back; within seconds he was asleep. He dreamed he was riding Mrs Korotchenko in a ceremonial pro-cession through the streets of Northampton; almost documen-tary realism, he was to reflect when he called this to mind later. After an unmeasurable time somebody said something to him.

'What?' he said, waking.

'Have you thought of a plan yet?' She was sitting on the edge of the table, absently swinging her legs.

'Plan? What sort of plan?'

'You know, you said you'd think of a plan to make my hus-band look a fool.'

'Oh, yes, of course. Well, as a matter of fact I have.'

'What is it?'

'Well, the idea is for you to get hold of a list of the people who are secretly working for the Directorate, a complete list if pos-sible, and then I'll write them all letters saying I'm on to them and Deputy-Director Korotchenko doesn't keep a proper watch on his office. Or his tongue.'

After apparent thought she said, 'That might do a bit more than make him look a fool.'

'Yes, I suppose it might. Do you mind?'

'No. No, of course not. They might send him home. The very thing. I can't stand this country.'

'Really? What about that list? Is it possible?'

'It shouldn't be difficult. No problem, in fact. There's a man in Korotchenko's office who wants to do things to me, but I haven't let him because I don't like him, but now I could easily tell him I'll let him do them to me once each after he's brought me the list. I shouldn't mind. It'd be worth it. I'll probably need a few days.'

'What are these things he wants to do to you?'

'Oh, all sorts of things.'

'Er . . . Sonia, it can't really be all sorts of things, can it? Astronomical things and gastronomical things and . . .'

'Oh, all right. Things like fucking me and so forth.'

'Things like –'

'But why should I? I've told you what I could do to get the list, but I didn't say I would. Why should I? You tell me why I should.'

'Very well. Listen to me. Your behaviour so far has been bad enough in all conscience, not only in deceiving your husband, in committing adultery, and with a much younger man at that, but in these evil perversions that, your appetite for normal healthy sex glutted and jaded, you positively insist on!' Resonance was in his voice and dignity and authority, or approximations to them, in his manner. He lifted a forefinger. 'Just try to imagine how your husband would feel if he could have seen you a few moments ago, sitting across a soldier in his uniform and jogging up and down like a drunken gypsy! You're revolting!'

He had hardly begun his tirade before she was fidgeting and catching her breath, her features turning coarse and brutal with glee. When he lowered his voice to a deeper pitch of gravity and his manner became grimmer yet, she made a bleating noise and settled herself clumsily at his feet.

'But all that, even that,' he was saying, 'pales into insignificance beside your proposal to submit to the most ignominious indignities in order to be able to deal a deadly blow to

153

your husband's pride and honour! Your foulest cravings are innocence itself in comparison! But justice will be done, and you will receive fitting punishment!'

Mrs Korotchenko had taken off one of his boots and was in the act of taking off the other; they were really high shoes, finely but stoutly made by Lobb of St James's, called boots because the name had never been changed in regulations. Now she halted her movements and gave him an eager glance.

'You mean I can put these back on?' she asked indistinctly.

'No, Sonia, I can't punish you for something you haven't yet done. When you've brought me the list it'll be a different matter, I promise you. This afternoon I'm just going to correct you for your vicious sexual behaviour.'

She gave a submissive nod, finished taking off the second boot and, with a longing look at them, put the pair aside. Moving on hands and knees, she went to a corner of the large Wilton rug that covered most of the floor of the room and threw it back, uncovering a surface of bare boards scattered with dust, fluff and a few dead insects. Here she lay down on her back, her limbs spread. It was Alexander's part to trample on her mildly for a few minutes, as he had learned to do last time. Then as now he had resisted her desire that he should carry out this exercise with his boots on. He had very little objection to causing her physical pain, since she so clearly had none herself to suffering it, but it would not do to cause her any kind of actual physical injury or leave an obvious mark on her. As before, too, he tried ridiculously to make himself weigh less as he put his feet down, cursing silently at the boredom of it, trying to find it funny and not succeeding at all.

After a while she ceased to squirm about and make her ambiguous noises. Guided once more by previous experience he stepped off her at this point and waited while she got rather groggily to her feet. What now? She mumbled something about two minutes and the same room upstairs and slouched out. Yawning, he went back to his chair. He noticed for the first time that there were representations of human figures wherever he looked, on plates or mugs, as parts of clocks or candlesticks, in the form of dolls, puppets, statuettes. They had been collected without regard for consistency of material, scale or period, let alone style. Their presence seemed to make it less, not more, likely that two people lived here, ate, slept, saw friends, played the music-sounder, read newspapers, watched the PP projector, gave orders to servants and were waited on by them. It was not after all impossible that Mrs Korotchenko was domiciled somewhere else altogether and kept this place entirely for use as a sexual gymnasium.

What was the matter with her? That was no way to put it; that implied that there was one received norm of erotic behaviour from which other modes were deviations, and if the twentieth century had achieved nothing else it had finally put paid to that last and greatest citadel of bourgeois morality. At the same time it was hard to love someone who ignored endearments, who attempted no caresses, whose interests reached no further than one's hands, feet, penis, not even mouth. Of course Latour-Ordzhonikdize had put it on record that he who had obstacles placed in his path to love deserved ten times more credit than he whose progress was unimpeded. What of it? Alexander felt he could do without credit (credit from whom, anyway?); he wanted Mrs Korotchenko to kiss him and stroke his neck and not even say she loved him, just tell him that he was a very sweet boy. He looked out of the window at the brilliant day and felt his spirits droop a little. Then he told himself not to be childish; a mature man took what came his way in the form it was offered and wasted no time fretting that it was not otherwise. The signal to move on would be that he was starting to tire of the lady's charms, and for the moment there was no sign whatsoever of that.

The loud screeching of a pig from the other side of the house had the effect of recalling him to his immediate situation. The two minutes must be up, perhaps twice over. He went out, up the stairs, along the passage and into the end bedroom. Here Mrs Korotchenko proved to be spreadeagled on the bed with her wrists and ankles tied to its corners and a gag, in the form of what looked like a substantial scarf, tied round her face. Within the limits open to her she was jerking about. Alexander started to unbutton his tunic. At once she shook her head fiercely and made antagonistic sounds into the gag. He too shook his head and told her it was his turn this time. As he stripped he wondered briefly and shallowly how she had got herself tied up like that. A slip-knot, he assured himself; for her second wrist she had used a slip-knot. It was some time later that he had leisure to reflect that a hand might secure another hand with a slip-knot, but would find it remarkably difficult to secure itself, especially when the binding material was not rope or string but (as he now saw) handkerchiefs or further scarves. So as not to chafe. He sat on the side of the bed and undid the gag.

For the first time since they had met, Mrs Korotchenko laughed, a comfortable, almost happy sound. Her glance moved over his shoulder and he heard a similar laugh behind him. A girl of about twelve stood there; she was naked. He recognized her immediately without knowing who she was. Where had he seen her? In the photograph he had noticed on his previous visit to this room; a year or two younger there, but the same. And then, when she came and stood in front of him and looked him up and down, grinning, and he observed her large ill-shaped ears, he knew who she was.

'Merciful God,' he said in a low voice, and snatched up what had been the gag to cover himself.

'There was no point in that,' said Mrs Korotchenko. 'Dasha's seen dozens, haven't you darling?'

'Of course I have, mummy.'

Alexander pushed the child aside and began collecting his clothes.

'What are you doing? Wouldn't you like to be nice to Dasha?'

'No thank you. I don't think I could be.'

Mrs Korotchenko laughed again and waited till he was almost at the door before she said, 'Do you really want me to get that list for you?'

14

'God save the Queen!'

  'Long live the gracious Queen!'

  'Hip hip hurray!'

The sitting-room with the hanging plants, with the conservatory at its further end, resounded with cheers, laughter and general loud talk. It was getting late at one of Ensign Petrovsky's soirées in Dr Joseph Wright's house. The vodka had long since begun to circulate and everyone was sweating in the late-summer humidity. The fattish young officer called Leo, the one with the flabby mouth, said heavily to Wright,

  'I could not see – I don't think I saw you drinking that toast, doctor.'

  'I have an early call in the morning.'

  'No doubt. I meant you deliberately and formally put your glass aside. It wasn't just that you didn't drink – you refrained from drinking of set purpose.'

  'All right, but please don't let's discuss the matter.' When the other assumed a look of theatrical puzzlement he hurried on, 'Because I know from experience that it's quite impossible to explain to a Russian how we feel about that. After what happened . . . there's no point.'

Leo's expression changed to theatrical surprise. 'She poisoned herself. Is that so mysterious?'

  'Please. Please have another drink.'

  'Oh, very well,' said Leo, all ruffled feelings now, 'I won't pester you any more. I just thought the more our people understand the English the better. I was only trying to be helpful.'

  'Your best way of being that is to shut up. Please.'

  'I will. I'm sorry, I'm sorry.'

Left blessedly alone for a moment, Wright thrust his line of thought away from him and surveyed the main group of three Russians and four Englishmen – no women; this was a serious-drinking night, not a screwing night, and that was an end of the matter. All seven faces shone with goodwill as well as drink; any number of them might be running with tears or blood before the next round was even poured, but for the moment the balance held. The three regarded the four much as the four the three, with tolerance, shallow affection, limited trust and that faint contempt likely to persist between parties of different nationalities even when long known to each other. And such were their fixed attitudes; at other times their feelings would be less whole-hearted but not essentially different. Wright could not have spoken for the Russians, nor did he particularly want to, but he was sure the English view of them would never change much. Peter Bailey, builder, hard-working, talkative, generous; Jim Hough, water engineer, not very bright, close with his money; Terry Hazelwood, farm engineer, fattish, re-liable, well dressed, knowledgeable about the local fauna; Frank Simpson, draughtsman, a great teller of stories, a great one for the women; all under forty. If the units of supervision were to be withdrawn (as one day they were presumably bound to be) in their lifetime, they would be sorry. For them, things worked well enough as they were. English is a language, thought Wright to himself; England is a place.

The person primarily responsible for the festivities had so far taken very little part in them and now sat apart looking as black as thunder. Wright went over in the hope of a chance to elicit vexation. He said as bracingly as he could,

'You're not looking too pleased with life, Ensign Petrovsky.'

'It's not life, it's myself. I did something the other day that made me very ashamed and I can't seem to get it out of my mind.'

'How annoying. Perhaps telling me about it would give some relief.'

Wright had been looking forward to turning down an unex-pressed invitation from Alexander to coax the story out of him and was quite surprised when he shook his head decisively. 'It probably would, but I'd have to tell you everything for it to mean much, and I can't do that because there are confidences in it. Still, thank you for asking. Even these few words have helped a bit. But this is boring. How's Kitty?'

Kitty's part in these sessions was traditionally limited to preparing sandwiches and other cold foods beforehand. By the time the guests arrived she was not only out of the way but out of the house, to spend the night with a neighbour. So went Alexander's own decree; he could not be responsible, he said, for what his brother-officers might get up to when drunk. Wright considered this to be eyewash. The chance of even an attempted rape, given the hefty opposition it would arouse, was surely negligible. No, what the fellow wanted to do was prevent his mates from getting so much as the most distant glimpse of his girl, not to have to use up the smallest part of his drinking-time guarding her against invitations to badminton-parties. But (Wright reflected) many young men were less confident than they usually appeared. He said,

'Kitty's in very good form. She sends you her love.'

'Thank you for relaying it. Please give her mine, for what it's worth.'

Soon afterwards Alexander said it was dull of him to sit about with a long face, poured himself a drink and joined in the singing that had started up. Wright had been on the point of thinking that for once something other than the incomplete fulfilment of his wishes was troubling the young man; now he suspended judgement. Ten minutes later, with the complete transformation of Alexander into a breezy, simple, honest Russian officer who had taken a drop too much (having more than once in the past appeared as a melancholy, troubled, bitter Russian officer who was killing himself with drink), Wright discarded his new ideas. At the sight and sound of the red sweaty faces and their stylized expressions, the arms punctiliously flung round shoulders, a boredom edged with hopelessness filled him. This was warmth, high spirits, good fellowship. What else was it? If this was not it, what was it like? Where was it to be found? Then a new song began and he felt hatred, less keenly than when Leo had proposed his toast but in the same direction.

> *'And the waters as they flow*
> *Seem to murmur soft and low,*
> *"You're my heart's desire, I love you . . ."'*

Somehow or other the evening was brought to an end without anybody actually punching anybody or being sick or falling down, though Victor said he needed physical support to get him to and into the transport. This, one of the eight motor-vehicles possessed by the regiment, was the 'B' Squadron stand-by waggon, a 500-kilogram Borzoi truck. It was of course forbidden under the direst penalties to remove it from quarters except on Major Yakir's personal order but, since its use was just as strictly confined to emergencies and there never were any emergencies, it was in practice removed quite often. Victor was shoved into the back along with Dmitri, the fourth member of the party, Leo went behind the wheel and Alexander sat next to him. When it started up, the engine sounded very loud, Pinking horribly on the inferior fuel, the waggon lurched down into the village high street, past the grocer, the barber, the saddler, the dozens of houses. All were in darkness, as was the street itself; only the central parts of the larger towns were lit. Holding to the centre of the carriageway, Leo increased speed.

'That was a splendid party,' said Victor's voice from behind.

Leo made a scornful noise. 'How would you know? You're too drunk to remember it.'

'That's how I know it was splendid – great bits of it are missing already. That shows I must have had enough vodka. Did we sing?'

'Why do you get so drunk?' said Dmitri.

'What else is there to be?'

'For you, not very much, perhaps,' said Leo.

'Well, tonight at least it was a very sensible thing to be. That's what we went there for, isn't it? We went there to get drunk, not to talk or sing. Did we sing? Anyway, if we did it was in course

160

of getting drunk, not for its own sake. I can't think why you went there, unless it was to sneer at the English.'

'The alternative was sitting in the mess with George and the major.'

'You'd have missed a marvellous party if you'd done that. Do you know how I know it was marvellous? Because already I can't remember much about the later bits. Did we sing?'

'We sang,' said Dmitri. 'Now shut up and go to sleep.'

The Borzoi followed its headlights along stretches of straight road, round wide curves, up and down gentle slopes. Now and then Alexander was visited by the illusion that, instead of the car following the road, the road moved about to suit the car, that it was wherever the car went. He had had the same fancy a couple of times before, he remembered, but only when very tired. Was he very tired now? Certainly he had not slept well the last night or two, whether because thoughts of Mrs Korotchenko had actually kept him awake he had no way of knowing, but he had thought the thoughts all right. Some of them had been fruitless self-questionings about why he found them so disagreeable, even what precisely he found them. He shut his eyes now and tried to imagine he was riding Polly.

He was just beginning to doze when he was jolted back into wakefulness by a momentary uncharacteristic movement of the car. 'What was that?'

'I think we hit something,' said Leo, driving on as before. 'There was nothing to see.'

'We'd better stop. Go back, in fact.'

'Why, for Jesus' sake?'

'Because our number-plates are illuminated. Have you forgotten what happened to that corporal in 3 Troop who knocked a child down and didn't report it? And he was riding his horse and carrying out an officer's order.'

'I agreed with him,' said Dmitri.

'*Fuck all,*' said Leo violently, and trod on the brake.

Some minutes later Alexander said, 'Here. Just at the start of the bend. It was on my side, wasn't it?'

'There's nothing there,' said Leo.

'Wait.'

Taking the torch from its clip under the dashboard, Alexander got out, walked across the road and at once saw a roughly circular pool of blood a dozen centimetres in diameter. A trail of button-sized drops led into the verge, where it virtually disappeared among the grass, so that even if he had wanted to he would not have been able to follow it. Without thought he raised his head and listened, and at the same moment, as if in response, Leo switched off the engine. In the huge stillness and darkness Alexander heard a cry, very faint or distant. He could not identify it, but then, as he realized, he could not have done so if it had come from five metres off. It was not repeated. He went back to the car.

'You were quite right,' he told Leo. 'There's nothing there.'

The rest of the journey back to quarters passed in complete silence. The presence of a light in the squadron ante-room turned out to indicate that Boris the commissary, unusually for him, was neither working nor sleeping but instead drinking a glass of beer and glancing through an out-of-date newspaper. He had unfastened his collar to be comfortable and on the entry of the others went hastily to hook it up again before deciding that it was best left as it was. Smiling and nodding his head to them, he got to his feet.

'What on earth are you doing here, Boris?' asked Leo. 'At this time.'

'He's been bringing the accounts up to date, haven't you, Boris?' said Victor.

'He might tell us if we give him a chance,' said Dmitri.

Boris gave an amused laugh. 'I can't see what you fellows find so extraordinary. There's an audit next week and naturally I need to clear my desk. George was playing billiards at the regiment and the major wanted an early night. So I worked late and dropped in for a final beer. Is that so strange?'

'Not a bit, Boris, not a bit,' said Leo. 'You make it sound as natural as breathing.'

There was a short pause. Then Boris said, 'I suppose you four have been out raising hell somewhere.'

'We had a tremendous party,' said Victor. 'Really tremendous. I think there was singing but I can't remember for certain. That's how I know it was a tremendous party. And now what I need is another drink.'

'Not long ago you were going on about having had enough,' said Leo.

'Was I? Well, that was not long ago, you see. Not long ago isn't the same thing. As now. What I need now is another drink. Where's that confounded Ochotnitscha?' Victor began to root clumsily in a cupboard behind the little bar. 'That thieving peasant of a mess waiter must have taken it to bed with him. Oh, I beg his pardon.' He poured himself a drink and held up the bottle. 'Anybody else? You are a miserable lot. I say, Alexander, would you mind signing the chit? I'll give you the cash in the morning.'

'Well, gentlemen,' said Leo loudly, 'there's obviously only one way for men of spirit to round off the evening, eh, Victor?'

'A morsel of Russian hide-and-seek?'

'Correct. Who'll join us? Dmitri? Alexander?'

Dmitri agreed; Alexander declined. They all knew him here, had what was by now a settled view of his attributes. And the presence of even the highest grade of visitor (that most worth impressing, in other words) would hardly have got him out into the dark to be shot at. Appearing reckless was one thing, being it very much another. The other three were about to fetch their weapons from upstairs when Boris said indignantly,

'Isn't anyone going to ask me?'

'I'm sorry, Boris,' said Leo, sounding quite unrepentant, 'but I've rather got out of the habit of thinking of you in this connection.'

'I'm not a man of spirit, is that it?'

Swaying slightly, Victor patted Boris on the shoulder. 'You've got lots of other very fine qualities, old chap.'

'I'll show you who's a man of spirit,' said Boris, who had flushed deeply. 'Can any of you lend me a revolver?'

'Don't go, Boris,' said Alexander, 'don't be a fool.'

'Kindly be quiet, young man, this is no affair of yours. Yes,

Boris, I can and gladly will supply your requirement. We'll be down directly.'

As soon as they were alone, Alexander said with real urgency, 'Change your mind. You can still get out of it. Who cares what they think, those idiots?'

'I do. I can't get out of it without tremendous loss of face.'

'Better lose face than ... All right, but now listen. The only reason that lot are still alive is that they all break the rules. Listen, Boris. You're supposed not to move after you've called out. But you must. Move like hell. Run, call out and keep going. Or dodge into cover. Have you got that? If you stand still you'll die.'

'Don't worry, Alexander, I can take care of myself.'

'I'm not sure you can, not in a thing like this.'

'Whereas I'm absolutely invulnerable when it comes to wielding a pen. Thank you very much.'

'Oh, merciful Heaven, I wasn't – '

'I'm only joking. Keep on the move, I got that. Now don't worry. Honestly, I promise you I'll be quite all right.'

'See you stick to that.'

When his four brother-officers had gone off together, Alexander stood listening till they were out of earshot. Then he strolled to the bar, poured himself a vodka and downed it in one (he had not drunk as much as he had affected to at Wright's), poured another, took a cigarette from the imitation-sandalwood box on the counter and lit it from the large metamatch that also stood there. After marking up the chit he had signed a little earlier he settled down to wait in a chair by the window. The lights on the ante-room dial showed twenty-two minutes past midnight; not really late at all, and he felt wide awake now, just incredibly tired. He reached across for the newspaper Boris had laid aside.

All at once terrible screams began to be heard, coming from a point some hundreds of metres away but evidently so loud at their source that none of their overtones was impaired by the distance. No identification was possible; indeed, no one could have told by the sound alone whether they came from a man or a woman or even a large animal. They had a grinding, perhaps a tearing quality, as if the throat that uttered them would soon have destroyed itself.

Within five seconds Alexander was out of the ante-room door and running at top speed down a grassy slope in the eventual direction of the lodge. The screams continued unabated but other voices were being raised too, murmurs and shouts of inquiry, puzzlement, horror. The sky was clear and there was a quarter moon, and this was quickly supplemented by lights being turned on in buildings and by the beams of torches. Figures in ones and twos were converging on what, as Alexander drew nearer, he saw to be one of the pillared structures of which there were several in the park and in another of which, weeks ago now, Theodore and he had sat and plotted. He caught a glimpse of a shallow flight of stone steps and a grey-uniformed man lying on them, but by the time he was ten metres off his view was blocked by dozens of excited soldiers, many of them half-naked in the heat. Somebody was shouting and shoving at them from the far side, trying to keep them off: Victor. Beyond him the man on the steps, still screaming, was being lifted into a carrying position by two others. The nearer of these looked up and saw Alexander as soon as he broke through the chattering circle.

'It's Leo,' said Boris. He had to speak at the top of his voice.

'But Boris, I was sure it was you,' said Alexander, though no one could have heard him. Someone who had might have thought he sounded disappointed.

'Get back there, you pigs.' Victor was striking out with his fists. He appeared perfectly sober. 'Sergeant, move these men along. Let's have a little discipline. Alexander,' he called, catching sight of him, 'fetch Major Yakir.'

Major Yakir, as it proved, was already on his way, in shirt, undress trousers and slippers, hatless, hurrying down the slope on his short legs.

'Well?'

'Leo's been shot, sir.'

'Shot? By whom?'

'I don't know, sir.'

'How bad is it?'

'I don't know, sir.'

Officers and NCOs had begun to drive the protesting troopers back to their quarters. Leo's screams came now from the small one-storeyed building next to the place where he had been struck, a store-house full of tents, flags and festive decorations. He lay writhing about on a roll of bunting, not perhaps much better off than where he had been before. A blanket, already soaked with blood, had been thrown over him and a grimy pillow put under his head. He seemed altogether unaware of the others' presence and indeed of anything in his surroundings. Regularly, he drew in his breath with a lugubrious moaning noise and let it out again at what must have been the loudest pitch of which he was capable. Now and then he put his hands over his mouth and muffled his cries somewhat, but each time after a few seconds moved them down again and pressed them against his middle; the lower part of his face was smeared with blood he had brought there from his wound. During one of these intervals Major Yakir drew back the blanket. From a point just below the breast-bone to the lower part of the belly the front of the light-grey uniform was soaked with blood – with other fluids too, Alexander was to say when he told the story. Blood was still flowing – Alexander could see it flowing – out of a hole in the material. The major restored the blanket, moved to a point where Leo could not have seen him without altering his whole position, and beckoned and then held out his hand to Victor; without delay Victor put his revolver in it. After the briefest of glances the major held the revolver a few centimetres from the top of Leo's head and fired. There were two sounds, one a kind of percussive sigh, the other that of the smashing of bone, and Leo just stopped.

Major Yakir's rather fine dark-brown eyes were usually most expressive, but at the moment they offered no clue to what he was feeling or thinking. He gave Victor his revolver back; he pulled the blanket up over Leo's face. Then he went to the intercom that stood on a packing-case in the corner and made three short calls. Finally he gave the other three a look that was also an order and led the way out of the room. He had said nothing to them, nor they anything to him, since entering it.

There was no great flood of talk back in the ante-room either. It was soon clear that the major would not be the one to start. Boris looked too stunned to speak, Dmitri (curly-haired, smooth-cheeked) too frightened. Victor's head was bowed so that his face could not be seen. Alexander said in a shaky voice,

'Those screams. Think of the pain he must have been suffering.'

'He was in pain all right,' said the major, his voice and manner perfectly prosaic, 'but that wasn't why he was scream-ing. If it had just been the pain he'd have been moaning, not screaming. No, he knew exactly what had hit him and where and what that would mean. He was screaming with fear.'

'But that's no better.'

'No,' agreed the major, and added curtly, 'come on, one of you.'

Still not looking up, Victor said, 'Leo suggested it – the others will confirm that. He always did.'

'Always?'

'Yes, sir. We've played this ... we've done this I suppose twenty times.'

'This being . . .?'

'We take it in turns to call out and be shot at by the others. They fire at the voice. Leo invented it.'

The major laughed through his nose. 'It's a hundred and fifty years old at least, in our army anyway. Have any of you any idea whose bullet hit him?'

No one had. Alexander, who had been included in the ques-tion, said with great meekness,

'It couldn't have been mine, sir, because I took no part. I was in here. The others will – '

'Why didn't you inform me of what was going on, tonight or on a previous occasion?'

'I was on my honour to say nothing.'

'Military necessity take precedence over private arrangement, as you know. However. Your powers of recall are deficient, like

167

the others'. It must be the shock of losing your friend. Allow me to run over what has really taken place in the last half-hour. The victim had been drinking to excess and had become boastful and offensive. He laid claim to courage; the rest of you were spineless, cowardly, not men at all. That was his contention. You would not dare, he said, to undergo mortal danger voluntarily, for instance by submitting to being shot at in the course of a mere game, as it might be then and there in the park. In vain the four of you pointed out the illicit nature and indeed the foolishness of such a course of action; he would not desist from his taunts. At last, stung by the continuing assault on your integrity, you took a collective decision you now bitterly regret and strongly deprecate but which you believe your judges will comprehend, each of you vowing to aim wide and to end matters after the first round. The victim had behaved aggressively before but never to anything approaching the same effect. You will throw yourselves upon the mercy of the court. Are there any questions?'

'Yes, sir,' said Alexander. 'You mentioned the four of us as having taken part in this affray.'

'Well?'

'Well ... my revolver hasn't been fired, sir. The investigators – '

'Fire it. Anything else? So. Even stupid troops conduct themselves better when told something of the reasons for their orders. The amended version of these improper events, then, is likely to bring you less displeasure from authority than the tale I heard earlier, but be advised that that in itself interests me not at all. If my officers were seen to be at such a low level of training, morale and esprit de corps as to risk their lives habitually in a fatuous prank, or to think that a thing like that is too ordinary to be worth mentioning,[2] – here Major Yakir stared grimly at Alexander – 'I should rightly be charged with unfitness to be their leader. This I naturally mean to avoid. Good night, gentlemen. I hope by all the saints I never have to command you in war.'

15

'Repent ye, for the Kingdom of Heaven is at hand! St Matthew, chapter three, verse two.

'I will arise, and go to my father, and will say unto him, Father, I have sinned against Heaven, and before thee, and am no longer worthy to be called thy son; St Luke, chapter fifteen, verses eighteen and nineteen.

'Enter not into judgement with thy servant, O Lord; for in thy sight shall no man living be justified; Psalm 143, the second verse.'

These words had not been heard for considerably more than the fifty years since the Pacification, neither where they had just been spoken nor in most other places of significance. It was of course unknown to Commissioner Mets or to any of his advisers that about the middle of the previous century various amended forms of prayer, supposedly more accessible to the congregation of the day and certainly disencumbered by hard words like 'ye' and 'unto' and 'thee', had begun to be used in English churches. The choice between one or other of these and the 1662 text had therefore fallen to the Rev. Simon Glover. He had scarcely hesitated. His best-loved uncle, an archdeacon of honoured memory, had never countenanced the smallest deviation from the old style, on the argument that any slight gain in literal intelligibility would be much more than offset by a loss in the power to win and enhance faith or even (as it must often be) merely to engage attention. Such an argument had gained force over the years. Glover knew too that he could bring to the wording he had learned in childhood a naturalness and warmth impossible to attach to the brisk, cheeky assertions and admonitions of the modern paraphrases. And, not very clearly, he felt he was offering the Commissioner a kind of defiance in spirit by going against what he would undoubtedly have preferred if he had known it was there to prefer.

The church showed no trace of the confusion Alexander had found when he strayed into it those weeks previously. The pews were up, the choir-stalls were up, the pulpit was up – not only up, but with the appearance of having been up for an indefinite time. The renovators' orders had been to produce something as indistinguishable as could be from the interior to be seen in the photograph given them as their guide, and they had accordingly attacked the pine boards with chisels, drills, hammers, adzes, had stained them, rubbed ash and tea dregs into them, stained them again; relays of men in cleated boots had run up and down the pulpit stairs. Above, missing or damaged panes of the Victorian stained glass had been replaced by window glass (of indifferent quality) overlaid with semi-transparent emulsions. Great care had been taken, on the whole rather successfully, to duplicate the tints and shades of the surviving parts, but if those craftsmen of old could have seen the reconstructions of the non-surviving parts, all supposedly conceived in a spirit of scrupulous adherence to the pictorial and devotional values of their period, they might have been very much surprised. The organ, on the other hand, having been left more or less undamaged except by rot and rust, closely approximated to its former self, in appearance at least, though erratic wiring behind the pistons had produced some sudden loud noises when soft ones had been expected and vice versa, together with unintended moments of complete silence, in the opening voluntary. Still, it led the choir safely enough into the first hymn.

> 'He who would valiant be
> 'Gainst all disaster,
> Let him in constancy
> Follow the master ...'

The choir, trained by Russian masters, stiffened with Russian singers, performed well, keeping the voices balanced, giving full value to every note, holding the tempo at the end of each verse.

Scattered among the congregation some old voices began to join in, most of them with the air, one at least with the bass part, powerfully and accurately rendered. Bit by bit others picked up the melody. To Joseph Wright, standing near the back with Kitty at his side, it seemed something he had always known, a part of his childhood, even though he could never have heard it in public after the age of three. The tune he understood, felt thoroughly at home with; the words were a different matter, set out in full as they were on the replicated sheet before him.

> *Who so* [sic] *beset him round*
> *With dismal stories?*
> *But they themselves confound . . .*

Why was it thought interesting that the kind of man who would be brave however disastrous the situation became would also be proof against mere discouragement and dismal stories? And why was the question of the identity of the dismal-story-tellers raised only to be instantly dropped? And the line about the people cursing (confounding) themselves was . . ; but the main drift was clear. Brave men were being encouraged to make a pilgrimage, to travel to some spot where a saint was said to have been executed or a miracle performed, the pilgrimage being under the direction of a priest or parson known as the Master. Such pilgrims were evidently subjected to verbal abuse and disheartening accounts of conditions on the journey. Well . . .

> *Then fancies flee away!*
> *I'll fear not what men say*
> *I'll labour night and day*
> *To be a pilgrim.*

Of course! The pilgrimage was frowned on by the authorities, perhaps actually forbidden, but the doughty Christian would make good his right to go on it just the same, undeterred by the fear that reports of this might reach their ears. So the poem was not so much about a literal pilgrim as about the duty of following one's convictions, which, Wright supposed, made it a religious poem even though it nowhere referred to God. Admirable as its theme certainly was, if it was at all typical of what his parents' generation had sung in church some of the early Russian measures had at any rate not been reasonless.

What had others in the congregation made of the hymn? They had clearly enjoyed the singing as such, producing, along with the choir in unison, a quite impressive body of sound in the last verse. Their expressions as they settled back in their seats were comfortable, pleased, expectant of further sober enjoyment. He could see no hint of triumph at a freedom restored or a gesture of defiance, however small, however permissible, offered the oppressor. Jim Hough, Frank Simpson and their families, the rest of them and their families, looked to Wright very much as their forbears might have looked when at evensong, in one sense peculiarly so, for the dark suits the men wore, the bowler hats and gloves they carried, the women's long dresses and wide-brimmed hats, had been carefully copied from another photograph, one taken almost a century before, in 1937, of a crowd of people leaving this church after a service. The clothes had been mass-produced by local labour from cheap sub-materials and in some cases were already starting to come apart.

'I believe in the Holy Ghost, the holy Catholic Church, the communion of saints, the forgiveness of sins, the resurrection of the body and the life everlasting. Amen.'

There was a prolonged rumbling and rustling as, one after the other, members of the congregation caught on to the idea of kneeling. Glover spoke alone from the chancel.

'The Lord be with you.'

'And with thy spirit,' responded those of his hearers who could read.

'Lord, have mercy upon us.'

'Christ, have mercy upon us.'

'Lord, have mercy upon us.'

To Kitty Wright, what then followed was relatively familiar, a piece of old church ritual in which people gave particulars of what they expected God to do for them every day. What had been said earlier interested her more: the list that began with the Holy Ghost. That was the third Christian god, about whom

172

even less seemed to be known than about God the Father; a sinister figure, even scaring if taken seriously, but she remembered reading somewhere that a great point of religions had been their scaring parts. The holy Catholic Church puzzled her for no reason she could have named, so she went on to the communion of saints. Communion of course had been another old church ritual, with which saints had no doubt had something to do. The final three items were plain enough in a sense, though the inclusion of the resurrection of the body was another mystery, given that it could actually be seen to be impossible in a way that the forgiveness of sins, for instance, could not. But the whole catalogue was very odd – remote and fanciful. It made sense to believe in keeping oneself to oneself, in divorce for unhappy couples, in a hot-water-bottle on cold nights; to do so might be of use in each case; that could be argued about. But what difference could it make to think the Holy Ghost advisable, to be in favour of the life everlasting? How had they come to recommend things like that? And yet men and women had died for the right to say they thought well of them. Incomprehensible; though it should be said that these days no one died for anything.

A girl who Kitty rather thought was Glover's granddaughter went and led him to the foot of the pulpit stairs and put his hand on the rail. Slowly but without a false step he completed the ascent and faced the congregation. The nave was full of flowers: yellow, bronze and orange chrysanthemums, white and pink dahlias, gladioli of all those colours. Glover could not see them as such; he saw vague variegated patches, but he had been told of their presence often enough. What he had not been told (because there was nobody to tell him) was that by the standards of another time the blooms were puny and undergrown, not diseased, just uncared-for. If he had known this he would still have been glad they were there. The church was almost completely silent, but he was necessarily unaware of that too. He tried to pitch his voice at the level established as satisfactory at the run-through the previous evening; one could not be expected to carry that sort of thing in the mind after fifty years.

'We are the children of God; the Epistle of Paul to the Romans, the eighth chapter, the sixteenth verse. As some of you will know, what you are about to hear is called a sermon, that is to say an address, a talk about religion, about God and ourselves. It won't be a long talk. Please listen carefully, because what I have to tell you is very important and very interesting.'

Already Glover was into his stride, speaking confidently and clearly; training, habit, whatever it was had told after all. He had dictated the whole thing to his granddaughter, who had read it back to him sentence by sentence till he had it by heart. Not once was he to make even the smallest slip.

'St Paul never met Our Lord Jesus Christ, but he knew a great deal about him, and about God the Father too, probably more than anybody else has ever done, and he handed on what he knew in as straightforward a way as he could. He was a very direct man. He meant what he said. So, when he said, "We are the children of God," he wasn't using the phrase in the vague sentimental way in which people used to talk about children of light or children of love. No, St Paul was speaking precisely. We – by which he meant the whole human race as long as it lasts, including all of us here this afternoon – we were created by God, put in this world by God. We are the children of somebody who is not a human being, somebody who is infinitely more powerful than any human being can ever be, and also infinitely more loving, that is, his love is without limit and without end. We are the children of our parents too, and we all know how loving they can be, but we also know that their love is not without limit, and quite right too: limitless parental love would be unreasonable. God is not only infinitely loving but also infinitely wise, and again we all know from our ordinary experience, some of us as parents ourselves, how necessary it is that love should be accompanied by wisdom.'

Glover spoke for a few minutes about these and others of God's qualities, avoiding with practised skill the ticklish problem posed by a divine love that apparently tolerated what could be severe affliction being experienced by the objects of that love. He hoped he was making some sense to some of his listen-

174

ers, even that he had some listeners; he sensed that, deprived of the stimulus of perceiving the effect of his words, he was delivering them with less animation than he would have liked. At least no loud objection or other response was being voiced; now and then he fancied he caught movement towards the back of the church, but it was too dark there for him to be sure. He ended by saying as earnestly as he could,

'*A world without purpose except that of survival is a miserable place. It's also a sinful place, but I'm not going to pursue that today. The freedom we once enjoyed is gone for good, and England will never be happy again. But there is one certain way of triumphing over whatever may be done to us, of turning our defeat not into victory but into defiance, of resisting the oppressor in a place he can never subdue, our minds and souls. It is the one way to recover our pride as a nation and our sense of purpose as men and women. And God is the way. More than at any time before we need God, need him not as a man with holes in his clothes needs new ones, but as a man with only one leg needs a crutch, or even as a drowning man needs air. God is our father; he wants what is best for us; and he knows what is best for us. Wouldn't most people give a lot to know the best way to live their lives, something more attractive and enlivening than just hanging on to them? What we must do is ask God. He always listens. Pray to him; he always answers. If you don't believe in him, pray to him just the same; if you want to believe in him, he will help you to. Of course he will. We are his children. All of us.*

'*We will sing the hymn "Jesu, Lover of my Soul".*'

Although he had nothing to go on beyond surmise, and despite the assurances of Commissioner Mets that no official interest would be taken in any part of the service, Glover was quite sure that a full text of his sermon would soon reach the authorities, had probably been relayed to them already. But he found it hard to care. He had glorified God. The doubts he had had earlier, whether, there being no bishop anywhere in the land, his own service of reconsecration had proved efficacious – these quite fell away from him. In his mind he thanked the young Russian officer who had pressed him into doing what he had done today.

After the Blessing, his granddaughter came and led him out of the church. He failed to hear the closing voluntary stop abruptly in mid-bar as the blower broke down. Nor had he any way of knowing that, of the more than two hundred people who had been present at the start, only eleven remained. Some had left in the earlier stages, but the largest exodus had been in the first few minutes of the sermon. They had made as little noise as possible and no fuss; they had too much respect for that.

Kitty was one of the eleven who had stayed, because her father had stayed. She looked with approval and some affection at the old clergyman as he slowly made his way down the aisle. Under his dark jacket he wore a curious undivided collar-like affair without tie and what was evidently a black shirt. He was smiling. So was she; it had been a very pleasant occasion, arousing tranquil feelings in those capable of appreciating it, sadly above the heads of most.

Joseph Wright was not smiling. He had started pestering Kitty to be ready to go to the church over an hour before the service was due to start, had driven them there in the little Russian-made Badger runabout in a style that sent horses scattering, and had sat through the open organ voluntary at a high pitch of expectation, all this to his own surprise. He had had no idea what he had been expecting, but he knew plainly enough that it had not taken place; he had stuck it out to the end from pure obstinacy. He realized that he had begun to put a growing emotional stake on the service ever since the evening Glover had in effect agreed to officiate. And nothing had happened, so unequivocally and with such finality that the chance of any significant event, any change, was ruled out for ever. That was the day Wright finally despaired.

16

'What a glorious day.'

'All put on specially for you, my darling. You look your
loveliest in the sunlight. It brings out the colours in your hair.'

'It also brings out the freckles on my skin. I suppose you're
going to say you hadn't noticed them.'

'You underrate me. To say I hadn't noticed them would be to
slight them. In fact they constitute one of your great beauties.'

'Dearest Theodore, I really think you should try to be a little
more selective in your flattery.'

'Now you do me an injustice: I'm highly selective. Should I
ever come across a piece of you I don't find beautiful I intend
to keep silent on the matter.'

'You'll have plenty to choose from.'

Nina had spoken without thinking. When she did think,
desire made her catch her breath and turn her head away. She
had on the instant such a vivid sense of lying naked in Theodore's arms that she found it hard to believe that it had never
happened, that their closest physical intimacy had been a kiss,
an embrace that no one living could possibly have found improper, or rather a fairly crowded series of embraces. Hearing
of this from her, Alexander had shown or feigned surprise and
indirectly (but clearly) intimated that it could be nothing but
the result of deficient erotic drive, especially on Theodore's
part. As if he had read her thoughts the latter got hastily to his
feet at that moment and strolled up the ornamental steps to the
small summer-house, containing a likewise small sarcophagus,
near which they had been sitting. On every side were assorted
saplings and the stumps of cedars, oaks and pines.

'Whose tomb is this?' he asked.

'I don't know, darling. But is it a tomb? It isn't big enough, surely.'

' *"To the memory of Pug,"* ' he read out, ' *"who departed this life June 24th 1754."* Presumably a young child, though it seems odd to give just the nickname. And to bury it here, or rather not bury it . . . Do you want to get married in a church?'

'Well yes, if we can, but perhaps we can't.'

'M'm.'

She certainly followed his thoughts at that point. 'I hear the *evensong* wasn't a success.'

'We had some people in for interview today. They said they enjoyed the singing but didn't know what the *parson* was talking about.'

'Oh dear. He's very old, isn't he?'

'The attendance at the exhibition of visual arts has been very bad, almost non-existent, in fact, and some of the paintings have been defaced or ripped from the walls. I'm dreading the music recital.'

'When is that?'

'Tomorrow night. I wish I knew what we've done wrong.'

'You've all had something else on your minds.'

'Yes.' He spoke without conviction.

'Is everyone ready for Sunday?'

'As ready as they'll ever be.'

Suddenly Nina felt a dreadful incredulity like a void in the middle of her life and emotions; could it be another involuntary message from Theodore? At any rate, she found herself facing as if for the first time the concept that in a single day the whole world was going to be changed. She was being asked to believe that within a few kilometres of her there were hundreds of respectable-seeming people, including the mild young man she was talking to, who after a morning and afternoon just like any other would start pulling out guns, arresting important officials, occupying public buildings, giving orders. And being obeyed – that was the hardest part. Surely Director Vanag would just smile, shake his head and go on as before if anybody tried to tell him what do do. She started to speak and stopped again.

'I suppose . . .'

'What? What is it?'

'This isn't all a joke? There is going to be a revolution?'

'No joke. Whether there's going to be a revolution or not is largely a matter of words. By now it looks more as if there'll be just a peaceful and orderly transfer of power. The important part, the real work will come afterwards.'

Before she could say anything to that her attention was caught by the sight of Alexander a hundred metres away leading Polly up the shallow incline from the churchyard, moving purposefully, not at his more usual dreamy stroll. Nina waved to him and he raised his hand rather stiffly in reply. He was hitching the mare to the little temple when, as though by pre-arrangement, the figures of Elizabeth Cuy and a brown-liveried manservant of the house emerged from the hall door on to the top of the steps. On seeing Alexander she hurried down them and embraced him with much zeal; even at the distance of the summer-house the lack of real warmth in his response could be seen. Before she had released him he shouted a quite sufficiently curt order to the servant to take the mare to the stables; then he set off towards the waiting pair with Elizabeth unregarded at his side.

'She keeps coming back for more,' said Nina. 'I couldn't if it were me.'

'Why does she do it? Assuming you're right.'

'It's funny, it's as if she positively wanted him to turn her down. I suppose in one way that's easier than ... And even the bad language ...'

'What? How beautiful you look. What on earth am I saying? How beautiful you are.'

She was certainly looking her best, happy, healthy and altogether young; there were indeed freckles enough over her jaws and temples but of lines none at all. By some trick of chance her sleeveless dress had been cut right and its two shades of green suited her colouring, which was brighter than ever in the sun. Without a word she stepped up into the summer-house and, out of sight, they kissed. Although he was nothing but gentle with her he seemed to her infinitely strong.

They were sitting on the steps when the other two arrived.

Alexander's expression was curious. It was serious and even troubled but Nina thought she read a kind of elation in it too. Addressing himself directly to Theodore he said,

'The information was not forthcoming.'

'Any reason given?'

'The person who was to have supplied it to my source is proving stubborn. Or so I was told.'

'That sounds rather fishy, somehow.'

'I thought so too. Delivery is promised for Friday afternoon without fail.'

'Not much more than forty-eight hours before we go into action. Fishier and fishier.'

'Agreed.'

'*Fucking hell*,' said Elizabeth, looking from one man to the other.'Don't try and behave as if we're not here – I won't have it.'

The general topic under discussion was clear enough to Nina. 'You can say anything you like; I'll vouch for her.'

Theodore said rather wearily, 'As you'll have gathered, we were expecting some information that has failed to arrive. There's an old principle about being kept in ignorance of what you needn't know.'

'Of course,' said Nina. 'So that there's much less for you to be able to give away under interrogation.'

'Or not under interrogation.'

'How do you mean?'

'Well . . . voluntarily. Willingly. In the course of duty.'

Nina crossed her arms and clasped her shoulders, frowning. 'But that wouldn't apply in this case. In Elizabeth's and my case.'

'You never know,' said Theodore, still wearily.

'You never know? Are you saying you can't be sure I'm not one of Vanag's people? That you've no way of being sure?'

'What way could there be? How can anybody be absolutely sure about anybody?'

'About anybody. Dear God, what a terrible world we've made.'

'I'll go if you like,' said Elizabeth with some violence, turning her head to include Alexander specifically in her audience. 'I was just passing. I didn't come for anything in particular.'

'Shut up, Elizabeth,' said Alexander; 'life's hard enough as it is.'

'You'll have a hard life, my lad, about the day the King of England gets to sit on his throne.'

'We are helping to run a revolution, you know.' Theodore's tone now was querulous rather than weary. 'It's a heavy responsibility.'

'I can see it must be. Locking up a few policemen. Very responsible work.'

'There'll be more to it than that. Certain persons will have to be killed.'

This was accompanied by a glance at Nina that showed awareness of having contradicted the reassuring forecast he had given her a few minutes before. To her, he sounded like someone organizing a garden party who complains of a shortage of good servants. Again she was visited with incredulity: had she somehow misunderstood everything, childishly mistaken a sophisticated game for a serious proposal to overthrow the administration by force? She hoped she was not looking as shaken as she felt.

After staring at Theodore in a parody of amazement, Elizabeth said sarcastically, 'Killed!' and gave a great snort. 'But not by you or the gallant soldier here, that's for certain.'

Alexander went red. 'You don't know what you're talking about,' he said in a shrill voice.

'Oh yes I do. You haven't got the guts, my lad. Not for a killing in cold blood, which calls for a lot.'

He said, this time in a furious, rapid whisper, 'Perhaps you'll change your mind when I shoot my father.'

'Impossible!' exclaimed Theodore, but after much too long a pause to carry conviction.

'Are you mad, Alexander?' Elizabeth turned to Nina. 'Did you know about this?'

'No,' said Nina, still trying to take it in but experiencing only a sense of monstrous unreality.

'What did you go and blurt that out for?' Theodore was quite as angry as Alexander had been.

'They'd have known soon enough.'

'Why?' said Elizabeth with great determination. 'I want to know why you think you have to . . . WHY?'

'It'll have great moral effect,' said Theodore.

'That's no justification.'

'I can assure you it's necessary.'

'Necessary for what?'

'For the revolution.'

'What will it achieve for the revolution?'

'Don't argue with her, Theodore,' said Alexander. 'You won't get anywhere, and the thing has to be done whatever anybody thinks about it.'

Elizabeth looked steadily up at him. 'To shoot an unarmed man is a terrible thing to do, and for you to shoot that man is revolting.' She was wise enough to say no more of not believing in his ability to kill in cold blood. 'You'll be using your position to get close to him without him suspecting anything, so you won't be giving him any sort of chance. And what's he ever done to you or anyone else to justify the least violence against him? He's always treated you kindly, too kindly for your own good perhaps, but I'd be willing to swear he's never done you an injury. And this is how you repay him.' She looked away and paused and then spoke in a new tone. 'I've been in love with you for two years while knowing you're rather a fraud. Now I think you're rather evil. But I still love you. I don't suppose you can be bothered to try to imagine what that's like, so I'll tell you — it's hell.'

Bursting abruptly into tears, Elizabeth turned and ran towards the house. Alexander gave a cheer and clapped his hands, but so quietly that she could not have heard. The other two had moved a little way off and Theodore was talking in gentle, serious, explanatory tones while Nina listened attentively, nodding her head from time to time, by the look of her not far from tears herself.

17

The music recital, which included works by Dowland, Purcell,
Sullivan, Elgar, the composer of 'Ta-ra-ra-boom-de-ay', Noel
Coward, Duke Ellington (taken to have been an English noble-
man of some sort), Britten and John Lennon, fell a long way
short of the disaster Theodore had feared. The audience remained good-natured throughout and even applauded after several of the items. They disappointed the organizers, however, by
talking loudly and continuously from start to finish, or rather
for all but the first five minutes, when the strangeness of the
experience almost silenced them. Somebody pointed out afterwards that they had not been told of the custom of keeping
quiet at such shows; somebody else said this might have been
just as well. The performance the following evening of 'Look
Back in Anger' was an out-and-out success. Only very rarely
in the past could the theatre have rung with so much happy,
hearty laughter. Afterwards the members of the cast had been
chaired round the neighbouring streets by an enthusiastic
crowd.

The night after that (Thursday) was to see the production of
'Romeo and Juliet' that had earlier interested Alexander. He
made preparations to attend. These included obtaining through
unofficial channels not only a ticket but something called a
dinner jacket and a dickey with a small black bow-tie clipped to
it, made specially for the occasion like the church clothes. He
also got one of the servants to make him up a bouquet of
flowers from the garden and arranged for its delivery at the
theatre. A couple of days earlier to do as much might have
seemed too troublesome, but the recent decline in his passion
for Mrs Korotchenko, consequent on her persuasions in the

matter of her daughter, had allowed his interest to move in other directions.

He changed in Theodore's office, had a *pint of best bitter* and a cheese-and-pickle sandwich at the Marshal Stalin in St John's Street and strolled round the corner to the theatre. It was a fine September evening, unusually hot and sticky for the time of year. A few people passed in the streets; most had already gone to their homes or to the lodgings that served as their homes in this cut-off island. Two military policemen, noticeable for their blue cross-belts and gaiters, moved slowly by in step, hands clasped behind backs. All was quiet. And yet in seventy-two hours, more like seventy-six hours to be exact, the revolution was to be launched and everything would be changed, set off by his shooting of his father. Was he going to be able to do it? He must; not to would be admitting to himself, and to others, that he was a trifler, a poseur, a *booby*. No going back now.

The foyer of the theatre was crowded with expectant English, none of whom had attended the play the previous evening (it had been a question of one or the other), but they had obviously heard all about it. Some were reading parts of the programme aloud for the benefit of illiterates among their hearers. A doubt or two was expressed whether a story of the kind summarized there could be very funny, but the doubters cheered up a little on finding that the characters called Mercutio and the Nurse were considered by experts to demonstrate Shakespeare's powers of comedy at their best.

The appearance of many of the men present would have struck most observers as odd. The *dinner jackets* they wore were just that; inefficiency and shortages had prevented the matching trousers from being ready in time. There were those like Alexander who had managed to find something not too incongruous among their own (usually very small) stocks of clothes; others had settled for tweed-like patterns or corduroys of various colours. The women looked strange too, though collectively rather than singly. A further set of shortages had caused them all to be wearing the same dress, a garment with a narrow and on-the-short-side skirt (to save material), no sleeves (same reason; hard on the not-so-young) and an unfetching round neck. By a stroke of petty lavishness, at the last minute so to speak total uniformity had been averted; exactly half the dresses were electric blue and the others emerald green, giving their wearers the appearance of opposing teams about to engage in some little-known sport. Not many younger people turned up and those that had were mostly in the bar downstairs. Nothing stronger than beer and stout was on sale, but a certain amount of spirits was being drunk, having been illegally distilled and brought along in pocket-flasks, or rather small bottles of all sorts. Here and there a mild rowdiness was beginning to show itself.

The ringing of a bell immediately produced something of a hush. When a bell rang, it meant authority was calling for attention, and plenty of those in bar and foyer could vividly remember the time when it had been wise to respond to that call without reserve. But the word soon got round that taking one's seat was as much as was asked for. This process went on longer than would once have been usual, given the number of parties and couples with no member able to read. In the end it was done and there fell another relative silence, in which this time an immense rustling of paper could be heard as several hundred boxes of chocolates, one to each seat, were torn open and their contents explored. A Russian researcher of unusually wide reading had come across the remark (sarcastically intended) that chocolates seemed to be compulsory at English theatrical performances. Those of tonight contained sweet pastes of uncertain flavouring, but they went down well enough with men and women who had had an early supper of (typically) cabbage soup, belly of pork with boiled beets, and stewed windfalls. After another pause the house lights were dimmed.

A tubby old man came on to the stage in front of the curtain. His painted face and his clothes, which were hard to imagine as the attire of any person in the real world, combined with the circumstances to suggest at once that here was an actor. Applause, led by a small claque, greeted him and he bowed. Confirmation of his histrionic status was soon given by his manner of speech, monotonous but unnatural, the voice dropping at the end of every line of verse. When he came to the words 'the hour's traffic of our stage' there was of course nobody to remark this notice that the text of the production had been cut by something like half or the metrical deficiency of the altered line. The man soon finished his say and, to more applause, withdrew. The curtain rose.

A loud sigh of pleasure and wonder arose from the audience. The wonder at least was understandable: the sets were the work of a Russian artist or artisan whose instructions had been to portray sixteenth-century Verona in a style the twenty-first-century English would appreciate. (He had conscientiously read the play in a recent translation and had put in many a touch he thought was Shakespearean.) Two men carrying swords, more fancifully dressed than their predecessor, came in and conversed for a short time. Two other men followed. The attention of the audience was held at first by the sheer unfamiliarity of everything before them, then by the excitement of the fights, which had been well arranged and thoroughly rehearsed, then by the (to them) dazzling opulence of the clothes worn by the Prince and his train. The exchange between Montague and Benvolio was cut almost to nothing; the good-looking young man playing Romeo was a natural actor, with a command of expression and gesture that enabled most of those there to catch the drift of those passages he understood himself, and it was found generally inoffensive.

Alexander had naturally not bothered to read the synopsis in the programme (an unnecessary demand on his English, for one thing), so he was almost surprised when, just after the start of the third scene, the tall dark-haired figure of Sarah Harland walked on to the stage. She was wearing a blue-and-white dress that miraculously both fitted and suited her and altogether she was looking even finer than he had remembered. After she had made a couple of brief remarks, two other females chatted for a few moments; she moved away and looked out into the auditorium and immediately, or so he fancied, caught sight of him. If she had, the way her face changed boded ill for his chances after the show, chances which seemed further diminished when he turned his eyes away and found himself looking straight into those of Kitty Wright. She and her father were sitting remarkably near him not to have noticed them before. It was going to be tricky, making for Sarah without Kitty seeing, but short of cancelling Sarah it would have to be done. An old Russian proverb said a rabbit in the snare was worth two in the field, and someone with far less experience of women than his would still know full well that infidelity even in remotest intention drove them wild with rage, in sad contrast to his own view that they could do what they liked provided they were available whenever he wanted them. (This may well have been his expressed view; his practice on learning of such conduct was to turn wild with rage and walk out at once, unless indeed nothing else was fully available at the time.)

The audience had some trouble with the Nurse's maunderings about Lammas-eve, which the writer of the adaptation had not dared to shorten because of what the experts had told him. There were attempts to laugh at it, but they soon died down when it went on being incomprehensible and, more important, when the other characters present went on either showing impatience or refusing to listen. But enjoyment of the occasion and the fair amount of goodwill accumulated in the first few minutes saw the Nurse through. What caused the first stirrings of resentment was Mercutio's Queen Mab speech, again uncut for similar reasons, and again for similar reasons the initial laughter was short-lived. By the end the house was audibly restive, and cheers greeted Romeo for finally shutting him up. Capulet's ball, what with the music, dancing and costumes, and a new set of great singularity, quietened things down for a time, though the Nurse drew an outburst of catcalls.

By the middle of Act II the conventions had been firmly established. Romeo and Juliet themselves were to be respected, or at least allowed to speak their lines in comparative silence. Mercutio, the Nurse and, as soon as he appeared, Friar Laurence were picked out as the enemy, to be subjected to jeers, abuse, threats and all manner of wordless yell. Jubilation at the death of Mercutio in the first scene of Act III stopped the show for over five minutes. A personal appeal from Romeo got it going again, but it never fully recovered. Muttering grew audible in Juliet/Sarah's speech at the beginning of the next scene; she was without the support of Romeo's presence and her dramatic powers were inferior to his. One passage, however,

> 'Come, gentle night, come, loving, black-browed night,
> Give me my Romeo; and, when he shall die,
> Take him and cut him out in little stars,
> And he will make the face of heaven so fine
> That all the world will be in love with night
> And pay no worship to the garish sun,

she seemed to understand and spoke with some conviction, not that that made any difference to the muttering.

The end came, or began, with the re-entrance of the Nurse. The prospect of more of her was suddenly too much to bear. Unlike the church congregation, the people here had thought they had an idea of what was in store for them and been disappointed. They had been looking forward to enjoying themselves and had been bewildered and bored. They had been told over and over again that this was a great play by a great Englishman and there was nothing in it. They had put on these ridiculous clothes and come all this way to be made fools of. It was what some of them had been calling it from the beginning – just another *Shits'* trick.

In what followed almost no one took no part and there was no opposing faction within the audience. Shouting, gesticulating, assuring one another that it was no joke and not good enough, they stood up en masse and slowly made their way to the space between the front row and the orchestra pit. The half-dozen Russian-trained stewards were swept helplessly along. The riot police had already been summoned by electronic alarm but it would be several minutes before they could arrive. The crowd appeared indignant rather than menacing and at first contented itself with verbal aggression. Fsom behind the footlights Romeo, Juliet, Capulet, Benvolio, Prince Escalus pleaded and apologized in dumb-show; words would have been wasted. Then some of the younger men from what had been the audience set about climbing up the barrier surrounding the pit with the evident purpose of getting on to the apron and so to the stage proper. Those questioned the next day said they intended no personal harm and meant only to do some damage to the set and properties, but anybody could have been forgiven for deciding to be on the safe side and making his or her exit before it was too late. The players did that.

Alexander, standing in the central aisle half-way down the front of the house, had an excellent view of all this and even more of the events that followed. For a moment the stage was empty. Then Romeo and Benvolio hurried back on to it and down on to the apron. They were shouting violently though inaudibly, inaudibly not only to Alexander but, as it seemed, also to anyone in the crowd; nobody looked at them. And they were shouting a single word, a monosyllable to judge by the movements of their mouths. He wondered very much what that word was. Nor did he have to wait long to find out. In the most spectacular fashion, a cloud of smoke, dense and spreading with remarkable rapidity, drifted into his view from behind the flats of Capulet's orchard. Very briefly it was his view alone. During that interval the concealed door next to the stage, the one by which Aram Sevadjian and Theodore had come to join him at the rehearsal he had visited, was opened from the far side. Actors among others began to come through that doorway, a minor Montague, a minor Capulet, one of the Prince's train, a man recognizable as Mercutio. He was certainly recognized by some of those milling about near him, but before he could be assailed or otherwise abused others had seen the smoke, much thicker and more widespread than when it had first appeared.

The shouting stopped, or rather changed into unnecessary but understandable cries of 'Fire!' Alexander looked at the stage again. Romeo and Benvolio were nowhere to be seen; they could only have descended into the auditorium. One after the other Prince Escalus, a man who might have been a stage-hand, a girl who might have been anything, Capulet came into sight and clambered down from the stage, presumably unable to make their way to the pass-door Mercutio's party were using.

Where was Sarah? Here at last she was, still dressed as Juliet, running, coughing, carrying a hold-all. In her turn she reached the apron and started to negotiate the gap between it and the barrier, but she was impeded by her hold-all, lost her footing and in a flash had fallen through the gap into the orchestra pit. Alexander acted nearly as quickly. He had moved along one of the rows of seats so as not to be in the path of the multitude surging up the aisle; now he scrambled over into the next row down and repeated the process until he reached the front. It was no great business for one of his physique to force his way through the press and haul himself up on the barrier so as to be able to see over it.

The floor of the pit, into which smoke was rapidly drifting, was perhaps two metres below him. Sarah Harland, coughing and gasping, half lay on it struggling to get up but, no doubt because of her fall, without success. She saw him at once, recognized him and silently but unmistakably entreated him to help her. He considered. He would have no trouble getting in and very little trouble getting her out. The trouble would come when he tried to get out himself. She could not help him, nobody else would and there was no furniture in the pit at all, nothing to stand on. He would have to rely entirely on the strength of his arms, and whether he could make it would depend on how far he found he had to reach up. From where he was it looked as if it might be too far. It just might be; that was enough. His decision must have shown in his face, because on to hers came a look of totally unsurprised contempt, a terrible look that was to haunt him till the day he died. He turned away to search for Kitty, for whom after all he was much more responsible.

Huge rounded masses of smoke piled on one another were sailing up the front of the house. The safety curtain, its mechanism failed or its operator fled, was less than half lowered; flames were moving down stage towards it. To be sure, it would not have saved Sarah Harland even if it had come all the way. She died of asphyxiation a few minutes after Alexander had left her, the only fatal casualty of the 'Romeo and Juliet' fire. It was soon established that this had been started deliberately, but the perpetrator was never found, nor even his motive placed beyond dispute. An adverse critic of the performance so terminated would have had no time to assemble his materials; a straight saboteur of the Festival might have been expected to pick a time when the building was empty. The most popular theory was that the culprit had been a crazed pre-war set on punishing the cast, the theatre staff, the audience and everybody concerned for having, in different ways, collaborated with the oppressor; he would have counted (rightly) on giving them all a good scare and could not have been expected to shed any tears if many more than one person had died. Again, no evidence for this view was discovered.

On the night of the fire Alexander returned to quarters; troop inspection 0800 hours on the morrow. Although it was still early the mess was deserted. This displeased him; for once he hankered for companionship. At the bar he took a bottle of beer from the shelf, put it back and poured himself a stiff vodka. The following afternoon would see his vital session with Mrs Korotchenko; his thoughts were soon fixed entirely on that. She had her imperfections, but for capturing and holding the attention, even at a distance, she was most effective.

18

At seven o'clock the next morning four officers were break-
fasting in 'B' Squadron mess: Alexander, Victor, Dmitri and
Vsevolod, the aggressive Byelorussian who had been flown in to
replace Leo. Boris had already eaten and left to start his day's
work; Major Yakir and George, the second-in-command, were
not yet down. The sunlight streamed in through the farmhouse
windows cheerfully enough, and yet the prevailing mood was
not in the least cheerful: restless, even nervous, under the
influence perhaps of the high humidity, the falling atmospheric
pressure and the unnatural stillness of the air, all unalleviated
by a heavy downpour in the small hours. Dmitri seemed to be
the least affected by these intangibles, helping himself to a
second coddled egg from the folds of a napkin in the basket
before him, skimming through the day's edition of 'Angliskaya
Pravda' and finding matters of interest in it. An item on the
back page drew a grunt of surprise from him.

'Listen to this, you fellows,' he said. 'Apparently there was a
big fire in Northampton last night. In the theatre there – they
were putting on some old English play or other. Seems to have
been quite a blaze.'

'What of it?' asked Vsevolod. He had a red face, bristly hair
and pop eyes, all of which went almost too well with his
manner.

'Well, nothing very much if you insist. I just thought somebody might like to know that, against all expectation, something
does sometimes happen in this depressingly unimportant part of
the world. No more than that.'

'And quite enough too, thank you.' Victor had his elbow on
the table and his forehead in his hand. His breakfast had con-

sisted of three glasses of mineral water and a cigarette, 'Not worth shouting your head off, anyway.'

'Sorry. A girl was killed, it says here. English. She'd been acting in the play. Trapped and overcome by fumes. Isn't that terrible?'

'Nothing like as terrible as what you're doing to the inside of my skull.'

'Alexander missed a chance there.' Vsevolod grinned as he spread cherry jam on white bread and butter. 'If he'd been around he'd have charged in through the flames, snatched up the girl in his powerful grasp and ridden off with her over his saddle-bow.'

Alexander said with great earnestness, '*Ballocks to you*. Fuck your mother, you pig. In this outfit we serve for a while before we start trying to be funny. Have you got that?'

'Yes, Petrovsky.'

'See you remember it. Well?' he said to the mess corporal, who had just come in.

'Your orderly is at the door, sir.'

Without another word Alexander threw down his napkin and strode out. There was a ripple of relief and amusement round the table.

'Can't he take a joke?' asked Vsevolod.

'Usually he can,' said Dmitri. 'Another time he'd have roared with laughter. It depends entirely on how he happens to be feeling. He's probably worried about the court-martial. I don't blame him. I certainly am.'

Victor scowled. 'Why don't they get on with the confounded thing? The prosecutor's been here a week. What's he doing?'

'Getting drunk?' suggested Vsevolod.

'That depends how much sense he's got,' said Victor.

Dmitri gave an admiring chuckle and said. 'You never miss a chance, do you?'

'*Horse-shit*,' said Victor. 'I think I feel strong enough now to try some tea.'

There was no relief from the humidity outside. In the remotest distance, greyish clouds moved sluggishly. The orderly, a bony, bullet-headed youth with a twitching eyelid, drew himself up and saluted – smartly, many would have said, but not Alexander, not this morning.

'As you were! Again! All right, I won't waste my time. What is it?'

'Sergeant Ulmanis's compliments, your honour, and this has just come by the CO's orderly.'

Alexander took the proffered envelope. It was grubby, but he noticed nothing; envelopes were always apt to be grubby. This one contained an informal, hand-written note from Colonel Tabidze inviting him to tea and after-lunch drinks at two o'clock that afternoon. If the party went on much above half an hour he would be late for Mrs Korotchenko. Well, that could be endured.

'Is there an answer, your excellency?'

'No, and get those trousers pressed before you go on parade or you'll find yourself on a charge. Move!'

The inspection passed off without incident. Alexander lunched early at the squadron and rode out in good time for the Tabidzes' house, where the colonel more and more preferred to spend those hours not absolutely required by duty. It was a handsome Victorian red-brick building with a turret at each corner and a porch largely constructed of wrought iron, and must have made an impressive sight in the days before the surrounding grove of Scotch firs was chopped down. From a staff on the roof of the porch the regimental standard hung limply in the motionless air. A servant took Polly's reins and led her away; another opened the front door as soon as he knocked, led him down a rather dark passage smelling strongly of furniture-polish and slightly of excrement and showed him into a room at the far end. This was the library, so called because part of one wall was given over entirely to bookshelves; elsewhere, sporting trophies, maps, photographs of rows of stern men in uniform and other objects of unimpeachable soldierliness were to be seen. Alexander had happy but sketchy childhood memories of it all.

'Ah, my dear boy, how nice of you to come.' Wearing a

belted civilian jacket that showed off his slim figure, Tabidze hurried over to meet him and shook him warmly by the hand. 'What appalling heat. I shouldn't wonder if there's a storm on the way. I must say I hope so. Let me make some fresh tea; this stuff's only fit to be thrown on the rose-beds. Do help yourself to a drink. And try one of those oatcakes with it – it's an old Northampton thing, I'm told. Well, how's my worthy friend Major Yakir?'

Pouring out a small glass of Dufftown-Glenlivet while the other busied himself with a quick-kettle, Alexander answered the question and others that followed. He answered them carefully because, from being quite certain what was in store for him and quite unperturbed about it, he had moved to a state of painful anxiety. It was normal for his commanding officer not to be short of things to say, but his normal style was a slightly remorseless pursuit of one point at a time, not this directionless chatter – he had turned now to incoherent reminiscence. Just as uncharacteristically, he had not yet looked his visitor in the eye.

They soon made themselves comfortable (physically at least) in a pair of imitation-leather chairs, one each side of the empty fireplace. Within Alexander's reach stood a small round-topped table loaded with tea, whisky, oatcakes, chocolates and cigarettes. Tabidze sipped a glass of white wine.

'Have a chocolate, Alexander – they go well with the whisky too.'

'No thank you, sir.'

'Have a cigarette, then.'

'That I will – thank you, sir.'

'Let's get down to business at once,' proceeded Tabidze, though his tone was less ready than his words. 'I have things to do later today and I'm sure you have too. First of all, this is nothing to do with your court-martial, so we can have that out of the way to start with. But I will tell you that the proceedings are fixed for Tuesday and, in confidence, that the tribunal is disposed to take a lenient view, at least in your case as the most junior. You're to be awarded a severe reprimand.'

Alexander said nothing, because he thought nothing, about

the principle involved (or the one flouted) in determining the sentence before the start of the hearing. The gloom and uneasiness that had lain upon him ever since waking lifted slightly. The court-martial would never take place, but it was pleasant to be vindicated, even in so unimportant a way. He muttered something and looked suitably humble, grateful and so on. Then, looking anxious instead, he asked, merely because it sounded right,

'What about the others, sir?'

'Rather less leniency there. Nothing harsh, however.'

He had just started to look relieved when Tabidze thoroughly disconcerted him with the offensive query.

'What really happened that night?'

(It was offensive because it took for granted that he had been lying before.) He was soon himself again reflecting as before that none of this was going to matter in a couple of days. He said with the utmost seriousness,

'I wasn't there at all. I stayed away after the first time. Oh yes, it was a favourite diversion of Leo's. He talked the others into it. He must have been mad.'

'He was a gambler. And you're not, of course; it doesn't go with being a dedicated young officer. Which puzzles me a little. I can't see why you didn't have to go and tell your squadron commander what was going on. Surely it must have been ... entailed on you.'

Colonel Tabidze's manner had relaxed somewhat, perhaps because he had evidently deferred business after all, unless indeed this discussion of motives was business. At any rate, he now glanced directly at Alexander, who said, with the merest touch of holy simplicity,

'But I'd given my word of honour, sir. They refused to tell me anything about the game until I had.'

'But your oath overrides any such commitment.'

'Major Yakir made the same point. I'm not looking for a justification, your excellency. I only mean to give you my reason.'

'So you go in for chivalry too. You certainly make life

difficult for yourself, don't you? I mean we must face the fact that a dedicated young officer is constantly being forced to behave in ways that a man of chivalry would find intolerable. And the other way round, of course, as here. Tell me, do you also practise chivalry in your dealings with women?'

Before answering, Alexander crushed out his cigarette in a silver ashtray that was brightly polished in those parts where the plate had not worn away or become corroded. He could not see what the other was up to. Was this elaborate straightfaced ridicule? On all previous form, unlikely. And yet that chatter at the beginning . . .

'Well, sir,' he said finally, 'perhaps I might put it like this. In that sphere I practise chivalry as far as possible.'

'That's not very far, is it?' said Tabidze with a chuckle, putting his glass down. Then his gaze shifted and he frowned. 'Which brings me to . . . My boy, I've known you since before you can remember, since I was a dashing young captain, just appointed adjutant to old Colonel Khvylovy. You might remember him. A very upright old chap with teeth that stuck out and a way of snapping his fingers when he was making a point. Anyhow, what I'm trying to say is that I'm an old friend, an old friend of yours and of your family. You must know how highly I regard your father. And your mother too. So, just for a moment, try to forget I'm your commanding officer. And another thing: there's no reproach or disapproval in what I'm about to say. It's just advice. A word of warning from an old friend. Can you accept that?'

'Yes, Uncle Nick.' Alexander was as full of curiosity as he had ever been in his life.

'Ah, how many years since! It doesn't do to think about it. Now this will only take a minute. I'm told, and we needn't waste time going into who told me – I'm told you've been mixing with some exceedingly disreputable company.'

This last phrase happened to coincide with one of Alexander's periodical previsions of what he was going to be up to almost as soon as this interview was concluded, and struck him as a very useful description of it. His forebodings fell away; the old fool had had his *prick* throttled in his corsets for so long that he was all of a dither at having to remember what it was for. And that interfering bitch of a wife had indeed been spreading the tale, as he half guessed at that Friday reception. Even after years of trying he had never actually managed to blush at will, but he had got so good at all the accompanying facial and bodily movements that a positive change of colour would have been a concession to purism. He produced one of his best-ever now and muttered something intended as before to be inaudible, having without conscious thought discarded denial as unlooked-for and therefore unproductive. The next words proved the soundness of his instinct.

'We all go against our better judgement from time to time in our youth. I'm not so sunk in age that I can't remember behaving foolishly myself. It's understandable and forgivable; perhaps it's even necessary. But what's none of those things is persistence in foolishness. Being swept off one's feet, carried away, is one thing; to embark on a course of mistaken action and pursue it deliberately is quite another. Are you with me so far?'

'Yes, sir.' What sort of person would it have to be who had been unable to keep up with this?

'Good. Sooner or later, you know, we have to go back, and it had better be sooner than later. There is such a thing as common prudence, after all. You must consider the immense weight of what is after all accepted as how things are supposed to be run. Will you – I beg you – will you give up this disastrous adventure? Please don't force me to be more specific.'

Alexander hung his head, or more precisely allowed it to droop. 'You know, sir,' he said in an interested tone, 'it's funny sometimes, the way things work out.' As he spoke he was telling himself that next week he would be able to bang Mrs Korotchenko in the middle of Northampton market square at midday if he felt like it and if she felt the enterprise would not be too humdrum. 'You know you ought to do something,' he twaddled on, deliberately not thinking ahead or back in the interests of verisimilitude, 'in fact you want to do it very badly, but you just can't bring yourself to. Lack of will or energy or something. And then, out of the blue, when you think it'll never happen, something turns up and gives you a nudge and in a flash you're the other side of the gap. You've taken the decision and you'll never go back on it. Well, that's what happened to me while you were speaking just now. I'll break it off, Uncle Nick. In fact I already have; it's just a question of letting it be known.'

Having followed this with a series of eager nods and a spreading smile, Tabidze came over and embraced him. 'I'm delighted! What a relief! Sensible lad, to step out in time, before you do anything really foolish. You'll never know how glad I was to hear you say those words. Which of course are confidential, like everything I've said to you. Have another drink, my dear. No, I insist. I'll join you.'

A few minutes later, Alexander said, 'Well, you were quite right, sir, I have things to do,' and sniggered inwardly.

'You must just have a word with Agatha before you go. She'd never forgive me if you didn't. In the garden, need I say it? Never out of it when the weather's half tolerable.'

Mrs Tabidze was out at the back of the house kneeling on a mat of some rubber-like substance, doubtless in the interests of comfort, since her green denim trousers could hardly have been dirtier; she seemed to be attacking a long row of various smallish plants with a pair of clippers. When she saw Alexander she smiled delightedly, got to her feet and took off her equally dirty gloves. They hugged each other; he was quite fond of her, in so far as he was fond of anyone. After the hug he looked about him, or feigned to.

'The garden's looking absolutely marvellous, Agatha,' he said, trying to ram sincerity into his voice. 'You have done well.'

She glanced at her husband and laughed. 'Coming from somebody who doesn't know a daisy from a hollyhock, that's a handsome compliment. There's nothing so ignorant as a man when he's not on his subject.' She turned. 'What are you looking so pleased with yourself about?'

'Oh, Alexander has made a very satisfactory report to me.'

'By the way you're beaming he must have reported they're going to make you a general.'

'Nothing like that.'

During this exchange, a matter of the barest particle of genuine interest came to Alexander's mind. 'I've been meaning to ask you, Agatha: you remember you told fortunes at that party at our place? The last one was a certain lady,' as he felt at the moment he was able to speak with unexampled naturalness, 'and at the end something happened that surprised you very much. What was it?'

Her face had changed at the mention of the lady, but it had changed back by the time she answered. 'Yes, it was most odd. You see, I'd turned up the seven of hearts in the active near-future position, and there it means, as you heard, that the subject will soon do a deed of resounding virtue. Well, in a way of course that isn't at all remarkable, theoretically any card may come up at any time, but what shook me was that I was quite certain I'd turned up the seven of hearts before, when it was what we call a dead card and didn't signify – so certain I'd have wagered all I possess on it. But when I looked back to where it had been before, where I thought it had been before, it wasn't there. Nicholas says it must have been the seven of diamonds I saw, but then ... Still, that's what it must have been. Very strange. Mark you, the whole thing's strange, fortune-telling by cards, I mean. Did you know it's a recognized form of proper divination? Oh yes. Cartomancy, they call it. Goes back centuries. You're going to laugh at me, but I think there's something in it. Yes, I do. It'll be interesting to see how that prediction of mine turns out. Not that one would really have expected ... But I mustn't run on. How's everybody at home?'

Alexander told her how and shortly afterwards took his leave. At one point in their conversation he had felt puzzled, but could not now remember the circumstances. As he rode away he dismissed the matter from his mind. Yes, he thought to himself, there might well be something in – what was it? –

cartomancy. There might or might not be more in it than in faith-healing, clairvoyance, palmistry, flying saucers, telepathy, evolution, water-divining, time-travel, the unconscious, religion, the flat-earth theory, art, astrology, relativity, the Loch Ness monster, dreams, racialism, socialism, vegetarianism, spiritualism, reincarnation and the belief that Earth was colonized by beings from outer space. But there was something in it, something in all of them, something for everybody.

Whatever that something was, wondering about it on the way to the house of Korotchenko at least helped Alexander to shut out as far as possible any thought of what lay ahead. This was not only because of the inherent unwisdom of allowing in any such thought while in the saddle of a moving horse; earlier that afternoon, he had found his normal joyfully lecherous expectation becoming tinged with a certain grimness as the hour approached, an almost sullen curiosity best stifled. The English had a phrase about *being put through the hoops* to describe the experience of having an elaborate ordeal forced upon one by another. To judge by the escalating unconventionality of the ones provided on previous occasions, today's *hoops* would have to be rather special.

It took some time to establish what they consisted of, even longer than expected. After a ten-minute search, in which he sagaciously included a checking of all cupboards and wardrobes, plus under the beds and even a none-too-large trunk in the corner of a box-room, he concluded that the house was empty. At that stage he remembered that there had been no cock and balls pictured on the front fence; perhaps Mrs Korotchenko had taken down her sign and moved on. Then in the silence he heard a pig squeal, as last time, and decided there was no harm in making absolutely sure.

Outside the back door there were quite a few pigs loitering about in a three-sided enclosure which also held a number of chickens, a number of ducks, a duck-pond, a dung-heap in an active state, a waggon with three wheels, a trap or dog-cart with one and a great pile of cardboard boxes, still saturated after the rain in the night. At the other end stood a large barn with a tiled roof and an open doorway in its middle. Alexander walked over, picking his way with some care, and looked inside.

His quest was done. Mother and daughter, naked as usual, were sitting side by side on the edge of what looked like a kitchen table near the middle of the building. As soon as they saw him they moved, mother getting up on to the table in her ungainly fashion and daughter getting off. He noticed a rope that had been thrown over a beam below the roof and was looped at one end, and speculated whether the arrangement might be that he should hang Mrs Korotchenko, or perhaps she him, during the act of love. When he got nearer he saw that there was a loop at the other end of the rope too and that she was engaged in putting one of them over her shoulders and under her arms, a task she finished in time to extend a courteous helping hand to him. The table moved a couple of centimetres as he climbed up on to it; he guessed it was on castors, which struck him as mildly odd. Very soon the second loop was round him and not long after that the act just mentioned had begun. It continued when the table had been moved out from under their feet (so that was the point of the castors) and they dangled together in mid-air, continued further, though with much effort, when Miss Korotchenko, showing some of her mother's bodily strength, sent them swinging to and fro in wider and wider arcs. Up to within a few metres of the end wall they zoomed, were suspended for an instant at rest and almost horizontal, plunged downwards again. By shoving them at angles to their original path the girl put them into a curved course that bore them out towards the side walls, and also cleverly imparted a spinning effect, so that they hurtled round the barn in a succession of vast unique elliptical orbits. Alexander thought it might never end, but it did; it had just started to when there was a slight jerk and he found himself flying through the air with an altogether different motion, out into the sunlight still locked with Mrs Korotchenko, now bawling her loudest near his ear, across the farmyard over the pigs and poultry and straight into the pile of cartons, which thanks to the soddenness of the cardboard adequately broke their fall. If they had come down anywhere else (except the dung-heap) they would have suffered severe injuries at least. When he had somewhat recovered he said,

'That was taking a bit of a risk, wasn't it?'

'What do you mean?'

'Well, you couldn't have been anywhere near sure we'd land on this stuff.'

'You mean you think I made the rope break on purpose? But we might easily have been killed.'

'Yes, that's right.'

'You think I'd take a risk like that? In God's name, why?'

'Why not? I admit I can't see you designing and installing the necessary release-mechanism, but you're perfectly capable of the rest of it.'

'What nonsense,' she said, not offended, not amused, not puzzled, just making a denial.

The daughter had been delayed by collapsing with laughter, or a pretence of doing so. Now she came up to them, still giggling. 'That was terribly funny, mummy. Did you mean to do it?'

'Of course not,' said Mrs Korotchenko as before.

'Do you mind if we go indoors now?' said Alexander, standing up and taking off the loop of rope. 'I think I'd like to sit down for a while.'

They went through the kitchen, where there was a lot of dirty crockery and cooking-pots and a lot of flies, and into the drawing-room, previously unvisited by him. He sat in a chair with a torn floral cover and the two females looked at him with expectant interest, as if he had come by appointment to sell them insurance.

'Can I have a drink?' he asked.

'Certainly. I'm afraid there's only vodka.'

'That'll do fine.'

'Dasha, bring Mr Petrovsky the vodka from the kitchen. And a glass. On a tray. Quickly, there's a good girl.'

When the girl had gone, he said, 'Have you got that list?'

'What if I have? What can you do with it now?'

'Until I know you've got it I can't punish you, can I?'

'It's upstairs. Will you keep your boots on this time?'

'If you insist.'

She shut her eyes and moaned softly.

'But it'll be just the two of us,' he went on. 'No audience for this one.'

'Agreed.'

He was left alone long enough to puff out his cheeks, rub his eyes and swear a couple of times, but no longer. Dasha came back with his drink, which she proceeded to serve efficiently enough. After considering him for a time, she said,

'Are you in the army or the police?'

'The army.'

'I thought you were in the police.'

'Well, I'm in the army.'

'Do you fuck a lot?'

He threw down the vodka in one. 'Quite a lot.'

'How often? Twice a day?'

'I suppose if you averaged it out it would come to something like that.'

'Have you got a nice horse?'

'Yes,' he said neutrally, curious about where this might lead.

'What's he called?'

'Oh. It's a mare. She's called Polly.'

'My pony's called Frisky.'

'Is he?'

'Yes. And he is frisky, too.'

'Really.'

'Yes. That's why he's called Frisky.'

'I see.'

Their colloquy was interrupted by the return of the girl's mother carrying an envelope. He held out his hand for it but she kept it away from him.

'Before you can have this I want the answer to a question.'

'Fire away.'

'What are you going to do with it? You're not the sort that plays jokes.'

He had rehearsed this one till he was word-perfect; not only

that, but blink-perfect and shrug-perfect too. First the slackening of muscles to indicate relief, then pressing lips together –
momentary resolve not to tell, followed by a glance at the envelope and away again – wavering, on to lowering the head –
touch of shame, finally the blunt statement in a be-damned-to-
you tone, 'Sell it.'

'Who to?'

'I don't know. Of course I know who to deliver it to. I should
think the man who's buying it is an enemy of Director Vanag's,
wouldn't you? But there's a lot of those, so we're not much
further forward.'

'But why? You can't – '

More shame and defiance in tandem. 'Money.'

'I was just going to say, you can't need the money.'

'Oh can't I!' he said with great but not too great bitterness.
'You try a few evenings of backgammon at a thousand a point
with the luck against you and see whether you start needing
money.'

'How much are you down?'

'Nearly six million.' He stared into space, stricken at the very
thought of so much waste.

'That's quite a lot of money, even these days. But surely your
father would let you – '

'No. Can I have that now?'

'It's very lucky that man came along just when he did, and
also when you'd got friendly with me.'

'He came along originally six weeks before I knew of your
existence,' he said indignantly. 'The luck was that he hadn't
found a seller in the meantime. And getting friendly – well, I
can't make out it was your idea and not mine, but I didn't start
it . . . Thank you.' While he was opening the envelope he went
on, 'Did you have to have a lot of things done to you to get
this?'

'Yes. Well, rather a lot. Some of them revolted me.'

'Merciful God.'

He drew out a document and unfolded it. What he saw made
him jump to his feet without having consciously intended to,

205

something that could have been said of very few other bodily actions of his since early childhood.

'Christ in heaven!'

'What is it?'

'Where's the telephone?'

'In the hall. What's the matter?'

He hurried out to the instrument, which apart from being of inferior manufacture was virtually identical with the one in use here half a century before. As he spoke into it Mrs Korotchenko watched him with mounting anxiety and annoyance. After a very short conversation he slammed the handset back into its cradle and turned towards the front door. She barred his way.

'Where are you going?'

'I have to leave. Something very urgent has come up.'

'I knew you were in the resistance.'

'Nonsense. Now, if you . . .'

'What about my punishment?'

'I'm afraid that'll have to be deferred till next time.'

She threw a punch that would have knocked him out if her weight had been properly behind it. As it was he staggered back and crashed into the table where the telephone stood, dislodging a mug of the anthropomorphous sort he had noticed in the dining-room on his last visit; it broke in two on the tiles. When he came back at her she was waiting for him with her guard up. Swearing afresh, he feinted with his fists and rammed his knee into the pit of her stomach; she bent double and started noisily trying to breathe; he stepped past her, turned and, his eyes gone distant, fetched her a kick in her bare arse that brought her head against the frame of one of the glass doors hard enough to daze her and laid her sprawling on the chequered floor. Her child appeared from the drawing-room in good time to see this and be reduced once more to what might have been helpless laughter. Alexander banged the front door behind him.

He set off at a fast trot for the Northampton road and the stables where Polly was. What had Latour-Ordzhonikidze had to say about situations of the kind just concluded?

Save that brought by death, there is no true grief in love. All partings of lovers are willed by both, and that will was present in the very impulse that drew them together.

Something like that.

19

His office had said that Theodore would be in a *pub* in George Row near the former county hall, now of course the seat of the civil administration. Although the street was only a couple of hundred metres long, Alexander had trouble finding the place. At last he registered the fact that two men were in process of changing its sign; from having been the Marshal Grechko it was that moment becoming the Jolly Englishman, an imaginative stroke, a bold stroke, a stroke that had not been cleared with authority in all its forms. Loud singing was coming from within. It was ragged and some of it was out of tune, but it sounded unnatural, forced, like low-life, rather drunken singing in a movie of sixty years and more earlier. At least it might have sounded so to an Englishman of that time, jolly or not. Certainly it meant nothing at all to Alexander.

> '*Get on well, for I must leave you,*
> *Do not let this parting grieve you,*
> *And remember that the best of friends must part, must part.*
> *Good-bye, good-bye, kind friends, good-bye, good-bye, good-bye,*
> *I can no longer stay and sigh, stay and sigh.*
> *I'll hang my harp . . .*'

He threw Polly's reins to a middle-aged labourer who had perhaps paused to listen to this and strode into what had been the public bar.

Through a cloud of tobacco-smoke (the Festival made its own rules) he had a brief impression of men in check shirts and neck-scarves with pewter tankards in their hands sitting on hard chairs round an upright piano. Theodore, who was at the keyboard, gave a startled look and came over to Alexander as soon as the chorus ended.

'What's the – '

'Shut up. Let's go.'

After a longer look Theodore called to a young man standing by the piano, 'Take over, Henry. Go on to the end, then start again at the beginning. Don't forget the cheers and the clapping. I'll probably be back before you've finished.'

'Yes, Mr Ivanov. What about the dirty stories?'

'We can run through those in the morning.'

Outside, Theodore said, 'You and I were meeting anyway in less than an hour.'

'This won't wait,' said Alexander. 'Keep walking.'

'What about your horse? Is that your horse?'

'I haven't forgotten her. Here.'

The proffered sheet of paper bore the faint diagonal red lines required by law on any replicated matter, which would otherwise have been indistinguishable from an original. It ran, in part,

FROM THE OFFICE OF THE HEAD OF OPERATIONS
88TH CHIEF SECURITY DIRECTORATE
TOWN HALL, DYCHURCH LANE, NORTHAMPTON,
ENGLAND
AGENTS IN FIELD IN ORDER OF SENIORITY AS AT
1 SEPTEMBER 2035
1 Col-Gen V. S. Alksnis ('Michael Mets')
2 Brig Ch. I. Kluyev ('Aram Sevadjian')
3 Lt-Col Y. N. Tchernyavin . . .

That was enough for Theodore for the moment. He had stopped dead on catching sight of the first name, or rather the first supposed pseudonym; a small bespectacled man carrying a tattered parcel had barged into him, apologized lavishly and not been noticed doing either. Alexander saw that clouds had moved over the sun in the short time since he entered the Jolly Englishman. The streets were littered and grimy; every few metres there was a broken paving-stone or a pot-hole filled with rubble that had strayed over the road-surface. People were hurrying home mostly as single individuals, heads down, silent, looking neither to right not to left. Everything was normal, in fact.

'Come on,' said Alexander.

'Where are we going?'

'We're not going anywhere. We're going to walk the streets, keeping with the crowds. It's probably the least suicidally dangerous place. I take it Mets is our leader?'

'I don't know for certain; I strongly suspect so. Nina and I talked to him for a second in your garden the night we were engaged. I thought he was drunk and Nina thought he was frightened.'

'Well?'

'Wouldn't you be frightened if you had an important job under Vanag?'

'Naturally I would,' said Alexander a little irritably, skirting a pile of empty tins and shoddily-lettered cardboard containers outside a soft-drinks shop, 'but I'd be even more frightened if Vanag was after me. Look, Sevadjian gave me the job of getting that list himself.'

'He had no alternative. It was a decision of the committee.'

'Did he support it? Was there a vote? And don't forget he had an alternative – killing me before I was within a kilometre of the list.'

Theodore had slowed in his walk and was further studying the document in question. 'Well, things aren't as bad as they might have been,' he said as he refolded it.

'How?'

'You and Nina and Elizabeth don't appear.'

'Better not tell Nina you checked that.'

'Aram a brigadier in Intelligence . . . It must be a trick.'

'I hope so.'

They turned right into Abington Street and began to move past the ruins of the great shopping-centre, not the result of any concerted effort, just vandalism and the passage of time. Here the passers-by moved slowly for the most part: housewives

210

facing a long walk home, idly chattering groups of school-children, strolling whores. A black Jaguar carrying some high official, perhaps from out of town, perhaps from London, weaved its way among the horse-traffic. After a few metres Alexander put his hand on Theodore's shoulder and halted.

'Let's go back,' he said. 'I know what to do.'

'I wish I did,' said Theodore, turning. 'It doesn't seem to me to make much difference whether it's a trick or not. Either way we're hopelessly exposed.'

'Not necessarily. I've had longer to think about this than you have. It does make a difference, perhaps a big difference. If that list is genuine, we are well and truly done for. If it's a fake, aimed at setting some of us against others, it need mean no more than that they've correctly identified a number of our leaders. They may still know everything, of course, but there may be things, quite important things, they don't know. For instance, although they know about me . . .'

'How?'

'Oh, Theodore. They get word a chap's trying to get hold of a list of their agents, never mind the reason he gives. What would you have thought? Or at least gone along with to be on the safe side?'

'Then she . . .'

'Yes. She believed it, I'm sure. She'd believe anything. No, that's not quite right. The little bit of wiring that enables you to decide what to believe and what not to believe somehow got left out of her. Together with numerous and extensive other bits.'

'Well, maybe. But it still can't have been a plot from the start. You and I had hardly spoken by the time she made her dive at you.'

'No, we all underestimated her, including Sevadjian. It was just a sort of joke on her part. She was stirring things up by telling her husband what she and I were up to and then doing just as he said. Holy Christ, I'd punish her now if I had the chance. Anyway: this is all assuming the list is a fake. If it's genuine they don't know about me through her . . .'

211

The two parted momentarily to allow plenty of room for an unshaven, ragged man with a bottle who was coming towards them in a series of arcs. When they were side by side again, Alexander, who seemed to Theodore almost to be enjoying himself went on as before,

'... but they still know about me because they know about everybody. And either way, alas, they know about you too. But one thing they don't necessarily know – if the list is a fake – is when we ...'

He stopped in the middle of the pavement and stared at Theodore with what anyone might have said was real consternation. Theodore made a puffing noise.

'No more shocks, for heaven's sake,' he said. 'I don't think I could stand another.'

'That *silly bugger* of a CO of mine.' Alexander got moving again. 'He summoned me this afternoon and gave me a rather cryptic warning. A good half of my mind was on Mrs K, and so I assumed he was warning me off her – not bad advice when you come down to it – and was being cryptic because the subject embarrassed him. But then he said something I didn't really take in till just now. When I said, quite falsely as you understand, that of course I'd do as he suggested and drop her – no, not drop HER, drop the enterprise or the involvement or something – he said he was glad I was getting out in time. Before what happened? Now with Mrs K, after you've decided to follow her up, which admittedly might be thought a bad move and also irrevocable in a sense, you just get more of the same, well no, not the same, but roughly similar. It would only be not in time, too late, if I ran away with her, something of that order, which needless to say I never contemplated. Or if her plan for our next meeting included me cutting her head off, which wouldn't surprise me totally, but I don't see how Colonel Tabidze could have heard about that. And then – yes! Afterwards we chatted with his wife for a couple of minutes, and he said he and I had had a good talk, and she had no idea what it had been about. Now you've only met them a couple of times, haven't you? but can you imagine him warning me off Mrs K without his wife not only being a party to it but probably drilling him in what to say? He was being cryptic because he was leaking a deadly secret at great risk to himself, the old idiot. And the secret isn't that they know about me, though I think it does rather prove that, don't you? No, Theodore, the secret is that they know when. They know about Sunday.'

They had made their way back to the Jolly Englishman, from which came voices raised as before in professionally-simulated amateurish song. Theodore fancied he also heard a faint roll of thunder. He looked a little distractedly at a passing boy and girl, then at Alexander again. What made the fellow so cheerful, so obviously in good form in these unencouraging circumstances? Was this what was meant by being at one's best in a crisis? How could he know? – he had never been in a crisis before. He said in a helpless sort of way,

'What are we to do? Give up?'

After a small hesitation, Alexander said violently, 'No, we can't do that now. My advice to you is to take that list to the most senior member of the organization whose name isn't on it. I'm certain as I can be that it's a fake, but we daren't take the risk of letting anyone see it who's on it, like Sevadjian. Now from the way Tabidze was talking, they've decided to wait for us to move, to reveal and incriminate ourselves. The only thing to do is seize the initiative by moving when they're not expecting it. Added to which they may change their minds and pull us in at any moment.' He glanced at the dial on his wrist. 'I'm advancing zero fifty-two hours. I'll see you at the rendezvous at seven o'clock.'

Theodore literally gasped. 'You're mad. How could I warn people in the time? And ours isn't the only revolution, you know. Even if we – '

'You'd better get a move on, hadn't you?'

'But this is ... What chance do you think I've got?'

'About none. But I must try it. Any other way we have no chance at all.'

'Assuming all your deductions are correct. At least wait till we've consulted somebody.'

213

'I've decided.' Alexander's manner had changed to a heavy obstinacy. 'This is the only thing to do.'

Squaring his shoulders, he moved off. Uncertain, fearful, exasperated too, Theodore could still not forbear from calling 'Good luck' after him. He turned at once and came back and the two young men embraced warmly.

'*You're a good pal, old boy,*' said Alexander.

'*And the same to you with knobs on.*'

20

The land was darkening under a sky that, though covered with a yellowish haze, still seemed bright. The buildings, the trees and bushes were drained of colour, differing only in their tones of what was no longer green, grey or brown; a patch of vague shadow surrounded each of them. Little tremors, too brief and shifting to be called breezes, stirred in the air and made the parched leaves rustle, but it was still intolerably hot and humid. At the horizon the thunder muttered and rolled, like an artillery barrage in a kind of war nobody remembered or would have taken the least interest in. For fractions of a second at a time, pale flashes showed there. So much vapour hung in the atmosphere that human voices out of doors sounded hollow, as if contained by more solid barriers. A sweetish, sickly odour drifted about, derived from hot grass bruised by the feet of men and animals, fallen flower-petals and some spice used in cooking, at one moment teasingly elusive, at the next almost too strong to bear. Minute seeds, singly or in clusters of four or five, floated to and fro, swinging abruptly aside as the currents caught them.

To Trooper Lomov, walking briskly up the gentle slope towards the main house in the park where his regiment was quartered, it all had an unreal quality, though it would not have occurred to him to describe it in any such way. The rough material of his collar, damp with sweat, chafed at his skin and the horses' harness jingled and creaked. All five of them were shaking their heads and lashing their tails against the small brightly-coloured insects that darted about them. Lomov's pack-horse whinnied sharply at no perceptible stimulus and he reached across and stroked the animal's forehead. Nobody spoke.

The party reached a level space about the size of a tennis-court near the corner of the house. Here, in some degree hidden from view by a rough line of straggling laurels, they halted. Lomov stayed with the horses while the other two went into the house by a side entrance.

With Corporal Lyubimov at his side, Alexander reached the hall, the basement door and the sentry and Security NCO, the latter a dumpy Muscovite with stupid, calculating brown eyes. Good, thought Alexander, watching the man's parade of con-scientiousness in checking the photograph on the proffered identity-card against its owner's appearance, with which he was perfectly familiar. Miming satisfaction for all he was worth, he waited for the next move, the handing-over of some document of authorization. When this failed to follow, his expression became first puzzled, then worried. Alexander waited ten seconds, then said briskly but pleasantly,

'Open up, please.'

Now the sergeant's expression was one of acute discomfort. 'Sir, with the most profound respect, your honour, my standing instructions are not to let anyone past that door who hasn't produced – '

'My mission takes priority over that regulation,' said Alexander as before. 'Temporary removal of stores for the purpose of emergency training. In a real emergency there would almost certainly be no written orders. I had mine directly from the commanding officer, by word of mouth. Now.'

The sergeant had been slowly and wretchedly shaking his head. 'I just daren't risk it, your grace,' he said hoarsely.

Alexander was prepared for this. He stared grimly at the man with his eyes dilated; he had practised this many a time in front of a mirror and knew it made him look alarming, even a little mad. Without averting his gaze he picked up the handset of the intercom on the table between them and stabbed his finger in the direction of the row of call-buttons. Then he waited.

'Valentine, it's Alexander. Is the Colonel still there?' He looked fixedly at the ceiling fifteen metres above them while he listened, or appeared to listen. After half a minute he spoke a single word of thanks, hung up, glanced at his wrist-dial and stared at the sergeant again, this time with the corners of his mouth slightly downturned. Another pause followed. At last he said, in a heavy, dismal tone, 'Two hours. They think,' and slowly put his hands on his hips. 'What do you suppose will happen to you then?'

If the sergeant had been brighter, if Alexander had done the expected and raved at him, if he could have counted on his own officer to support him, if anything to justify the security procedures, anything in the least out of the way had ever happened to him or even been heard of since before he was born, above all perhaps if he had been trained as thoroughly to insist on the strictest observance of standing orders in all circumstances as he had been trained to do what officers told him to do, he might have held out. As it was, he hesitated for only a moment or two before saying,

'Very well, your honour – about turn, if you please. You too, corporal.'

So at least the intruders never learned the secret combination they now had no need of.

A quarter of an hour later they were trundling a loaded handcart back the way they had come. These eight metres or so were the most dangerous of all their journey: their cargo was covered with a waterproof sheet, but a cart meant stores, and hereabouts they could only have been security stores, and security stores on the move were seen rarely enough and never without a heavy escort. One piece of inquisitiveness would have been too much, but there was none; they emerged safely into the gloomy daylight and made their way towards the horses, the metal wheels clattering over the grassy irregularities in the ground.

As they approached, Lomov peered at them and past them under lowered brows, blinking. 'Sir, who was that with you just now, as you came out?'

'With us? With me?'

'With you, sir. That man.'

'What man?'

'After a few paces he turned round and went back into the house. I saw him.'

Lyubimov started to speak but Alexander shushed him. 'What did he look like, Lomov? Was he one of us?'

'No, sir. He was . . . He was a civilian.'

'What else? How was he dressed? Was he an English servant? A gardener?'

'He was a civilian, your honour. I only saw him for a moment.'

'You saw nothing, you stupid rookie,' said Lyubimov with good-natured contempt. 'Where have you hidden the bottle?'

Lomov was still looking rather oddly at Alexander. 'Are you all right, sir? Are you well?'

'Fuck your mother!' snarled Alexander, his considerate protective manner vanished. 'Don't try and play games with me, you son of a whore, or I'll break your back. Now shut your mouth and get this stuff loaded.'

It was soon done, a projectile-launcher and its mounting on the near side of each pack-saddle, the projectiles themselves with their red-painted nose-cones in bandoliers on the off. With Polly already ridden hard that day, Alexander had taken his orderly's horse, in effect his own second mount, a big stallion (black, needless to say) with nothing of the mare's kind temperament, but he was a good straight mover and had plenty of heart. Earlier, there had been an emotional farewell to Polly at the troop lines; not that Alexander had any settled expectation of not seeing her again, or of anything else, but one never knew, and it sounded good.

Down to the main gate they moved in file: Alexander, Lyubimov, Lomov. Little Lomov was possessed by excitement, also by fear, beyond that by a deeper, more unreasoning fear, by dread. Even considering the state of the light, he had been able to make out remarkably little about whoever it was had walked those half-dozen metres out of the house and then back again. He had had a brief impression of extreme thinness and a great many teeth. Perhaps the other two had failed to notice the stranger because he had not in fact drawn level with them, had

218

followed them to tell them or ask them something, thought better of it and removed himself. Perhaps. Lomov tried to forget it.

Thunder, much nearer now, crackled round the sky behind them. They were going to get soaked to the skin very soon, he thought to himself; the light cape each man carried attached to the rear of his saddle would be poor protection against the kind of downpour that impended. As he glanced about him at the grazing horses, the hurrying or strolling groups of men and the assortment of buildings that housed them, he could not believe he was about to leave the place that was all he had known of home for the past three years, very likely never to return. No doubt that disbelief was the cause of his almost total lack of regret at the prospect. Or it might have been the excitement. That seemed real enough. He was riding off on an operation that had been only sketchily described to him, and even parts of that description he found obscure. Other parts, however, had been quite plain, plain enough to justify moderate fear in anyone of moderate prudence, and Lomov easily fitted into that class. On the other hand, he felt that until a moment ago the whole of his life (he was twenty-three) had been spent passing time, getting through the day, waiting for something to start. Well, something had started now. If he had felt any differently, he would not have been where he was at this moment. How Lyubimov felt was another matter altogether. He was unpredictable. A good soldier, Lyubimov, a good NCO and a good friend, but inclined to be unpredictable. Impulsive, too.

They clattered through the gateway, across the road and on to the broad verge, riding east. Alexander ordered a trot. Just afterwards, thunder came from almost overhead and with the utmost abruptness; the noise was like the ripping of an enormous sheet of canvas. All the horses started violently and Lyubimov's pack-horse reared for a second or two; not having the reassuring presence of a man on his back, he could hardly be blamed. Still no rain fell, though the light was getting worse all the time. They had rounded a bend and gone about a kilometre when Alexander swung his right arm in an overarm bowling motion – 'Follow me'; a spoken order would not have been heard for the thunder, now continual. He put his horse into a gallop and easily cleared the low fence into a large field of pasture. As soon as the others had completed the jump he gave the signal to halt, then the one to dismount. Leading his horse he walked over to Lyubimov. For what was to follow, words would be preferable if they could be heard at all.

'Put up One!' he shouted.

'Put up One, sir.' Lyubimov turned away to his pack-saddle.

'Direction west six!'

This time there was no acknowledgement.

'Direction west six, you pig!'

Turning his head so that he spoke half over his shoulder, Lyubimov bawled, 'The regiment's thereabouts, sir. Is that the target?'

Most of the reply was drowned in thunder, but its drift was clear: the order was to be obeyed and no questions asked. There was a short pause. Lightning flashed ceaselessly over the surrounding fields. Then Lyubimov swung round holding his pistol pointed at Alexander's middle. Next he depressed a stud in front of the trigger-guard, thus switching from single-shot fire to automatic and by the action threatening not to kill or maim but to rend apart; Alexander understood that well enough. Finally Lyubimov shouted,

'I'm sorry, sir, but I won't do it, and I won't let you do it either. Are you with me, Lomov?'

'Yes!'

'Do as you're told!' screamed Alexander.

'I'm sorry, your honour. We'll blow up Vanag and his men for you and welcome, but we won't see our own lads harmed. Make up your mind to that.'

Alexander raved for nearly five minutes. His main theme was that the two were behaving in this way, not out of comradeship or humanitarianism, but as an expression of the envy and malice which vile creatures like them must naturally feel for anyone of his exalted state. Much of his tirade could not be heard, and much of what could be heard was unintelligible to Lomov, who even so decided that some turns of phrase would not have been disowned by the regimental farrier-major. He felt embarrassment too, and at one point acute alarm, when it seemed that the officer would strike the corporal and be blown in half for his pains (there were limits to Lyubimov's unpredictability). But the moment passed.

Suddenly it was all over, and Lomov found himself looking at the back view of a man on a horse moving away from him at full gallop.

'Come on!' yelled Lyubimov. 'There's no knowing what he might get up to in that state.'

It had sounded rather like an excuse, but Lomov ran for his mount as fast as he could.

Now, as the early-autumn evening closed in, a long chase began. One after the other Lyubimov and Lomov jumped the fence into the next field, and the next, and the next, then into a lane which they crossed into a patch of thin woodland. The thunder receded, returned and once more receded without bringing a drop of rain. In his grey uniform and on his black horse, Alexander was not an easy figure to spot among the shadows, and twice they almost lost him in the woods, but he had not had much more than a hundred metres' start and the more intensive training of his men had made it possible for them to narrow the gap. On the flat, things were more equal; even so, when the woods were behind them and they entered on a wide expanse of level grass with patches of scrub, the pursuers had the advantage of being able to traverse the chord of any arc traced by the pursued. Here Lyubimov gained slightly on Lomov. Strands of lightning came into view and were gone so fast that the reactions of the retina could not keep pace and vision became fogged.

It may have been this impairment which prevented Lomov from seeing the man on the grey horse until he was almost level with him. The horse was grey only in the language of horsemen; other people would have called it white, or rather not exactly white, nor any shade of grey; there was no naming its colour satisfactorily. Lomov thought he had never seen a horse stand so still. It's rider, a tall man in black, wore a hat that shaded his face, though his posture indicated that he was watching the chase, more particularly the one being chased, with intense interest. He did not return Lomov's wave.

The going became less even. A boy and a dog were moving a flock of sheep with predictable difficulty; the thunder had returned for the second time. Soon a road came up on the right. The three men and five horses, by now almost a single party again, tore along it at top speed until they reached a small church standing back from it. Here Alexander reined in cruelly hard, causing his mount to stagger, and proceeded to dismount. Lyubimov did the same, then Lomov.

'Are we to consider ourselves back under your command, sir?' asked Lyubimov.

'You can consider yourselves what you please.' The strenuous ride had done nothing to cool Alexander's rage; he was still moving his lips about and glaring. When he went on he tried to control the way he spoke. 'I have an errand here that will take two minutes. If you decide to come with me after that I can hardly stop you.'

'Where are we, sir?' asked Lomov curiously. 'What's in the church?'

A short man in a dark suit had been standing near the church door, as if waiting for someone, when they first rode up. He had not looked at them then. Now, whether at Lomov's question or by chance, he turned his head. Alexander saw the face of a man of fifty, rather heavy in the jowl and baggy under the eyes, with an expression of mild curiosity, nothing more, not the slightest hint of menace. But Lomov screamed.

Alexander turned on him savagely. 'What is the matter with you, you dolt, you imbecile? What did you see this time, you madman, Hitler's ghost?'

'I didn't see it, your honour. I didn't see anything.'

'Of course you didn't,' said Lyubimov gently. 'We all know that. You just thought you saw something, that's all.'

'Yes, I made a mistake. I . . . made a mistake.'

'Of course you did, but saying so once is enough.'

'Forgive me.'

With a great effort, Lomov unclenched his hands and straightened up to his full small height. No good would come of trying to puzzle out what he had seen or could not have seen in the last hour; the images, never clear, had already started to fade, and whatever was to come, he felt sure, would call for all his attention and capability. Sighing deeply and swallowing, he took off his cap, smoothed his hair and put the cap back on. His officer was just going on foot round the corner of the church. The man in the dark suit was nowhere to be seen. For the time being the skies were quiet and had even grown a little lighter over to the west. After a careful look at his companion, Lyubimov said,

'I could do with a beer, I don't mind telling you. Still, I can use up some of the time making room for it, can't I?'

He handed Lomov the reins of the three riding-horses, went into the churchyard and set about urinating; it was against regulations to do so in the open street.

'Lyubimov, what is this place?'

'Search me. No, wait a bit, it's probably his dad's house behind this, if we're anywhere near where I think we are. You know he's a big noise in the government side of things round here.'

'Of course,' said Lomov thoughtfully. 'I expect he's got a –'

Afterwards he always swore he actually heard the great bare pillar of lightning come into being over and beyond the church, but varied on whether it did so with a click or a fizz. At the time he shut his eyes automatically and after no apparent interval flinched at the tremendous detonation that seemed to reach right down to him and be everywhere about him. Neighing loudly, the horses stamped and plunged and pulled him from side to side. Lyubimov, doing up his trousers, hurried over to help.

'That was close,' he said.

It had been closer still for Alexander, who had just passed the miniature temple when, with stupefying suddenness, the flash touched the lightning-conductor system of the house. Enormous sparks flew outwards and the air shifted and shook and tossed him to the ground. His fall, on to a patch of coarse grass, left him undamaged, but he lay there for a couple of minutes in a torpor, shocked and half-blinded, deafened too for the moment, inhaling the pungent refreshing odour of ozone. At last he got laboriously to his feet.

The lights were on in the drawing-room, but the curtains had been pulled and in any case the windows were too high off the ground for him to see inside. This business must be finished with as soon as possible; even as it was he had underestimated times and would be late at the rendezvous with Theodore and the others. If they came. As quietly as he could without loitering, he mounted the steps, went indoors and reached the little lobby. With his eyes on the engraved pane he wondered, not for the first time, how that other Alexander would have regarded the enterprise that this one was about to take in hand, and at once saw quite clearly, so clearly that he could not understand never having so much as glimpsed it before, that all his feelings in this matter were fabrications, that he and the dead Englishman were separated not only by time but also by another barrier just as impenetrable, a mental one, a moral one, and that their shared name was the product of a dreary, puny coincidence. How could he have supposed anything else?

Sergei Petrovsky sat in his high-backed Karelian armchair, looking very elegant in West of England tweed trousers, yellow cashmere sweater and light-green suède boots. He was feeling rather lowered in spirits, having that morning received from London the official redraft of his proposals for the reform of land tenure in the district. The first eight clauses, outlining the new system of labourers' co-operatives, the structure of these, their degree of autonomy, the procedure whereby their applications for possession were to be drawn up and considered by authority – all these items followed the very wording of his original memorandum. Clause 9, however, sanctioning the transfer of the specified properties to duly qualified claimants, was missing in its entirety. In other language, the English were entitled to ask for land but not to be given it. Those proposals of his had been toned down all right. Well, he tried to tell himself, it was a start. And it was certainly not the chief of his worries.

When Alexander came briskly into the room and shut the door behind him, he jumped to his feet with a delighted smile. 'Alexander, my dear . . .' Then his whole bearing changed and he said in the grimmest tone, 'So it's today, not Sunday, eh?'

'Not Sunday?'

'Don't trifle with me, Alexander. I know. I haven't really had time to take it in yet, but I know. How much I know doesn't matter at this stage.'

'You've got it wrong as usual, father. How much you know might matter a great deal to me, though admittedly I shan't have time to test your knowledge.'

'Well, I know enough, that's the point. Not everything, of course. But THEY do. Need I say whom I'm referring to? They know everything. Everything and everybody.'

'Not true. I proved the contrary less than an hour ago. A somewhat major particular has escaped them.'

'Believe me,' said Petrovsky earnestly, 'they know every name, every move, every item on the time-table, every – '

'Wrong again. I've changed the time-table. And why should I believe you, of all people? I never have in the past, and I can't think how many mistakes it's saved me from making. And you're begging for your life now, so naturally you'd lie. Who wouldn't?'

'I'll never beg, from you or anybody else,' said Petrovsky firmly. 'I just want you to know your cause is lost.'

'Why? Why do you want me to realize that? Because it might save your life. And what if my cause is lost? I've never thought it was anything else, right from the beginning. With any luck, I'll be able to achieve my object, do what I've always wanted to do as long as I can remember, the only thing I've ever really wanted. And that's merely to inflict some damage, to smash something. To register a protest. Oh, the world will never change, but in a short time from now it'll have evidence that at least one of its inhabitants hates it, hates it for its complacency,

225

its ignorance, its lack of love, its selfishness, its sentimentality, its lack of any guiding principle, its callousness, its superficiality, its philistinism, its illiteracy . . .'

Alexander, whose voice had risen, could think of no further grounds on which somebody might hate the world, and time was passing, so he took his pistol out of its holster. The sight of this weapon, with its long butt-magazine, daunted his father extremely; perhaps until now he had not started to believe that he might be going to lose his life. His voice had lost nearly all its firmness when he said,

'Not one of those bursts, please. At this range, one shot ought to be . . .'

'We mustn't inconvenience the servants. A liberal to the last. No, don't yell for help, or you get a burst in the stomach straight away.'

'I swear to you . . . I don't know what you've done in the past hour, but believe me it's allowed for, it can't make any difference.'

'I don't mind taking the gamble.'

'Alexander, if you surrender now, lay down your arms and give yourself up, the civilian police would do, it needn't be Vanag's men. . .'

'Oh, so we're doing deals, are we?'

'I'll never bargain with you. This is all so absurd. You and I should be on the same side. Why didn't you approach me, why didn't you try to recruit me?'

'You weren't worth having. As is now plain.'

That seemed to go unheard. 'It's not too late. Let me join you now. I could be very valuable to you. There are all sorts of –'

'You know, at first I wasn't sure I could do this, but a touch of your style works wonders. Time well spent. Good-bye, Controller Petrovsky.'

Alexander's glance had become remote when he pointed the pistol. There had been no more thunder since the mighty peal and everything was quiet. The Controller fell to his knees and lifted his clasped hands, saying loudly,

'You can't do it! Your own father! Who gave you life! You

must be raving mad! You'll never forgive yourself! What good will it do? They'll shoot you for it! You can tell them you couldn't find me!' Petrovsky in his turn was running out of things to say, but he battled on. 'Think of . . . think of your mother! Think what it would mean to her! To have her son murder her husband in cold blood! You may hate me, though I can't think why, I've always done my best for you, but she in her goodness and . . .'

Suddenly Alexander remembered Leo writhing and screaming with pain and fear on the roll of bunting in the store-house that night. He had no intention of giving his father cause to behave in any such way, but the memory was so vivid and distracting that he had begun to wander from his aim when the door burst open to reveal Lomov. Before Alexander could finish turning and raising his pistol at him Lomov shot him through the temple – a single shot. He was dead at once, though the impact of the small low-velocity bullet was slight and it took a moment for his body to finish falling on to the tiger-skin rug that had come from the shore of the Aral Sea.

Cautiously, Lomov advanced into the room, keeping his pistol trained on Alexander until he was sure he was dead. Then he burst into tears.

'Who are you?' said Petrovsky, getting shakily to his feet.

'He was my officer,' Lomov managed to say.

'What are you doing here?'

'He brought us. He told us . . . Forgive me, your honour.'

Petrovsky put his arm round Lomov's shoulders. 'Don't cry, my boy,' he said kindly. 'You did what had to be done. You saved the regiment's honour. Colonel Tabidze will be proud of you. You're an excellent soldier, quick-thinking and efficient.'

From somewhere very far away Lomov heard the deep note of a bell, but he was too distracted to take any notice. He dried his tears.

By then, others had come to the room, including the butler Anatol, the batman Brevda, Nina, Tatiana, Lyubimov. There was much talk and sound of lamentation. Anatol looked utterly bewildered, Brevda utterly discomposed. Nina went into a corner by herself. Tatiana knelt down and looked into Alexander's face; someone had already closed his eyes and the wound was not so terrible. Lyubimov talked quietly to Lomov.

After a minute, Petrovsky drew his wife aside, sending her a look of diffident appeal.

'What is it, Sergei?'

'Don't say . . .' He stopped.

'Say what? Why should it make any difference what I say now, rather than at any other time?'

When he made no reply, she turned away and went to Nina.

At last it began to rain.

21

Director Vanag sat in the passenger's seat of a converted Range Rover parked in a field about thirty metres from a thick wood; the trees were mostly eucalyptus, poplar, Douglas fir and other quick-growing species. His regular driver, a flat-faced man with closely-shorn grey hair, sat beside him. They did not speak. In eleven years they never had, except for the passing of instructions and functional information. The recent storms had lowered the temperature and the humidity, and the weather was now more seasonable, mild and sunny with cool breezes. It was seven-twenty in the morning.

Establishing this by a glance at his wrist-dial, Vanag climbed into the back of the vehicle. The uniform he wore today differed from the usual run in having large patch pockets. He rubbed his hands and looked expectantly towards the wood. The early sunlight sparkled on the many raindrops that hung about the boughs and leaves, making a pleasant picture. Then they started coming, half a dozen wood-pigeons in an irregular line, flying fast, climbing fast. But Vanag was ready for them. He sent three short bursts of 7.55-millimetre steel-jacketed bullets up at them and knocked one down with the second; the bird lifted as if kicked in the breast and fell turning over and over. For his second sweep he had to increase the angle a good deal and missed altogether, but by then a group of mallards, slower and nearer the ground, had turned up from the pond in the wood, and he got two of them.

The weapon was a replica of a 1950s Red Fleet anti-aircraft light machine-gun on a ring mounting. A contact who knew of his interest in such matters had picked it up almost complete in a Trieste museum and had it flown home. Vanag had had it stripped down and copied and the copy installed in the back of the Range Rover with a raised chair attached. The thing was ideal for his purpose: easy to handle, reasonably accurate and with a rate of fire too low for the hosing technique possible with more modern weapons, which in his view were not for the sportsman. The ammunition had to be specially made in Birmingham, but that was no problem, any more than raising volunteers to put the birds up for him was a problem.

He was changing magazines when his eye was caught by a movement at the edge of the wood. It soon resolved itself into a rabbit running from the approach of the beaters. Vanag clipped the fresh magazine into place as quickly as he could and swung the muzzle, but in those few seconds the rabbit had come far enough towards him not to be reachable by the machine-gun even if he depressed it to its limit. Instinct for shelter took the creature under the belly of the Range Rover. There it stayed. He got off the firing-chair, took from its hook the heavy old revolver he kept by him for just such unpredictable crises as this, and jumped to the ground. It was not an easy shot, with the wheels and differential casings to avoid, but the rabbit helped by immediately freezing, and quite soon it had no head. In that short interval he had lost a lot of birds; never mind, plenty more were coming.

His final bag, apart from the rabbit, was five pigeons, four ducks and a hen pheasant. The last was as much as he usually allowed himself on this shoot; the population was dropping and the birds, with their lumbering flight and low rate of climb, were almost too easy to bring down. This morning's kill lay not far off; it had taken the better part of a full burst and was almost shorn in two. Like the other carcasses, it would not be moved from where it had fallen; beyond a little veal at times, he touched no meat, and that was an end of it.

He got back into the front seat and the driver started the engine. They had finished here; they were going where they always went at such times. Where they went was Vanag's imposing Georgian mansion near Newport Pagnell. There his armourer took the machine-gun and the revolver off for cleaning, his valet helped him to change into a tunic of more conventional cut, a third servant brought him a cup of coffee and a rusk on a silver tray, and his living-in secretary went through the new Harrod's catalogue with him. By the time he was back in the forecourt the Range Rover had disappeared and the Rolls, gleaming in black and silver, awaited him. It was bullet-proofed, but that was nothing but a pleasing anachronism in deference to his position; he no more expected to be shot at than a ceremonial sentry expects to find himself bayoneting someone. He climbed in; the driver shut the door.

By eight-twenty-eight he was entering the former town hall, now the offices of the 88th Chief Security Directorate. His first stop was the information screen, but as he had expected there was nothing there that was both new and significant, and he waved away the print-out offered him by a clerk. Next, a call to his office-secretary; nothing there either. Then he took a lift to the second floor. Two armed guards were present on the landing, armed not with bayonets and such but with automatic weapons of the very sort he eschewed in his sporting activities, carried at the ready, too. Another pair stood outside a barred double door. Vanag walked past them and down a narrow corridor to a smaller door, also guarded. Beyond this door a flight of stairs led up on to a narrow stage; he ran nimbly up the stairs and made his way to a lectern near the back. On the reading surface of this he laid a single sheet of notes. The wall behind him carried a large map of the world with the union in red, allies in blue, unincorporated democratic republics in green and neutralized states in yellow.

He was standing in a lecture-theatre that held about a hundred and fifty people. The benches were filled with men (a few women, but mostly men) who were unshaven and tousle-headed and even dirtier than usual. Their expressions were frightened and hostile, mostly frightened. In case what hostility there was should take an active form, eight armed guards all told were stationed round the hall and actually pointing their guns at the audience. Their purpose was not to deter any kind of sudden concerted rush at Vanag by indicating that the first dozen or more to move would certainly die, but to make sure that they would all die long before they got their hands on him. He considered that such a rush was most unlikely; nevertheless, he had founded a highly successful career on the principle of always being on the safe side.

'Well, I must say I don't get a hell of a lot in the way of a sense of achievement when I contemplate you crowd,' he began without preamble (and without accent) in his clear, high-pitched voice. *'A bit too much like robbing the blind school for my taste. Shame to take the money, really.* But since I want you to understand me I won't go on in the language of the nation you were prepared to make such sacrifices for. Now I got some of you up here to have a proper look at you. I couldn't have seen you at all well in the basement. I'm afraid it isn't very comfortable there, but then you see it isn't supposed to be. That's not the idea. Anyway, it means you probably appreciate being up here instead for a short time. I'm sorry it will only be a short time. Even so we have had some rather tedious precautions to take, as you can see. But I thought it was worth it for the sake of getting a proper look at some of you.'

Director Vanag moved his eyes along the benches before him, no doubt conscientiously doing as he had said. As he did so he began to shake with laughter, then to utter peals of it, hunching his small body and banging with his fist on the lectern. He seemed to be venting an amusement that was quite untouched by malice, like one enjoying the antics of an exceptionally gifted comedian. At least one person in the audience had heard that laughter on a different occasion: Theodore. His present feelings were such that the behaviour of the man on the platform left them unchanged, as most things would have done.

After a not very short time Vanag elaborately pulled himself together, cleared his throat and settled his tunic into position. 'Here is what we paper-merchants call a situation report,' he said, consulting his notes. 'It has been quiet everywhere for over forty-eight hours. In fact in most places it has never been anything else but quiet. Moscow: what was known among you as a change of government did not take place. Now as to England.

232

Bristol: an explosion injured four Security personnel, one of them seriously. Sevenoaks: shots were fired at a high-ranking official and a member of his entourage was slightly wounded. Near Scotton, Yorkshire: two army vehicles were set on fire but there were no casualties. And that is all.

'Except in this district. Since three of the five who founded Group 31 were our men, keeping abreast of subsequent developments has hardly taxed our powers to the utmost, and correspondingly we haven't in general had more than meagre opportunities of displaying anything more than the barest competence.' He looked up and smiled. 'Rather dull, in fact. Nothing to push against. Well now, partly by chance, in this district something that was rather more fun became possible: a little conspiracy, using the term in its technical sense, a tiny scheme, a provocation and a deception rolled into one. A provocation is attractive because it has the effect of raising the stakes in a winning game. You'll understand the force of that in a minute. Anyway, the deception was successful. We succeeded in passing off on you as a list of our men in your organization what was in fact a list of your own leadership, whom some of you promptly murdered. The provocation was accepted in full.'

Until now his hearers had sat in silence, whether intent or indifferent, but now fierce murmurs arose among them. Vanag went on as before,

'That had a sort of elegance about it, though in order to succeed it needed stupidity on your part of a quality that you slightly astonished even me by providing. Oh, if you're wondering whether I'm telling the truth, ask yourselves why I should lie to you. What do I care what you think about anything?'

This took a moment to sink in. Then there were shouts and screams, and two figures were borne to the ground almost at once and hidden from view. At the very first move the guards had looked at Vanag, who held the palm of his hand towards them. It was not long before, at another signal, the bodies were dragged out and the prisoners driven back to their seats with some roughness, but without the use of more than an occasional gun-butt.

Vanag waited till all was quiet before shaking with laughter again, this time in silence. 'You are an amazing lot,' he said, shaking his head. 'Supposing that had been the conspiracy? Well, it wasn't, but it might have been, and what then?' He paused and seemed to consider. 'It's remarkable – no, of course it isn't in the least remarkable, no more than what anybody with the merest speck of sense might have expected. But then none of you have even that. I was going to say it's appropriate that your cover activity, that Festival, should have been as total and as miserable a failure as your true purpose. Giving back culture. What a bizarre notion. Especially since nobody had it to give in the first place. Not that some of you didn't take it seriously. Poor Sevadjian led our fellows a devil of a dance, at the theatre till all hours, dashing off to remote spots in search of actors and so on. Able man in his way. Just no sense. Let it be said in your favour that you didn't do as disastrously as some of the other Festivals. In the south-east, for instance, at a place called Glyndebourne, they put on an opera or a ballet or something using real wild animals, and everyone made such a row that they ran amok and killed five people. English, naturally. Unfortunate, though.

'Well, that's about all I have to tell you. I thought you'd like to know the position, and as I said I wanted to have a proper look at some of you.' He pressed his lips together and twitched a couple of times. 'I realize I'm very lucky, in that I know what to do. I have something to live by – the values and rules of the institution I'm part of and have been part of for many years. Traditions, if you like. Now some of you may argue that those rules and traditions leave a certain amount to be desired, and there may well be something in that. But for me, for us, for these guards, they're better than nothing, which is what you've got. By "you" I mean not only you who are here, or you and your colleagues downstairs, but everyone in this country who isn't part of Security: the administration, the bureaucrats and their families, all the units of supervision. The army is a bit of an exception but it hasn't got enough to do. We have plenty to do, and we can do it well or badly; our behaviour has meaning.

You, all of you, can't do anything, from keeping a secret to washing a dish. You can't even come up with a decent fortune-teller.' As he said this he looked at Theodore, who caught the look. 'By the way, I know you won't tell anybody I made those nasty remarks about the administrators and the rest. I'm sure I can trust you. Well, if no one has any questions . . .'

There was a wordless stir among those on the benches. The guards again looked at Vanag, who again showed them his palm. He said earnestly,

'Do feel quite free to ask anything within reason.'

'Please tell us what will happen to us,' said a voice.

'How terribly thoughtless of me, of course you want to know that. The trouble is, I can't really give you an answer. It doesn't rest with me, you see; it's a matter for the courts. But if you want, let's call it an educated guess . . .?'

'Please,' said the voice.

'Very well. This is where raising the stakes comes in – it really was intolerably feeble of me to forget that. I'm afraid that by accepting the provocation you've done yourselves a grave disservice. The judges are bound to take a serious view of those deaths, deaths of criminals, true, but still Russian deaths. Let's be specific. I think any form of execution can safely be excluded. Yes, I think so. But the setting of any limit to your confinement – almost equally unlikely. So we seem to be left with the question of what form of confinement. I'd rule out exile – for those of you who don't know, exile is enforced residence in one or another Asian locality. Yes, I'm afraid I can't honestly see it being exile. Exile is what your more fortunate counterparts in less violent districts will suffer. In my prediction. If you're very unlucky, if the prosecution press hard for it, it'll be strict régime – a strict-régime labour camp, where the weakest are the luckiest. But . . . No, my forecast would be a standard labour camp, not too cold. You're expected to work, not die. I'm told it's possible to have some sort of life in such places, rather depending on which one it is. Are there any more questions?'

There were none.

'Then that's all. I'd like to thank each one of you for being fool enough to play your part in the only interesting thing that's happened to me in eleven years. Not only interesting in itself, but the means of a much-desired promotion. I've been told unofficially that I'm to have Oxford. You people can imagine what a thrill that is for me. There are still colleges there, you know. The buildings, that is. Very cultured. You won't start blabbing that everywhere you go, will you? Thank you for your attendance. Dismiss.'

Now Vanag made a sign to the guards that sent them hurrying forward, but Theodore had time to raise his hand to him in a gesture of appeal. He nodded and beckoned to the nearest guard. Thumps and cries were heard as the audience were helped on their way out of the lecture-theatre.

Theodore found himself separated from the other prisoners. The guard Vanag had spoken to, squat but powerful, with sallow Mongolian looks, gripped him by the upper arm and bundled him to the landing. The man pulled him about as they went so that he constantly staggered and stumbled, giving the appearance of resistance while offering none. In the same way he was thrown into and out of the lift, although in both cases he was quite willing to do what was required of him. When he started to say so he was slapped hard and expertly across the face, twice, backhand and forehand. He ought to have learned better by now, his third day in custody. Well, sooner or later he would learn, there was no possible doubt of that. The object must be never to let him forget for a single moment that he was in captivity. He would learn that too.

On the lower floor he was dragged and pushed along a wide corridor and flung into a room opening off it, so violently that he almost fell. It was a small room, not only furnished sparsely but containing a remarkable paucity of objects: nothing on the walls, no cupboards, no files, no papers, just an open note-pad and pen on the desk at which Vanag sat facing him. The only other things on the desk were an intercom, a telephone with switches and a glass that had contained fruit-juice – lemonade, Theodore remembered. Also present was a fair-haired man of

236

about thirty in civilian clothes, sitting behind a bare scrubbed table at right angles to the desk. He said nothing and made no move throughout the interview that followed, and Theodore never had any idea what he was there for.

When neither of the other two spoke, he said, 'May I sit down?'

Vanag looked at him. His manner had lost some of the affability it had held during his address upstairs. 'Yes,' he said after a moment. 'Well, what do you want?'

'Nina Petrovsky,' said Theodore, settling himself on a wooden folding chair. 'Where is she, do you know? She doesn't seem to be in any of the cells here.'

'Of course I know where she is; I know where everybody is. She's in hospital, but she won't be there for long. Just a little concussion. Nothing serious.'

'How?'

'She resisted arrest.'

'But what could she do? She's only a girl.'

'Perhaps no more than verbally.'

'May I see her?'

'No you may not,' said Vanag sternly. 'Do you think I have men to spare for frivolous errands like that? There's still a lot of work to get through.'

'Will I see her again?'

'It's possible; it's also unlikely. You may be moved out at any moment. Is there anything else?'

'How was her brother killed?'

'Shot by one of his own men as he was about to shoot his father.'

'Oh.' Theodore reflected. 'How did the man happen to be there so conveniently? It doesn't matter – what about your man? Where was he at the time? Or – '

The other gave a conclusive nod. 'You have a point,' he said. 'Our man was snoring on his bed and the show woke him up. He only had three of the servants under his orders and he wasn't expecting anything to happen till the next day but one. Like everybody else, I'm only as good as whoever they send me.'

'Who was he?'

'No. There are some rules I never break.'

'Whoever he was, how's that episode going to look in your report?'

'Very different from how it happened.'

Theodore gave a sort of laugh. There was hardly any amusement in it, but it affected Vanag. The look he now sent Theodore was not friendly, but it was not contemptuous or irritated either; it acknowledged the intimacy brought them by having taken part in the same operation, even though on opposite sides. He spoke a single word into the intercom on his desk and seemed to relax a little.

'If there ever was a fool,' he said, 'it was the late Alexander Petrovsky, whom you recruited with such headlong alacrity. Only a fool of prodigious dimensions would pursue an affair with the Korotchenko woman. A vicious child and a destructive child too, that one. She has her uses, though, as you must agree.'

'I still don't understand that. Surely she wasn't under orders when she threw herself at Alexander.'

'No, no, she was following her own inclinations, as always. Some days afterwards, they led her to tell her husband about her latest adventure. No doubt he had displeased her in some way. And then again perhaps he hadn't.'

'But she ... but he might have ...'

'Your wonderment proclaims your ruinous ignorance of the world and of the human character. Young Petrovsky's evident failure even to consider the possibility that she might betray him in that way proclaims something even more crass. As he was in an unimprovable position to have known, that was exactly the sort of thing she likes doing. Well, one of the sorts of things.'

'He guessed that in the end. When it was too late.'

'Quite so. Actually Korotchenko had heard about her and your friend Alexander already, so she only thought she was betraying him.'

'Who told Korotchenko?'

'I did. It's important that a Deputy-Director of Security

should be informed when his wife has relations with a counter-revolutionary. Yes, the after-dinner conversation at the mess.'

'That fellow with the birthmark,' said Theodore bitterly. 'But I looked carefully and found nothing.'

'Having done which, you felt altogether safe from eavesdroppers, safer than if you hadn't looked, and of course, you didn't look further. Our man's conduct was slightly creditable.' Vanag made a note on his pad.

'Did you record our outdoor conversation? Or was that impossible?'

'We have the capability of recording any conversation anywhere, but even after all these years outdoor technique is still rather complicated and calls for a skilled operator. We're chronically short of them and so we tend to keep them for gathering material of some importance.'

'Weren't you rather taking a chance? We might have been planning to steal the projectiles the very next day.'

Vanag smiled broadly. 'You can't ever have thought seriously about that, as indeed about anything else. If you had, you'd have realized that it was out of the question for soldiers to be able to get their hands on real projectiles whenever they felt like it. Do you think a man in my position would trust Field Security? They're soldiers too. What your mate would have been shooting at me were dummies painted like the genuine article.'

'But there must be real ones somewhere.'

'Assuredly there are, and where do you imagine they'd be? The same place as the real TK gas. When real projectiles are needed for a practice, we dole them out, and we account for every one. Just like the KGB in days gone by. But you wouldn't know about them. That's one of the things that's so depressing about all you people. Because you don't know how to live in the present, you haven't the slightest interest in the past. You and I had a very brief argument once, about what happened when we Russians came here, about the Pacification. I remember you said that organized English resistance ceased on the third day of fighting and thereafter there were isolated pockets of resistance. Perfectly true, and perfectly misleading. And you are one of the great number of misled, of those willing or more than willing to be misled.

'Pockets of resistance. Wherever our soldiers went they ran into one of those, especially in the country, though they came across plenty in the towns too. There was a particularly capacious pocket in the village of Henshaw, not far from here, where naughty Alexander used to do some of his courting. The English slaughtered a company and a half of our boys and severely mangled the relieving force with captured weapons before they were themselves destroyed. Only a few of their troops were involved. Most of them were villagers, including women and adolescents. They refused to surrender even when the buildings they had occupied were set on fire. They went on shooting through the smoke. They weren't hitting much by then. Our side had to hush all that up as hard as it could. It would have done terrible damage to morale. Some things couldn't be hushed up.'

'The English must have suffered appallingly.'

'Yes, very appallingly indeed. It had been said earlier that they had gone soft. If they had, I'd be interested to know what they were like before. They went on after they'd lost – Henshaw was after that – after they knew they were beaten. In the name of God, why? Well, that's one thing we can safely say we'll never know. And it went on. There was a victory parade through the streets of Liverpool, one of a series that turned out to be called for, and a middle-aged woman took a carving-knife out of her handbag and put it through the heart of the man marching on my father's right. She was dead in a second, but so was he. Perhaps it was something to do with their queen being killed. It was an accident, but nobody ever came across one of them who believed it. She was supposed to be a shadowy feudal relic. Those who'd said that, or were said to have said that, underwent corrective training that proved fatal in most cases.'

There was a pause. The fair-haired man looked interestedly out of the window. Theodore scratched his armpit, waited a moment and said,

'Could I please have a drink?'

'Certainly not,' said Vanag, but without asperity this time. 'Nor a cigarette. What and where do you think you are? And isn't it rather early for a drink? So, anyway. There had been disorders here, runaway inflation, mass unemployment, strikes, strike-breaking, rioting, then much fiercer rioting when a leftist faction seized power. It was our country's chance to take what she had always wanted most, more than Germany, far more than the Balkans, more even than America. And she took it, after serious difficulty at first, after being on the point of having to withdraw entirely in order to regroup.'

'What did the Americans do?'

At that, Vanag gave one of his merriest and longest laughs. It died away finally in affectionate chuckles and little snorts of amusement. Then his demeanour changed again. He stared grimly at Theodore. After another pause he said,

'All that was new to you. But if you'd really wanted to, you could have found it out. Found out a little about the nation you were supposed to be ready to kill and die for.'

'You didn't exactly make it easy for me or anyone else to find it out.'

'How true, Markov; we didn't exactly make it easy. In fact I'll go further: we made and make it difficult in the extreme. But that's all. Nobody can bury the truth so deep that it can never be found, and I ought to know. The most that can be done is to persuade people there's no point in looking for it. People who are willing to be persuaded. The versatile Alexander also thought he was interested in the English. And in a way he really was – at least he fucked quite a few of them, which is more than you ever did. He had some acquaintance with that ancient clergyman, Glover, who conducted the pointless and profitless church ceremony in your Festival. You are an extraordinary lot. Well, Glover among others would have been quite a useful source of knowledge about the Pacification and events before and since if you'd ever wanted one. And I'm sure Alexander would have put you on to him if you'd ever told him you wanted one. But you didn't, so you didn't. That's the trouble with ignorance, it defends itself to the death against knowledge. Behind it lies absence of curiosity and behind that – absence of any reason to know. Intelligence is no help to those in your situation. A man can't behave intelligently when he doesn't understand anything.

'Let me ask you one last question. Did you believe that story about handing the country over to the English when things had settled down? You needn't answer. Of course you never bothered your head about how, and which English, and awkward questions like that. But in fact none of it arises, you see. It would only arise if we were talking about a real counter-revolution instead of the greatest Security operation of the last fifty years. I think it's good that you should know that, on the off-chance that you still have some pride left. Yes, Group 31 was all the brain-child of one of our men in Moscow. Quite straightforward: induce the disaffected elements to reveal themselves in apparent safety, arrange for them to commit crimes and then arrest them. There was a conspiracy if you like. More selective than a purge, excellent training for the organization, double deterrent effect – if you join a subversive movement we'll catch you and punish you, and more than that, if someone tries to persuade you to join one he's probably a policeman. I'll be interested to see what effect it has on the rather different operation planned for Poland, starting early next year. I shouldn't advise you to tell your colleagues about this part, unless you happen to fancy a broken neck. Some of them aren't as nice as you. That's another thing that's no help: niceness.'

Vanag's hands had not moved from the desk in front of him, but there was a thump at the door and the guard came in. Theodore said quickly,

'I was against those killings, you know.'

'I do know, and what of it? There won't be room for fine shades like that at the kind of trial you'll have. Niceness is no help. *You poor bloody little fool.*'

He nodded to the guard, who wrenched upwards at Theodore's arm even though he was already well on his way to a standing posture. In the corridor, lurching about as he was pulled and pushed at, he wondered dully if this was indeed the same man that had brought him to Vanag; he seemed a little taller, a little less broad. But whether or not he was the same man, he was beyond all doubt the same sort of man, the sort of man that treated all his charges with casual, inattentive brutality, that if ordered to would go much further, as far as anyone might require, not cruel, just wantonly merciless, the sort of man that had always been needed somewhere in the world since the beginning of civilization. This representative of that sort spat carefully and copiously in Theodore's face as they stood in the lift, and swung him into his cell with such force that he crashed against the wall and bruised his shoulder painfully.

The cell was no more than six metres square, but with only thirty-eight people in it there was at least room for everyone to sit down. Theodore found a place near one corner, and also inevitably near the slop-pails. He had been expecting to be asked, perhaps even sympathetically asked, what had been happening to him, but nobody so much as looked up. He clasped his wrists round his knees and shifted about on the stone floor; it was hard to find a not uncomfortable position. The place was at least dry and adequately ventilated. Slowly his mind went back to the last part of his conversation with Vanag. When asked whether he had believed that it had been intended to give England back to the English, the reason for his failure to answer had not been the result of unwillingness to betray himself one way or the other; he had simply forgotten what he had believed. Now he made an effort and tried again to remember. It was no good; he had never thought about the matter much and the last time had been too long ago. Had he believed that the revolution would succeed? That was easier; he had pondered about the matter now and then and in the end decided to suspend judgement and let events take their course. Or had he just got bored, left off pondering? He was not sure.

The long morning crept by. Every few minutes someone used one of the slop-pails, always having to step over him to reach it and sometimes kicking or hacking him in the leg. There was no conversation. A guard paced up and down the corridor outside, his footfalls very distinct on the flagstones. The cell was at the end of the row; Theodore could hear his regular tread receding towards the other end, turning, coming back. By estimating the length of his stride while he was in view through the bars and counting his steps, it should have been possible to calculate the length of the corridor, but that piece of information was not worth the trouble of acquiring; it had no point. How long to the midday meal? Nobody could know, all dials and watches, together with all other personal effects, had been removed by the guards before the prisoners had been taken to the cells. They were too far below ground to hear anything of the outside world.

Further questions, thornier questions, began to come lumbering up, presenting themselves to Theodore's reluctant attention. He conducted a slow-paced dialogue with himself.

Was the revolution a good cause? – or rather, was I right to think it one?

> Certainly. The English had been deprived of what was theirs by right and to restore it must be good.

What about Vanag's point? They'd have to be trained to run the country, wouldn't they?

> Yes. Yes, of course they would.

And they'd have to be given responsibilities a little at a time, as they became more experienced.

> I suppose so.

But that would have run directly counter to our declared policy of giving them full political control at a stroke.

> What of it?

Why was I in favour of that policy?

Wait. . . . Because Sevadjian recommended it.

Did I understand his arguments?

Yes. If the handing-over was done in stages it would never be done at all.

Why not? How does that follow?

What's the next question?

Do I care about the English? Enough to risk my life for them?

No. I joined the revolution because I wanted to fight for what I believed in.

What do I believe in?

Justice and freedom and so on

Do I care about them enough to risk my life for them?

No. I wanted an adventure.

Enough to risk my life?

No. I didn't think it would come to that.

This is a pretty squalid story.

Is it? Whatever my motives I was at any rate working for what I believed in.

What do I believe in?

I've mentioned justice and freedom. Then there's truth and art and perseverance and power and happiness and loyalty. All the things that matter.

What does 'matter' mean?

At this point Theodore broke off his internal colloquy. His cell was the first in the row, which meant that anybody arriving from upstairs was visible from it. And somebody was visible now, standing in a stooped attitude not five metres away while one guard showed another a piece of paper. It was Nina. She had a dirty bandage round her head and looked ill, listless and confused. He was going to call to her, then did not. He said to himself that it would have done no good, though he was far from clear about what he meant by that. In another moment she had gone. He let his head hang. It occurred to him that he ought to be feeling sadness, or remorse, or even a consoling awareness of duty done. But for a variety of reasons nothing of the sort was possible. All he could feel was some apprehension and a great indifference.

22

The little churchyard was crowded. A guard of honour from the regiment lined the paths and stood in a double line at the graveside. Across the road, 8 Troop were paraded under Sergeant Ulmanis, who at a signal from Colonel Tabidze ordered a party to dismount. Six men did so, went to the nearby waggon and, with Lyubimov in charge, lifted the coffin on to their shoulders. They moved carefully but not very smartly into the churchyard while a contingent from the regimental band played a slow march.

Lomov was not one of the six; he had not volunteered for the duty and was in any case too small. He sat his horse in a soldierly way, holding the reins of Lyubimov's. The last time he came this way he had wept a great deal, genuine tears produced by very genuine relief. He had broken military regulations, disobeyed an officer's order, had a hard ride, seen (or rather not seen) two strange things and come within a second of being a party to murder. Always a quick thinker, he had instantly and rightly guessed that to have saved Controller Petrovsky from death would square his account with the army; Lyubimov's too. Now Lomov congratulated himself on the native curiosity that had taken him up to the house just in time, and held back a smile of complacency at knowing what all but a very few besides himself would have given a month's pay to know. He was on the whole sorry that the ensign was dead, but he had been too changeable for a good officer, exciting to ride with, dangerous to cross, in fact dangerous at all times.

Some members of the regiment had attended the burial as private persons and stood here and there inside the churchyard: Victor, Boris, Dmitri among others. Major Yakir was there too, but in his capacity as the deceased's squadron commander. Victor had picked his station with some care, in a corner of the walls where everyone within reach would have his back to him and he would be able to wield his vodka-flask without being noticed. As the place filled up, other mourners moved quite close to him. The closest was a woman wearing a curious black dress and hat, evidently on her own. She was in her thirties and had a remarkable bosom which he glimpsed when she half turned and gave him a brief stare. After that, she took another step or two backwards until she was standing really very close to him. He had started to take a quick swig from his flask, thinking this an ideal opportunity, when he suddenly choked. His feelings of grief for the dead, never profound, vanished altogether.

The coffin was lowered into the grave. Colonel Tabidze rested at the salute for a minute afterwards and there was comparative silence everywhere. Then he lowered his hand to his side, took a pace forward and began to speak.

'We bury here today a gallant young officer who gave his life for his country and also, by an inspiring chance, for his father. In the midst of our grief we can only rejoice that the ruthless assassins responsible for this atrocity have been caught and punished. May their names perish in infamy. In their victim, Alexander Petrovsky, Russia and England have lost a good soldier and a good friend. His parents, to whom our hearts go out in sympathy and love, have lost the best of sons. Everybody who knows the family knows how Alexander revered his father and mother. As one who knew him all his life and was his commanding officer for the whole length of his brief career, I am perhaps specially qualified . . .'

By now, almost everyone had stopped listening. All but a few had paid close attention at first in the hope of picking up some clue to the truth about Alexander's death, which by common consent could not have happened as officially described. The general disbelief arose not from any inherent improbability in the story of the two masked gunmen who escaped after their assassination attempt but were captured later at some distant place; elsewhere there had been plenty of successful attempts of that kind within an hour or two. It was just that the notion of Alexander giving half an hour of his free time, let alone his life, for his country or his father (or any other entity) could not be a true one. Such persons were none the wiser, and likely to remain so. The others, the few like Lomov who knew what had happened, had listened with less curiosity to Tabidze's opening remarks, looking for nothing more than some inner amusement at the skill and extravagance of his evasions. Another of this party, Brevda, felt none of that. After the first shock he had settled down to a state of low-intensity panic that might run wild at any moment. He had not yet been brought to account for nearly letting the Controller get killed under his nose, but it could not be long delayed. No doubt the boss was waiting for the funeral to be over and things to get back to normal; then would come the summons to the Directorate. Of Alexander, except remotely, as the cause of the trouble, there was no thought in Brevda's head at all.

Tabidze was nearly at the end of his address. He had worked on it with characteristic conscientiousness, mentioning everybody who should have been mentioned, avoiding flat lies wherever possible in speaking of the deceased, enumerating his virtues without gross exaggeration, or at any rate without downright invention. And, because these things had to be done properly, and fiddling with pieces of paper at the graveside was not doing things properly, he had learned his speech by heart and had practised it. Naturally he kept to himself his own opinion of Alexander. This started with the observation that the young idiot had tried to be too many things. To take only his soldiering: from one moment to the next one never knew whether he was going to turn out to be a liberal or a martinet, a technician or a cavalryman, a rulebook pedant or an improviser, a dandy or a professional. Add to that his sex-life, his social life ... And then this final, fatal piece of lunacy. On the whole he had been a liability to the regiment, showy rather than brilliant, and too easily bored to be trusted. Life would be more comfortable with him gone, and not appreciably duller.

'So death has taken away Alexander Petrovsky,' said Tabidze

in conclusion. 'Everybody here must be distressed by the knowledge that he or she will never see him again. That's all.'

He came to the salute once more. His trumpeter, fluffing occasionally, sounded the meagre, sentimental dirge that served as Lights Out. The guard of honour rested on their arms, heads bowed. The firing-party discharged their old-style carbines across the grave and the English attendants started shovelling the earth back in.

On the other side, in the front row of mourners, stood the small black-clad figure of Elizabeth Cuy, one of the couple of dozen conspirators who had conspired to little or no purpose and had been released after questioning. She was crying bitterly, or rather with great intensity. She was thinking of herself as she wept, of herself as the girl who had had a hopeless passion for a young man who had now died. When she did think of Alexander it was of someone who had treated her with some unkindness and not a great deal of notice, and perhaps some of her tears were those of one who lays down a burden. Agatha Tabidze was next to her, and she too was crying, but then she always cried at funerals, even ones that commemorated people she had not particularly cared for. Tatiana Petrovsky, on the other side, was the only person present who was shedding genuine tears, being likewise the only person in the world who would have grieved for Alexander whatever he had been like. She was grieving for Nina too, also taken from her and yet still living, and so already beginning to occupy a larger place in her thoughts. Her surviving son, Basil, off the aeroplane from Manchuria only that morning, had her hand in his but was not weeping. Sergei Petrovsky was not weeping either. Nor was he grieving; he was entirely taken up with the bad time his conscience was giving him.

8 Troop was filing off at a slow pace, Polly next to Ulmanis at their head, her saddle and bridle hung with black. The guard of honour marched out into the road and the crowd began to disperse. It was a chilly day with, in the past few minutes, small gusts of rain. Kitty Wright had reached the gate of the churchyard when a young Russian officer approached her.

'*Good afternoon,*' he said; '*may I speak with you?*'

'All right, but it'll probably be easier if we use Russian.'

'Thank you. Aren't you Kitty? Alexander's girl? I'm called Dmitri. This must be a sad day for you.'

'Yes, it is.' A sad day it was; not an unpleasant day or a difficult day, but a sad one.

'I liked him. I didn't know him well, but I thought he was a good fellow. Are you coming up to the house for a drink? We're all invited.'

'I'm not.'

'Yes you are; I'm inviting you. Nobody'll mind. Things are getting easier all the time.'

'All right,' said Kitty again. 'It'll be funny to see it. He never brought me here, but he talked about it. I wonder if it'll be as I imagine.'

They waited for more people to leave, then slowly made their way against the flow towards the side of the church. As they passed the grave, now completely filled in, the turfs back in place, something she had heard that night at the theatre came half-way into Kitty's memory, something about somebody dying and being turned into stars and put in the sky. With more concentration than she had ever summoned before, she tried to remember the precise words, just some of them, just one phrase, but she was not used to efforts of that kind. She tried again; she nearly got it. No. It was gone.

More About Penguins and Pelicans

For further information about books available from
Penguins please write to Dept EP, Penguin Books Ltd,
Harmondsworth, Middlesex UB7 0DA.

In the U.S.A.: For a complete list of books available
from Penguins in the United States write to Dept CS,
Penguin Books, 625 Madison Avenue, New York,
New York 10022.

In Canada: For a complete list of books available from
Penguins in Canada write to Penguin Books Canada Ltd,
2801 John Street, Markham, Ontario L3R 1B4.

In Australia: For a complete list of books available from
Penguins in Australia write to the Marketing Department,
Penguin Books Australia Ltd, P.O. Box 257, Ringwood,
Victoria 3134.

Romance, intrigue, adventure
– it's all here in these unputdownable Penguins

The Feast of All Saints

Anne Rice

In the raw, sensual and legendary city of New Orleans before
the Civil War; amongst the waterfronts, the slave markets
and the quadroon ballrooms lived the *gens de couleur*, a fierce
and proud people, neither black nor white, but caught
between the two – free and yet not free. Out of this race came
Marcel, the mesmeric copper-skinned youth, adored by all yet
dreaming of distant cultures, and his sister Marie, who longed
for love and marriage in a world ready to sell her to the
highest bidder.

Exotic and exciting, the author of the bestselling *Interview
with the Vampire* has written a novel as colourful and
sensuous as the old French Quarter itself.

Manchu

Robert Elegant

The big bestseller from the author of *Dynasty* – it'll spellbind
and enthrall you to the very last page! The year is 1628, and
the fabulous court of the Ming is secretly penetrated by the
Jesuits and assaulted by the fierce and terrible Manchu. Here
we meet Francis Arrowsmith, an Englishman and exiled Jesuit
turned soldier-of-fortune; a genius with gunpowder, cannon
and shot; a lover, husband, father – and spy.

Delving back through the shifting sands of time, Robert
Elegant recreates the opulence of the Chinese courts,
the swift savagery of the wars, the porcelain eroticism of
the women and the last embattled days of the doomed
Ming dynasty . . .